SCALLYWAG LOVE

by
Jim Hall

Order this book online at www.trafford.com
or email orders@trafford.com

Most Trafford titles are also available at major online book retailers.

Note for Librarians: A cataloguing record for this book is available from Library
and Archives Canada at www.collectionscanada.ca/amicus/index-e.html

Printed in Victoria, BC, Canada.

ISBN: 978-1-4269-1082-1 (sc)

*We at Trafford believe that it is the responsibility of us all, as both individuals
and corporations, to make choices that are environmentally and socially sound.
You, in turn, are supporting this responsible conduct each time you purchase a
Trafford book, or make use of our publishing services. To find out how you are
helping, please visit www.trafford.com/responsiblepublishing.html*

*Our mission is to efficiently provide the world's finest, most comprehensive
book publishing service, enabling every author to experience success.
To find out how to publish your book, your way, and have it available
worldwide, visit us online at www.trafford.com*

Trafford rev. 06/29/09

Trafford PUBLISHING®   www.trafford.com

North America & international
toll-free: 1 888 232 4444 (USA & Canada)
phone: 250 383 6864 ♦ fax: 250 383 6804 ♦ email: info@trafford.com

The United Kingdom & Europe
phone: +44 (0)1865 487 395 ♦ local rate: 0845 230 9601
facsimile: +44 (0)1865 481 507 ♦ email: info.uk@trafford.com

10 9 8 7 6 5 4 3 2 1

Courtroom Dramas

Patrick Chapman's motto: If you're looking for a good fight, you've come to the right man, because I'll give you one!

"Bless me father for I have sinned, it is 25 years since my last confession".

"Welcome back"

"I have lived a life of sin and crime".

"Did this life of sin and crime not make you sick to your stomach?".

"It did, father, but I took something for it".

"And what was that, son?".

"Money, father!".

Scallywag Love

"Scallywag," Dr. Connolly began. "God loves you and so do I. Be confident no matter what because there is great goodness in you."

"Thank you Sir". No one had ever spoken to him like that before.

Dedication

I wanted to turn a tragedy into a triumph.
I wanted to turn a negative experience to positive account.
I wanted to turn a lemon into lemonade.
I wanted to turn a sorrow into a servant.
I wanted to turn a problem into a project.
I wanted to turn an obstacle into an opportunity.
I wanted to grow a rose on the dunghill of a bad experience.
I wanted to turn a difficulty into a dividend.
I wanted to harvest fruit from frustration.
I wanted to turn an adversity into an adventure.
I wanted to turn a stumbling block into a stepping stone.
I wanted to turn my pain into a parable of progress for my children, Lorcan and Michelle.

This is also for Kim and Susanne.

Unsolicited Testimonials:

"'The book you sent me is a masterpiece." (Rev. J.H. Belfast.)

"I am deeply obliged to you for your book which I enjoyed reading." (E.L. Alicante, Spain.)

"Thanks a lot for your interesting book. I highly recommend it to anyone."' (G.O. Genoa, Italy.)

"I congratulate you on your warm embrace of humanity." (P.F. Meath, Ireland.)

Contents

A Christmas Collage

Little did I realise on the day I collected my parchment from the Incorporated Law Society, to the enormous pride of my mother and father, that one day I would defend Santa Claus on a charge of murder.

When I went to see him in the cells of Ballyskerry police station he certainly looked like Santa Claus, even though he was wearing a three piece suit with a gold watch and fob chain. Two of his male friends from the retirement home were with him. One of them told me that their friend used to be called Spud Murphy but he had changed his name by deed poll to Nicholas Christmas. He had neatly parted hair, a pot belly and a Santa Claus beard. He was about seventy years of age and did not, in the first instance, want to talk about the charge levelled against him. Instead, probably because it was December and the effect that this month always had on him, he wanted to talk about the season of goodwill.

"I love the sounds of Christmas; church bells calling in the quiet of midnight on Christmas Eve; Christmas carollers singing for charity; the snap of the letter box as the postman brings greetings from family and friends; the tearing of wrapping paper as urgent hands long to find out what presents this Christmas has brought.

"I love the smells of Christmas; the Christmas cake and pudding suffusing the house with their own distinctive aromas; cloves and cinnamon in mulled wine; rain sodden coats steaming near a radiator; the turkey and stuffing roasting; cigars and sherry."

"If it's any consolation to you," I said, "your trial will probably come up close to next Christmas. The legal calendar is divided into four terms: Hilary runs from January to the end of March; Easter runs from mid April to the end of May; Trinity begins in June and continues until the end of July and Michaelmas beings in October and leads up to Christmas."

He smiled with an inappropriate air of satisfaction. "How very apt," he said, "for Santa Claus to go on trial in the Michaelmas term."

My secretary, Sharon, who is a statuesque brunette – lovely enough to be a model and always fond of black leather trouser suits – was with me and remarked on the unlikelihood of Mr Christmas committing a murder. She whispered this to me.

His friends smiled in approval. "Excuse me for not introducing myself earlier," the fat one said. "My name is Mr Hardy."

"And I," the skinny one proffered his hand, "am Mr Laurel."

"You changed your names by deed poll as well?" I asked.

"Oh yes," said Mr Hardy. "It's a wonderful thing to do as you retire and face the last lap of life – a sort of declaration that there can still be fun in the advanced years and an imputation of the hope that the best is yet to be."

"Have you ever heard 'The legend of the Robin'?" Mr Christmas again.

"No," I said. "I don't think so."

"The legend of the robin is a symbol of unselfish dedication to the Lord. When Jesus was born in Bethlehem, many came to witness the divine event, having been led there by a wondrous star that came and shone over the humble place where the Holy Family rested. A little robin, passing by that night, was also led to the stable by the star.

"There the robin saw the glorious Infant surrounded by worshippers. No one noticed the plain brown bird. By and by, when the visitors had left, the Baby slept. Joseph built up a fire to keep the family warm through the night. But Joseph and Mary fell asleep, too, and the fire died down. Seeing this, the robin swooped in and fanned the fire with his wings until the coals began to blaze warmly again.

"His breast grew red with the heat, but he stayed until morning, keeping the fire aglow. Once the Baby woke and smiled at the robin.

"And that is why, today, the robin is known for its cheery red breast – a symbol of faithful service."

Sharon smiled and said, "Isn't that lovely!".

Mr Christmas – obviously a man who liked his renditions appreciated turned to her and asked, "Do you know the story behind the poinsettia plant?"

"No," Sharon answered.

"Allow me to grace your gorgeous ears with the tiny tale. In 1825 Joel Poinsett was appointed American's first Ambassador to Mexico. In 1828 he discovered the red leaved plant which was named after him – the poinsettia. The reason he favoured the plant was because he saw the original miracle of the poinsettia taking place.

"It was the custom in prosperous Mexican circles for the children of the rich to bring special gifts to the baby Jesus in the crib on Christmas Eve. One poor Mexican child wanted to give something to Jesus so he picked a small weedlike plant. He presented it to the baby Jesus and the congregation laughed with derision. The child was so embarrassed that he blushed. The baby Jesus blushed! And the poinsettia blushed! The weed turned into a beautiful flower. The congregation was astonished. The miracle of the poinsettia made the little child smile. From that day on the poinsettia has become the favoured flower of Christmas."

Sharon was so touched that she gave Mr Christmas a kiss.

"Thank you so much, young lady. That is my first Christmas kiss this year."

His friends were smiling; I was smiling; Sharon was wiping a tear from her eyes and none of us mentioned the charge of murder levelled against him. We were caught up in a time warp of bonhomie and goodwill. The old codger had his audience in the palm of his hand and he was loving it.

"In addition to Joel Poinsett I would like to tell you about two more of my old friends – John Pierpont and Frank Church.

"Frank Church was a heavy drinking journalist who worked for an American newspaper titled The Sun. A little girl once wrote him a letter:

'Dear Editor,

I am 8 years old. Some of my little friends say there is no Santa Claus. Papa says, "If you see it in The Sun it's so." So please Mr Editor tell me the truth – is there a Santa Claus?

Virginia O' Hanlon.
115 West 95th Street."

"Frank Church wrote back as follows:
'Virginia, your little friends are wrong. They have been affected by the scepticism of a sceptical age. They do not believe except they see. They think that nothing can be which is not comprehensible by their little minds. All minds, Virginia, whether they be men's or children's, are little. In this great universe of ours man is a mere insect, an ant, in his intellect, as compared with the boundless world about him, as measured by the intelligence capable of grasping the whole of truth and knowledge.

Yes, Virginia, there is a Santa Claus. He exists as certainly as love and generosity and devotion exist, and you know that they abound and give to your life its highest beauty and joy. Alas! how dreary would be the world if there were no Santa Claus! It would be as dreary as if there were no Virginias. There would be no childlike faith then, no poetry, no romance to make tolerable this existence. We should have no enjoyment, except in sense and sight. The eternal light with which childhood fills the world would be extinguished.

Not believe in Santa Claus! You might as well not believe in fairies! You might get your papa to hire men to watch in all the chimneys on Christmas Eve to catch Santa Claus, but even if they did not see Santa Claus coming down, what would that prove? Nobody sees Santa Claus, but that is no sign that there is no Santa Claus. The most real things in the world are those that neither children nor men can see.

No Santa Claus! Thank God, he lives, and he lives forever. A thousand years from now, Virginia, nay ten times ten thousand years from now, he will continue to make glad the heart of childhood.

-The New York Sun, September 21, 1897"

"My Friend – John Pierpont:

"John Pierpont was a failure seven times over in his life. He was born in 1785 and, as a young man, chose education as his first career. He was a graduate of Yale University but failed as a school teacher because he was too soft on his students.

"Career number two was the law – but he failed as a lawyer because he never collected his fee up front and was a sucker for a hard luck story which could be remedied by justice.

"Career number three was as a businessman. He did not charge enough to make a profit and he extended too much credit.

"Career number four was as a poet. Although he was published he didn't sell enough volumes of his poems to make a living.

"Career number five involved retraining yet again. He became a Minister of Religion but he upset his eventual congregation by being for the prohibition of alcoholic drinks and against slavery. He was requested to resign or be sacked. He resigned.

"Career number six was in politics. He tried to be elected as Governor of Massachusetts for the Abolition Party. He failed.

"He ran for Congress for the Free Soil Party – he lost; so much for politics.

"The American Civil War broke out and he tried his hand as an Army Chaplain. He had to resign within two weeks because of failing health. So much for career number seven. He was seventy six years of age.

"Some kind person found him a job as a Government Clerk for the last five years of his life. He died in 1866, aged eighty one, with a lifetime of memories as a failure continuously dejecting his mind and spirit.

"However, on his gravestone today in Mount Auburn Cemetery in Cambridge, Massachusetts are the words:

John Pierpont
Born 1785 – Died 1866
Poet, Preacher, Philosopher, Philanthropist.

"Why are those tributes added to his name? The answer is really quite simple. John Pierpont wrote a song – a Christmas song. John Pierpont wrote 'Jingle Bells'.

Jingle bells! Jingle bells!
Jingle all the way!
Oh what fun it is to ride
in a one horse open sleigh!

"The legacy of a failure was a song of joy, which, it is estimated, one fifth of the present population of the world knows off by heart.

"Everything John dedicated his life to came true – slavery was abolished, the environment and organic produce currently enjoy favour; religion, education and the law are in a state of continuous reformation.

"Every year, come Christmas, we celebrate John Pierpont's success."

"Nice one, Nicholas," said Mr Laurel.

"Well done," said Mr Hardy.

"Do you have any more old friends Mr Christmas?" asked Sharon.

"Indeed I do," the old codger exclaimed. "My old friend Clement Clarke Moore spent his life writing a work entitled Lexicon Of The Hebrew Language. But it was for a much smaller work that he became famous. On 23rd December 1823 he published his poem:

A Visit From St. Nicholas
Clement Clarke Moore

'Twas the night before Christmas when all through the house
Not a creature was stirring, not even a mouse.
The stockings were hung by the chimney with care,
In hopes that St. Nicholas soon would be there.

The children were nestled all snug in their beds,
While visions of sugar-plums danced in their heads.
And mamma in her kerchief, and I in my cap,
Had just settled our brains for a long winter's nap -
When out on the lawn there arose such a clatter,
I sprang from the bed to see what was the matter.
Away to the window I flew like a flash,
Tore open the shutters and threw up the sash.
The moon on the breast of the new-fallen snow
Gave the lustre of mid-day to objects below.
When, what to my wondering eyes should appear,
But a miniature sleigh and eight tiny reindeer.
With a little old driver, so lively and quick,
I knew in a moment it must be St. Nick.!
More rapid than eagles his coursers they came,
And he whistled, and shouted, and called them by name.
"Now Dasher! now, Dancer! now, Prancer and Vixen!
On, Comet! On, Cupid! on, Donner and Blitzen!-
To the top of the porch, to the top of the wall,
Now, dash away, Dash away, Dash away all!"
As dry leaves that before the wild hurricane fly,
When they met with an obstacle mount to the sky.
So, up to the housetop the coursers they flew,
With the sleigh full of toys - and St. Nicholas too.
And then, in a twinkling, I heard on the roof
The prancing and pawing of each little hoof.
As I drew in my head, and was turning around,
Down the chimney St. Nicholas came with a bound.
He was dressed all in fur, from his head to his foot,
And his clothes were all tarnished with ashes and soot:
A bundle of toys he had flung on his back,
And he looked like a peddler, just opening his pack.
His eyes-how they twinkled! his dimples, how merry!
His cheeks were like roses, his nose like a cherry;
His droll little mouth was drawn up like a bow,
And the beard on his chin was as white as the snow.
The stump of a pipe he held tight in his teeth,

And the smoke, it encircled his head like a wreath.
He had a broad face and a little round belly,
That shook, when he laughed, like a bowlful of jelly.
He was chubby and plump - a right jolly old elf;
And I laughed when I saw him, in spite of myself;
A wink of his eye, and a twist of his head,
Soon gave me to know I had nothing to dread.
He spoke not a word but went straight to his work,
And filled all the stockings: then turned with a jerk,
And laying his finger aside of his nose,
And giving a nod, up the chimney he rose.
He sprang to his sleigh, to his team gave a whistle,
And away they all flew like the down of a thistle.
But I heard him exclaim, ere he drove out of sight,
"Happy Christmas to all, and to all a good-night!"

"What a wonderful catalyst old Clement was! He combined Scandinavian myths about Old Man Winter and the English Father Christmas with the Saint Nicholas of the Dutch and Americans ......

"Which brings me to my knowledge of the original Santa. He was born in Patar in AD 280; he died in December 345 in Myra – both places are now in modern Turkey. What a lot he blessed the world with, in one simple life! He urged the Emperor Constantine to release the condemned prisoners – he became the patron saint of prisoners.

"He saved the city from starving by commandeering a cargo of grain and nevertheless when the ship reached Byzantium, it was found to be full. That miracle made him the patron saint of sailors.

"Three lovely girls were so poverty stricken that their only way of making a living was going to be to sell their sexual favours. St. Nicholas heard of their plight and because he was a wealthy man, by inheritance, he decided to save the day. Without dowries the girls had no chance of attracting husbands.

"St. Nicholas, on a dark winter's night, got up on his horse and rode to the girls' house. He threw 3 bags of gold in through their open window. St. Nicholas is the patron saint of unmarried women because of this. Funnily enough because of his 3 bags of gold he is also the patron saint of pawnbrokers.

"It was the habit of an innkeeper in ancient Turkey to kill Asian children, pickle them in vats of brine and serve them to his customers as salted pork. St. Nicholas once saved the lives of 3 Asian children and pronounced a curse on the innkeeper – he died the same night. St. Nicholas has been the protector and patron saint of children ever since.

"I made up a little story about Santa myself. I call it:

Santa – the Hero of Justice!

Snow lay deeply around Santa's Home at the North Pole. Christmas trees and other evergreens provided the only colour. The snow would have been blinding in its whiteness if anyone had noticed. But the reason they didn't notice was because this was Christmas Eve.

The culmination of the year lay about the elves' feet as they parcelled each present in gaily decorated wrapping paper for all the little boys and girls of the world. Oh what fun would be had!

One by one the presents were tucked into Santa's magical sack. It defied reason and logic that one sack could hold all the toys needed but, of course, this was no ordinary sack – it was magical.

The little elves trooped off to lunch but when they arrived back to Santa's factory they noticed strange footprints in the snow. Who could it have been? Who would want to visit Santa's factory while the little helpers were at lunch?

It was a thief! All the year's toys for all the girls and boys of the world had been tucked into Santa's magical sack and stolen! What would Santa Claus do if the children of the world were not to be heartbroken?

Santa was told the sad news by the elves. Santa gathered all the people of the village into the town hall. He had placed a table with a sooty black pot on it in the centre of the room. "There is a rooster under this pot," explained Santa. "And I am going to turn off all the lights. Every person in the village is to touch the pot and when the thief touches the pot the rooster will crow!"

Santa turned out all the lights. Everyone touched the pot but the rooster did not crow. When the light was turned back on everyone had soot on their fingers except the thief who was too afraid to touch the pot!

Santa and the elves set off for the thief's house. There they found Santa's magical sack and all the toys the elves had made during the year. Soon every child will be visited by Santa and his magical sack!

The thief was dealt with on New Year's day. "Please Santa," he pleaded. "I'm really a good boy – it's just that I was tempted when I saw all the lovely toys in your magical sack. Please forgive me – I promise never to do it again."

Santa forgave the thief, gave him a hug and a lollipop and sent him home to his Mammy. And they all lived happily ever after!"

"I think you will find the Judge in the Central Criminal Court somewhat different to Santa," I decided to inject a note of reality into the proceedings.

"But surely," said Mr Christmas, "if my trial comes up in the Michaelmas term he can't fail to be touched by the fragrance of the season?"

"I'm sorry to tell you this – but, yes, he can."

"Good heavens – this is more serious than I thought. Come what may, with friends like Mr Laurel and Mr Hardy I will be able to keep my spirits up."

"Mr Christmas," I began. "The Central Criminal Court is to criminal trials what the Gaiety and Olympia theatres are to pantomime: it is the tops. It is an arena in which the most serious cases are tried; the greatest criminal barristers of the day argue before the most distinguished Judges. And you, Mr Christmas are going on trial there accused of murder. It is a very serious matter. I will need to brief a very brilliant Senior Counsel – I suggest Mr Arthur Guinness.

"The deceased whom you are accused of murdering was named Linda Shaffrey. She was the editor of a women's magazine entitled 'Femmyfirst'. You must tell me all you know about this woman and try to remember everything."

"I find myself feeling somewhat bewildered. I know I must try to remember but I simply can't at the moment. Perhaps tomorrow?"

"Try to get some sleep tonight and we'll be back first thing in the morning." I turned to Mr Laurel and Mr Hardy and said, "I will need statements from you two also."

Mr Laurel said, "Be assured of my highest consideration at all times." Mr Hardy was more simple, "Include me in."

When the case eventually came to court it transpired that the luckless Ms Shaffrey had written an article entitled, 'Santa Claus Commits Suicide'.

Mr Christmas had taken great offence principally because the bubble of children's illusions were punctured. He had gone to the building which housed the magazine to remonstrate with Ms Shaffrey. On the same evening she had had the misfortune to fall down the lift shaft from the fifth floor while the lift was broken down five floors below. There was some circumstantial evidence which foul minds interpreted to indicate that Mr Christmas had diddled the lift and thrown her down the lift shaft. Mr Arthur Guinness has having none of it.

Summing up speech of Mr Arthur Guinness:

"I suggest to you that my gentleman is a man of inviolable virtue. I suggest to you that my gentleman is a man who has lived a blameless life. I suggest to you that my gentleman is a man of excellent character!

"Must we bury the last vestiges of chivalry? Is this the death knell of the age of gallantry?

"Since when has it been enshrined in law that it is a crime for a gentleman to say to a lady, 'After you'?

"And how was Mr Christmas to know that the brassnecked Ms Shaffrey would fall to her unbemourned death as a result of a gross irresponsibility on behalf of the personnel officer of her magazine?

"No, my dear friends, this is not a case of murder. Rather it is a case of an innocent man being put through a grotesque ordeal. Ms Shaffrey was an honorary auxiliary policewoman. Therefore the death penalty is prescribed for your verdict of 'guilty'.

"The death penalty is a terrible thing and we cannot wish that fact away. The numb sick fear of the condemned man, the tired shivers of his warders, the forlorn anguish of the chaplain, the sweating of the governor glancing at the phone as he leaves his office, the impatience of the grey faced executioner, the ticking watches, the echoing footsteps, the pounding hearts, the slamming of doors, the mask, the lurch into oblivion, the groan of the rope, the doctor feeling absurdly in the dark for a heartbeat, a grubby note with a drawing pin on the gate.

That is what execution is always about. And that is why we can have none of it."

It wasn't long before the jury came in with a verdict of Not Guilty and Mr Santa Claus was released into the company of Mr Laurel and Mr Hardy to enjoy Christmas as best he could and to recover. As I shepherded them down the court steps they complained about how their sleep pattern had gone haywire. I thought my parting greeting was apt:

"God rest you merry gentlemen – let nothing you dismay."

"Shoplifter"

Dear Friend,

I received a long statement recently on arriving into the office one Saturday morning. Sharon had taken the statement from a well dressed young man, about 30 years of age, on Friday evening. When I came into the office that morning Sharon seemed to be subduing a type of excitement. She sometimes gets upset about the occasional case we have to handle. I think because of her past there are certain accused persons with whom she can identify and associate. Clearly the young man who had left the statement was one of these. (I enclose the full statement the young man made. Besides being some story in itself something else happened after we received it which to this day frightens me. However, I won't jump the gun). I will let the story unfold as it happened.

Statement of Robert Page

Introduction My name is Robert Page. I am 31 years old and I work as an Executive Officer in the Department of Economic Planning. I am married with three children, two living with me and one living in the spirit world. My wife's name is Gwen. At the time those events began we had only one child.

August 15th 1980 On this date I was arrested and accused of shoplifting in Grubby Street at about 5.30 on a Friday evening. That day at lunchtime I went into Rufus Records in Grubby Street and

13

bought an LP record entitled Sky I. Sky are a band of musicians featuring John Williams, the celebrated guitarist, who got together and decided to play classical music in a rock format.

I gave the girl behind the counter a ten pound note. The record cost six pounds, forty nine pence so she put the precise copy of the record I handed her into a plastic bag with Rufus Records written all over it, gave me a receipt and three pounds fifty one pence change. Since it was lunchtime and I had to go back to work I didn't have enough time to have a look at the charts of best selling records.

I went back to work and because a few months before this my young son gave my wife and I a fright by running out into the kitchen with a plastic bag over his head, I took the plastic bag off the record and threw it into the basket beside my desk. I then placed the record into a small briefcase which I carry to work. Unfortunately the record did not go all the way down in the briefcase. A part of it was left sticking up at the top.

At that time I worked in the Finance Division of the Department, looking after the payroll of £1.25 million and a few other accounts such as travel and subsistence worth another £0.25 million. That evening I left work and went back to the Rufus Records shop. I had a look at the charts and walked around the small shop with my record sticking up out of my briefcase.

As I was walking around the shop I felt the need to go to the toilet. Since 1975 I have suffered from colitis and various stomach ailments. In 1979 I was put on a high fibre diet and since then my health has considerably improved. The only problem is that I go to the toilet rather a lot. This is far easier to put up with than internal bleeding.

I walked out of the shop and ran down the street until I came to the corner of Nassau Street. I walked from Grubby Street corner to the Berni Inn and went to the toilet there. While I was in the toilet I decided to sort out some rubbish that was in my pockets and in my briefcase. I threw a used raffle ticket, the receipt for the record, a card that was stuck on the front of the record, a paper tissue and a few other odds and ends into the bowl and flushed them all away.

When I walked out of the Berni Inn I was accosted by two young men. One of them shouted at me, "You robbed that record from our shop." The other said, "You walked out of our shop with that record."

The first guy was of average height, slim and had a quiff that stood up on his forehead. He was the manager of Rufus Records. The other fellow was also of average height but had long hair and a bear. He was the security guard.

I said to the security guard, "Of course I walked out of the shop with the record. If you were watching me I also walked into the shop with it. I bought it there at lunchtime."

The manager fellow said, "If you bought it where is the receipt?"

I said, "I've only just now flushed it down the jacks in there".

He said, "If you bought it where is the bag? Did you get a bag with it?"

"Yes I did," I said. "I threw it out this afternoon. Look, I can assure you I bought the record, I didn't steal it."

"I don't know," said the shop manager. "What did you run for?"

"I ran because I was in a hurry to go to the toilet," I said.

"Will you come back to the shop with us, I just want to check something," said the manager.

"Why should I go back to the shop with you?" I asked?

"It's no hassle," said the manager. "I just want to check."

"Look," I said. "This is hassle enough for me, being stopped in the street and asked all these questions. Look, I've had enough of this. I'm going home, OK?"

The security guard said, "There's a Guard now." A Garda was walking along the street. The manager said, "There's an element of doubt. We'll have to give him the benefit of the doubt." Then he said to me, "You're a reasonable bloke. Good luck." I said, "Good luck to you too."

I then walked on and crossed the road at the new entrance to Trinity College. I park my car at a car park in Pearse Street, on the opposite side of the College, so I walk through there every day. As I was walking in the new entrance I heard running footsteps behind me. It was the two from the shop again and this time they had a Guard in tow.

"You robbed that record from our shop you bastard," the shop manager said. "Everything you told us was a load of bullshit and this proves it." He was holding up the soggy card which had been stuck to the front of the record and which I had thrown down the toilet.

The Guard said to me, "Hold it. These fellows say you robbed a record from their shop."

I said, "Look I've already told them that I bought it there at lunchtime. I also told them that I threw the receipt and that piece of rubbish down the toilet."

"We'll have to sort this out down the station," said the Guard.

"Am I being arrested?" I asked.

"Yes," the Guard said. "You've already been arrested by these two fellows."

"Give me a look at that card," I said to the shop manager. He was in a state of anger and panic. He reached to show me the card and as I took it he pulled it back and said, "No you might try to tear it up." In so doing he caused a small tear in the card.

The squad car came and I was bundled into the back of it along with the Guard. In the squad car I again explained what had happened to the two policemen sitting in the front. One of them said, "Oh you stole the record alright. You might as well admit it." When I was getting out of the car at the police station the driver said to me, "Good luck". I said thanks and went into the police station.

On entering the station the Sergeant shouted at me, "Prisoner get over here and write down your name and address." I went over to the desk.

"What's the story John?" he asked the Guard. The Sergeant was a small man who made up for his lack of stature by being a bully. He shouted all the time and adopted an aggressive and hostile attitude before he had heard a word from me.

"Right I've heard enough," he said. "You're guilty OK, you might as well admit it. There's stacks of evidence against you. You were caught red handed. If you plead guilty the Guard can speak up on your behalf and say you were cooperative. If you don't you're for it. Come this way." He led me down a corridor into the interrogation cell and proceeded to shout at me. "Right, what have you got to say for yourself?" As I was telling what had happened he interrupted me with remarks such as, "Nonsense" and "Rubbish" and "Not at all". "You're as guilty as hell," he said. "You might as well admit you robbed the record."

He carried on in the same vein for quite some time, shouting and heckling every time I tried to say something. He then left the room and brought in the two idiots from the shop. The manager chap was hysterical and kept shouting that everything I had to say was a load of bullshit. When they had trotted out their stories they were allowed to leave.

I was then left alone in the interrogation cell for about 30 minutes. As a parting shot the Sergeant told me, "You'll be in jail overnight and you'll appear in court in the morning." When I was alone one of the first thoughts I had, since I am a moderately religious person, was that I now understood why it was that Jesus associated himself with the least brethren and how he must have felt following his arrest. I then went over the day's events in my mind and I discovered in my pocket the £3.51 pence change I had received in the shop that day at lunchtime.

I went out to the reception desk and produced the money. "I don't want to hear anything about that," the Sergeant said. "Why didn't you show us that when the two fellows from the shop were here?"

"I've only now had an opportunity to go over the events of the day," I said. It made no difference. I was charged by the Guard. I pleaded not guilty and made a short statement. The statement I made was, 'I bought the record today at lunchtime. I gave the girl behind the counter a £10 note and she gave me back this £3.51 change. I did not steal the record'.

The time was getting on for 7 o'clock and the Sergeant asked, "If I let you out on bail will you turn up in court tomorrow morning?" I said I would. He then produced a few forms for me to sign. As I was signing them my wife, whom I was allowed to phone, and my brother, arrived at the police station. My wife was upset. Her eyes were red from tears.

My brother suggested that we return to my office and see if we could find the Rufus Records bag. We drove back up to Kildare Street and I galloped up the stairs to see if it was still in the basket beside my desk. It wasn't. I rushed back down the stairs and asked the doorman, Gerry, if he knew what the cleaning women did with the rubbish from the waste baskets. He said it was taken to the basement. He accompanied me down the stairs. Because the building is four stories high and fairly big there was about sixteen mailbags full of rubbish.

I told Gerry what I was looking for. He asked me had I left something in it. "It doesn't matter why I want it," I said. "But it's very important that I find it." I didn't know Gerry very well and so I didn't want to confide in him. The only thing I wanted to do was find that plastic bag. I upended the sixteen bags, one by one. I sifted through the rubbish as carefully as my state of panic would allow me but we did not find the bag. I left word for the cleaners who bale the rubbish to look for the bag first thing Monday morning.

That night I slept fitfully. My brother said he would contact a solicitor and that the solicitor would phone me. I brought the phone upstairs and plugged it in beside the bed. At about 2 o'clock the phone rang but it wasn't the solicitor. It was the first of many peculiar phone calls I was about to receive. There was noise in the background that could have been a police station. Either way he pretended it was a wrong number and hung up.

The following morning, Saturday 16th, August 1980, I went to Court with my brother. A solicitor was there waiting for me. The Judge remanded me on continuing bail and told me to come back on the 29th September (please note the date well).

The following Monday Matt the cleaning man, in the Department and in the building in which I work, found the Rufus Records plastic bag.

September 1980 Summons On 2nd September 1980 I was summonsed for failing to turn up on the 29th August. I protested to the Guard who summonsed me that I was told to turn up on the 29th September but he did a Pontius Pilate act on it and disclaimed all knowledge and all blame. I appeared before the District Court on 2nd October. My solicitor turned up late and made a balls of the case. He could have told the Justice that he had written down the date on a piece of paper. Instead of which he tried to look for lenience and said that I had made a mistake.

The Justice wasn't having any of it. He fawned over the Guard and fined me £30. We promptly appealed this conviction and on 20th November we won the appeal despite the Guard swearing that we were told to turn up on 29th August. This comedy of errors without the comedy was a draining experience. Despite being summonsed we turned up on 29th September but the case was not heard. It was a wasted journey for myself, my wife, my solicitors and Matt, the man who found the plastic bag.

October 1980 Slander and Defamation The day I was fined £30 for estreating bail I was in a state of shock. The Guard, John Smith, told me he wanted to reinstate the original case as soon as possible and that he needed to know where to contact me. I gave him my phone number and extension in work.

The following day in work I heard three girls behind me talking. One of them, Helen Carey said, "He was convicted and fined £30." One of the other girls said, "Still and all he is innocent until he goes to trial." Helen Carey said, "He wouldn't have been arrested if he was innocent. He wouldn't have been charged if he didn't do it. My John says he did it and that's good enough for me. John told me about it before but he didn't tell me Page's name. He's guilty right enough."

By a grotesque twist of fate the Guard who arrested me was engaged to a girl who sat two desks behind me. From that day on Helen Carey never missed an opportunity to make a knowing dig at me to the two other girls. They laughed like hyenas and thought the whole thing was great fun.

The tension and stress of working under these conditions built up in me. The next time we went to Court in November the Guard said he had an independent witness who couldn't turn up that day. Once again my solicitor, wife and Matt traipsed home without the case having been heard. The following morning in work Helen Carey got up from her desk, walked over to one of the other girls and said, "John's found a fellow who saw your man taking the record."

This set my imagination going and drove me up the wall. I thought that Smith and the Sergeant had got one of their regulars readied up to point the finger at me and have me convicted. After this incident and the fine I realised the only hope I had was to ask for a trial by Jury.

At the end of November we went to Court once again and this time I asked for a trial by Jury. The Justice – Mr Justice Goldberg – made a comment to the effect that this case was dragging out too long. He gave the Guard 10 days to get the Book of Evidence together. As you know this is a list of statements by the prosecution witnesses of all they are going to say against me.

Helen Carey continued her campaign of slander and defamation. I have pages of statements she made in my hearing. She constantly emphasised that the independent witness would be my undoing.

The night before 5th December I stayed back and told Helen Carey that if her Guard handed me a statement of a false witness the following day she and her boyfriend would be for it. She protested that she didn't know what I was talking about but I told her to deliver the message that I had given her to her boyfriend. She gave the game away on herself by saying, "I'm not carrying messages to anyone. Tell him yourself if you have something to say to him." By those words she proved, if proof be needed, that she was indeed Guard John Smith's girlfriend.

Office Life The following day I went to Court with my solicitor and received the Book of Evidence. There was no independent witnesses statement. Just the statements from the two Rufus Records idiots.

That afternoon I went back to work and my immediate superior officer – an old fart named Harry Desmond – asked me to come out to the corridor. He immediately went into a bullying routine to the general effect that I had attacked Helen Carey the previous evening and that I would be lucky not to find myself out of a job because of my behaviour. At this point in the game I made one of the biggest mistakes of my life. I thought that by telling the whole story in an honest and straightforward manner, I would get Helen Carey sorted out and that I would get some support from the people with whom I had worked for the previous three years.

After listening to the story up to that point the first thing Desmond did was to take my job from me. The second thing he did was to go mouthing the whole story to anybody who would lend him an ear. He told junior people, senior people, people in other Departments and for a few months made a career our of my misfortune. All the time he adopted a bullying stance to me whenever the opportunity arose. My working life degenerated to a shambles.

Home Life On the home front my wife and I kept up a brave face. We told our closest friends and one of them said, "Why don't we all go off to Tenerife on a holiday early in the New Year and forget all this?" I told him not to book the holiday until the trial was over but he went ahead and booked it anyway. He booked the holiday for the last two weeks in February.

I was changed from one room to another in work, away from Helen Carey but put sitting opposite Harry Desmond. I phoned my solicitor and told him about the holiday arrangement my friend had made. He told me not to worry about it. If the trial was fixed for that date we could ask for a change.

Desmond was 'all ears' while I was on the phone and strange as it may seem something happened which was a stroke of good luck for me. We booked the holiday with a company called Bray Travel. They went bankrupt and so the holiday was cancelled. However, I believe Desmond spoke to Carey and she in turn informed Smith of my holiday plans. I was off sick with a stress related illness in January and the Guard phoned me saying I would have to go to court again for arraignment.

On the fifth of February 1981 I went to the Circuit Criminal Court and was told by the judge that if my solicitor didn't turn up – he hadn't turned up for the arraignment – I would have to handle the case myself. The date of the trial was set for 18th February 1981.

My wife became very upset about the fact that all this seemed to be going on and on interminably. She was four months pregnant at the time and every night before going to sleep she became upset. On the 12th February she woke up at 3am. The blood was flushing down her legs as if there was a cistern in her stomach and someone had pulled the chain. She had an abortion that night and our baby went flying off to the spirit world. It was most distressing and upsetting for her and for me.

The abortion took place at home. The bed was swamped with blood.

I will never forget that night as long as I live.

There are some things about this whole matter that I can forgive and understand but I can never forgive the fact that all those bastards induced an abortion in my wife. It was a planned and wanted child.

Trial The trial lasted all of Wednesday 18th February 1981. Since it lasted all day I cannot give you a word by word account of it. Nevertheless, certain aspects of testimony stand out in my memory.

The first witness was the Guard. Because he was in front of a Circuit Court Judge and Jury and not in the District Court or in the police station, I think he realised the game was up. He was not going to notch up a conviction to impress his girlfriend or to help along his probation and promotion prospects.

There is a story in one of the Gospels where Jesus comes to a well at which a woman is taking water and they had a conversation. The woman was flirting with Jesus by saying that she didn't have a husband. Jesus informed her that she had five husbands. She was astonished by this, that a stranger should know her business. The reason that the Guard's evidence against me reminded me of this incident was when he was asked about the £3.51 change I showed him. He didn't deny it outright.

He said, "I think he showed it to another Guard." The facts of the matter were that I showed it to him and the Sergeant. Like the woman in the Gospel who denied having one husband he wasn't telling a direct lie. My barrister did not press the point and so it passed.

The evidence given by the shop manager – the man who started the whole thing – was in line with his statement in the Book of Evidence. He said he saw me walking out of the shop with the record sticking up out of my bag, that he followed me and arrested me. He didn't remember any of the conversation that took place and it was only on cross examination when it was suggested to him that he confirmed the conversation.

He frightened me as I sat in the dock and listened to him giving evidence because he was so sincere about believing that I had stolen the record. One of the things he said was that he had six copies of Sky I behind the counter and that the copy in the shop wouldn't' have been sold to me. He said, "I can't prove that I had six copies but I know I had." That sincere tone and honesty impressed the jury and frightened me.

The security guard was a different kettle of fish altogether. He told one lie after another with an air of desperation that was pathetic. On cross examination he was sliced, filleted and gutted.

The Guard, the shop manager and the security guard concluded the evidence of the prosecution. The shop manager's evidence was the most dangerous. The Judge decided that there was a case to answer and just as he was rubber stamping a form to that effect my barrister asked if there was time before lunch for one defence witness to address the Court.

<u>Defence</u> The Judge agreed and my family doctor took the stand and gave evidence of my colitis problem and the high fibre diet I was on as a result. When the Judge heard this evidence his whole attitude changed. This, of and by itself, was enough to constitute reasonable doubt.

Before returning for lunch the Judge cautioned the jury not to discuss the case. He said that if someone took up a position then, having heard only one side of the story, it might be difficult to make a change of mind once the full story was heard.

The Court was adjourned for lunch, we went across the road to a pub, had a sandwich and a drink, a little chat and returned to Court.

After lunch it was my turn into the witness stand. I was very tense and anxious that everything that had happened should have an airing. I don't remember a lot of what I said but I know that I went over the story I have outlined up to now. Cross-examination was another story again. The bearded prosecuting counsel adopted a tough stance and suggested to me that my actions in attempting to find the plastic bag was a charade and that I had planted the bag among the rubbish to support my story. I had no trouble denying that since it wasn't true. He asked me why I had taken or bought that specific LP. Was there a piece of music on it I wanted? I didn't realise at the time that there weren't many tracks on the LP but I had no hesitation in answering, "A couple of years ago I got up every Sunday morning to try to learn French from a series on the television. There was a piece of music that was often played as background music to a short serial within each programme. The week I bought the LP Mike Murphy had played that piece of music on his radio programme. He named the tune – Gymnopedie – I didn't know the name of the tune until then. I bought the record because of that piece of music."

Another thing I remember the prosecuting barrister suggesting to me was that I ran down Grubby Street that evening not because I wanted to go to the toilet but because I wanted to escape being caught for stealing. I replied to the effect that I attended a specialist, Professor Massey in the Richmond Hospital, in early 1979 and that he had put me on a high fibre diet. My family doctor had given similar evidence so there was no point scored against me.

I was on the witness stand for what seemed like an hour. It may have been longer or shorter but that's what it felt like. When I was finished giving evidence I was greatly shaken but glad that every detail had been gone into.

The next four witnesses corroborated various bits of my evidence. Gerry, who came down to the basement with me that evening and watched with amazement as I upended every sack of rubbish in search of the plastic bag told of the event as he saw it. My wife told the Judge of how our little boy had run out to the kitchen with a plastic bag over his head three months previously. My brother gave evidence of seeing the £3.51 change and of driving around to the office to search for the bag.

Above all I remember Matt's evidence with the most clarity. He began like this, "I arrived at work that Monday morning at about seven o'clock. I had various bits of work to do before going to the basement to bale the rubbish. I put new toilet rolls in the Minister's toilet and put in a clean towel for him. I cleaned out the ashtray in the Secretary's office and replaced them. I ...."

"Yes fine sir," said the Judge. "That is all very interesting but would you get to the point." Matt looked at the Judge sideways as if to say, would you ever hold your whisht. "At about half past eight I went down to the basement and made myself a cup of tea." This was getting to the point? The Judge looked up to heaven and the jury smiled. "It was then I saw it my Lord. Every bit of rubbish tipped out on the basement floor. Who in the name of Jaysus did this, says I to myself. Well, just then Robert Page came down and told me he was responsible for the mess. He told me what he was looking for and I sifted through the garbage until I found it. I brought it up to him in his office and he said, 'Thanks very much, you don't know what that means to me'. He gave me a pound for myself and I bought a pint with it. He's a generous boy M'Lord."

The prosecuting barrister didn't bother cross examining any of my witnesses, as he knew it would be a futile exercise. The Judge took well over an hour to sum up. He went through the evidence of the pair from the shop in good detail. He then asked the jury to use their common sense in deciding the issue. If I was not telling the truth then I would have had to conspire with all of my witnesses in order to pull the wool over everybody's eyes. Did this idea appeal to the jury's common sense? He continued with this line of thought for some time and laid emphasis on the fact that I had no previous convictions. Then he said, "It's been a long time since I mentioned this before. As a matter of fact it's only once in a blue moon any Judge ever mentions this and there'll be a blue moon out before I mention this again but in some cases even a verdict of not guilty is not good enough. If I was Mr Page I wouldn't be satisfied with a verdict of not guilty if I knew there was a chance of a better verdict.

"In this context I must inform you that it is possible to add an additional formula of words to a not guilty verdict such as, 'It is the opinion of this jury that there is no doubt as to the accused's innocence' ……."

After the Judge's excellent summing up in my favour, my barrister made a concluding speech during which he said that I was a young man of excellent character, who had lived a blameless life. The jury were out for about half an hour and then came back in with the verdict. "Not guilty without any doubt."

I was congratulated and hands were shaken all around. I made it my business to thank each member of the jury as they left court. I felt so up in the air that I was still operating on a high wire of nervous energy the next day. I didn't waste any time feeling sorry for the people who had lost the case. As a direct result of their petty evil my wife had had an abortion and I was out of work for eight weeks with stress-related illnesses. I used up all my annual leave attending court, it cost most of my life savings to hire a barrister and solicitor, for a week after the arrest I suffered internal bleeding and I was put on a limb in work where I was verbally attacked by the Guard's girlfriend and bullied by Harry Desmond.

<u>After the Verdict</u> You would imagine, having gone through this traumatic series of events, that I should have had a chance to return

to myself and regain my good health after the verdict. Unfortunately, what should be often never becomes reality.

The day after the trial when I was in work Harry Desmond received a phone call. I had informed him that I intended taking a High Court case against Rufus Records. During the course of his telephone conversation he assured his caller that he, Desmond, would keep the party at the other end fully informed about everything that went on. He told the caller that I had told him that I intended taking a High Court case against Rufus Records. Then he said, "I know he robbed the record. He might be able to fool a Judge and jury but he can't fool a pair of old hands at the game like us." Desmond was disappointed at the verdict but even though the trial was over he intended to stay involved in my business. His cynical malice shocked me beyond words.

The day after the phone call I let him have it. I threatened to take legal action against him and cleared out my desk. I had no intention of working for that malicious bastard again.

I told the Personnel Officer what had happened and what I heard Desmond saying to his police friend on the phone. The Personnel Officer told me I would have to continue working for Desmond. I informed that Personnel Offices that I would rather clean windows than work for that bastard again. I told the Personnel Officer that I would take all the annual leave I had left to give him the opportunity to find a new job for me.

My wife and I borrowed some money and went to Tenerife for a holiday. It cost a thousand pounds and while the complete break from our normal environment did us good, the complete collapse of my faith in the people with whom I worked stayed with me and grew as time went on.

On 13th May 1981 after I had gone back to work, in a new job, I received a threatening phone call. The man who threatened me said that if I took legal action against the Guards or Rufus Records, Ireland's Secret Police – the Special Branch – would get me. I remember that phone call particularly because it was the same day the Pope was shot. Many more threatening phone calls followed at home and at work.

Towards the end of June that year I suffered a mental breakdown. I spent a month in a psychiatric hospital. I had been told by my solicitor that legally I didn't have a case against Rufus Records. Everything the people from the shop said against me was 'privileged' and their defence against everything they did to me was to show that they had 'reasonable cause'. My solicitor said to me, "If there was negligence there has to be defamation, trespass or something else but without a witness there was no defamation. We can't sue them for malicious prosecution even though there was malice involved. You may be certain that your wife's abortion was directly attributable to your prosecution but one in every five pregnant women suffers an abortion, so you can't prove it. We can't sue them for anything. If you sue them you would probably win and be awarded 10p damages. It would only be a technical victory. You wouldn't be awarded substantial damages."

There was another matter to be taken into account and that was my mental health. My doctor and psychiatrist both advised me not to take anyone to court because it would amount to a retrial.

I was stunned by this advice but my wife agreed with the solicitor and the two doctors. However, it is now many years since I was first arrested and I still feel I want to sue Rufus Records. My son is growing up and I must show him a good example by following the best course of action. If this happened to him I would want him to sue with the best legal team he could find and afford.

I would like you to inform me – a second opinion – what my chances would be of receiving a substantial award if I sue now.

Yours faithfully
ROBERT PAGE

End of Statement

Sharon and I had a long talk about Mr Page and the tragedy that had befallen him all because he gave his custom to Rufus Records. Legally there was nothing I could do. The statute of limitations was 3 years – and that meant 3 years since his arrest. Sharon felt very sorry for him. It was a lousy outrageous thing to happen but the only comfort we could offer him was that a suit would indeed have turned into a retrial. Nevertheless it would have been good to go into the Circuit Court and let those bastards have it from both barrels. But this was not to be. The best thing Mr Page could do would be to try and forget all that had happened.

He told Sharon that he was still attending the psychiatrist and was still on medication. He hadn't received so much as an apology from anyone. He had been passed over for promotion in work because of his sick leave record and he still had nightmares about being arrested.

Sharon shook her head after I dictated a letter to Mr Page informing him that there was nothing we could do. "If only there was some way to force the owners of that record shop to pay compensation .... if only there was some way," Sharon said.

"The best we can do," I said, "is to find out who the owners are and send them a sophisticated begging letter informing them of how their prosecution has affected this young man and hope that they have some decency."

"I'll go down to the Companies Office in Dublin Castle first thing Monday morning," Sharon said.

"What he needs is a lever to force the directors of the record shop to pay him compensation," I said.

The weekend passed quickly and at noon on Monday Sharon arrived back from the Companies Office with the information we required. The shop was owned by a husband and wife team called Kennedy. Mrs Kennedy was obviously the one who had put up the capital for the business because she was Managing Director and Company Secretary. The husband, John Kennedy, was listed as a Director. In addition to their chain of record shops they were also involved in a construction company.

I wrote out a letter informing them what had befallen Mr Page, as a result of their employees' action. I told them of his wife's abortion, his illness, the expense of the litigation, the loss of income in the coming years because of his sick leave record and the suffering caused to his marriage and social life. I waited for two weeks for a reply but no reply was forthcoming.

I then decided to ring the Kennedys. When I did finally get through to them they told me to fuck off. I was surprised at their reaction and decided to have a chat with a barrister I regularly give business to. He said there was nothing he could do. The statute of limitations had run out and even if it hadn't, the shop personnel could claim 'privilege' for everything they said and 'reasonable cause' for everything they did.

I wrote a letter to Robert Page informing him of the outcome of my investigations on his behalf. Sharon typed it and expressed continued concern over our afternoon coffee.

"What that guy really needs," she said, "is a lever to force the Kennedys to pay him compensation."

"It is best not to get emotionally involved," I advised her. As usual other work had to be dealt with and I got on with it.

Imagine my surprise one week later when a very pale and distressed young man came into the office and was introduced by Sharon as Robert Page.

"The police are after me," he said. "I don't know what they are on about. I had nothing to do with it and neither had any of my friends."

I told him to slow down and tell me what happened. The police had called into his office. Seemingly they had asked him to accompany them to the police station and like a mutt he had agreed to go. The two police officers began to question him in the old one bully, one nice guy formula. The bully had begun to tell him that he knew what this was all about and if he came clean they would go easy on him. Mr Page said he didn't know what they were talking about. After a while the police 'nice guy' told him that one of the Kennedy's children had been kidnapped while out walking with his child minder. An anonymous phone call had then been made to the Kennedys informing them that if they paid compensation to Robert Page they would see their child again. If they didn't pay up they would not see their child again. The Kennedys had contacted the police and they began an investigation. Their first port of call was Robert Page's work place. Although of a nervous disposition Mr Page stood up to the interrogation fairly well.

I gave him one of my business cards and told him to inform the police that if they wanted to speak to him again they should do so through me. Sharon talked to him and calmed him down. By the time he left the office he was more in tune with himself.

Two weeks passed and Robert phoned Sharon and told her that he had received a phone call from the Kennedys. They wanted to pay him compensation. Robert told them that he would have to look into the legal position of accepting compensation under the circumstances. Mrs Kennedy had been close to tears on the phone and had implored him to tell them at the earliest possible moment that he would accept compensation. What a turn up for the books!

I drew up an agreement between the Kennedys and Mr Page which was signed by both parties and witnessed. Mr Page thought about the compensation he was due and settled for the equivalent of the top prize in the Irish lottery – a substantial sum.

The thing that frightened me most about this whole episode was the fact that I overheard Sharon making a phone call during the two weeks that the child was missing. She said, "...... He is only 5 years old and this morning he looked out at the orange juice and milk on the front door step and said, 'Look Aunty the juice man left some milk'. Isn't that cute?"

I never asked Sharon who she was talking about but it was enough to give me a nightmare that night.

Fruitcakes

Dear Friend,

I came in to my office one morning recently to find that Sharon was hovering over the post, flicking one letter through her fingers. After our usual morning greetings (sex under the desk on the deep pile carpet! How I sometimes wish it was!) She informed me of the curious letter that had arrived. It read simply:

Dear Mr Chapman

You have to do something about Michael Price. He shouldn't be locked up. He is as sane a man as you or I. His son and his son's wife have done it. They did it in order to take over his fortune. Greed is at the back of it, nothing but greed. He is locked up in Hillcrest Private Hospital, Swords, Co Dublin. You have got to do something about it. It's not right that a sane, sensible and kind old man should be locked up like that. Please do something.

Yours faithfully
Jonathan

Now it is not that I am an unsympathetic chap, but basically all I have got to sell is my services as a solicitor. I have no other income from any source and the Law Society tells me I have the right to bleed people white of their life savings to help them get out of trouble. I need the money to pay for the little luxuries of life such as the mortgage, bread, shoes and frills and fripperies like that. So when I receive a letter in the post from someone I don't know asking me to investigate God knows what, without enclosing anything resembling a fee, the only option to me is to either crumple the letter into a ball and consign it to the waste paper basket or to give it to Sharon and tell her to put it in the freaky file.

The freaky file is a file of, usually anonymous, letters which I receive from time to time. Often they contain threats from the relatives or friends of disconsolate guests of Mountjoy jail. Other times they are so far out that they defy description. I must send you a few sometime.

I forgot about Michael Price, Jonathan and whatever their problem might be until later in the week when Sharon informed me that Jonathan was on the phone. I told her to put him through.

"Am I speaking to Patrick Chapman?" the voice of a cautious middle-aged man asked me.

"Yes sir, you are," I said.

"Are you sure this phone isn't tapped?"

"It's more than likely that it isn't," I said and continued in order to put the man's mind at rest. "You see, in order for a phone to be tapped a warrant is needed and that warrant must be signed by either the Minister for Justice or the Minister for Defence. I very much doubt if either of these gents are interested in my business. You can safely tell me whatever is on your mind."

"Everything I say has to be in the strictest of confidence OK?" he said. He certainly was one frightened old bugger.

"All my business is strictly confidential," I said. "A solicitor and his client are like the priest in the confessional and the repentant sinner. So relax and tell me what the problem is."

"I have a friend. I told you his name in the letter. His son and daughter-in-law had him locked up in a looney bin but he is as sane as the President."

"I see," I said, sure that I had a right one on the line. "Why would they do that?"

"Because he is a rich man. They are after his money. You check it out. Check out every word I'm saying. If they knew I was ringing you they would probably have me knee-capped or worse. They are very dangerous people."

"I see," I said once again. By this time I was sure in my own mind that I was dealing with a man who needed a long rest, preferably under psychiatric care. "I don't think there is anything I can do."

"Yes, there is," he said. "Check it out. They took all his property away from him. They are the worse type of thieves imaginable. They robbed their own father and had him locked up."

"Right," I said. "First of all you have got to give me your name and address and all the relevant information about the case. Secondly, in return for a modest fee I will examine what has happened to see if any law has been broken and if so we can then talk about a course of action and the price of that course of action. You will appreciate I can't work for fresh air."

"OK," he said. "I'll send you some money in the post. It doesn't matter what my name is. Just call me Jonathan. The important thing is that you check it all out. Thanks." And with that the phone went dead.

I put it down and went on with the rest of my work. The following morning I received a crisp £100 note in the post. I decided since I was paid I might as well put in a little work for it. Sharon rang Hillcrest Private Hospital and found out that there actually was a Michael Price resident there. I told her to ring again and find out the visiting hours and make an appointment with Mr Price to see me. She did so and that afternoon I drove out to Swords to see Mr Price and to find out what exactly the problem was.

Hillcrest Hospital is situated in the rolling countryside of North county Dublin. There is one main driveway up to the hospital and it is guarded by a security guard who sits in a small gate cabin. The grounds of the hospital are extensive and encompass – would you believe it? – a game of crazy golf, a couple of tennis courts and a jogging path. The hospital itself looked, for all the world, like a four star hotel. The receptionist in the foyer paged Mr Price over the hospital intercom and within minutes a tall, plump man in a two piece suit with a flowing silk handkerchief from his breast pocket and a cravat came striding down the corridor to greet me. I introduced myself and explained the letter and phone call from Jonathan. He smiled with what seemed like fond affection. "Ah yes," he said. "Jonathan was my chauffeur for twenty years. When they locked me up here they put him out to grass also."

At Mr Price's instigation we went to the Writing Room. This was a comfortably appointed lounge with straight chairs and writing bureau. There was no one else there so we had the room to ourselves. I explained the reason I was there and that if anything illegal had occurred I was the man to attempt to put it right.

"They are not stupid people – my son and his wife," Mr Price said. "They planned the whole thing very carefully and executed their plan quite efficiently. You see Mr Chapman I am worth about £25 millions. I have been in property development all my life and my son knew that he was going to inherit all my wealth in good time. But unfortunately that money grabbing woman he married couldn't wait for my demise to get her hands on the loot so she devised this plot. They did it quite well." He smiled and I wondered was this the reaction of a mad man or of a chess player who admires the tactics his opponent used to defeat him. Was he out of his head or so laid back that he could admire the ingenuity of those who had knocked him for six? "They found out that all you need to get someone locked up in Ireland is the signatures of two doctors on the appropriate forms and you're in business."

"Mr Price," I asked quietly. "Have you ever had any mental illness before in your life?"

"Mr Chapman I have always had a bit of a temper but until this episode no one has ever called me insane. The only thing that is wrong with me is that I am the victim of other people's greed."

As we spoke I got the impression that I was talking to a nice elderly man who was, in the words of his old chauffeur, as sane as the President. He told me how his son and daughter-in-law had persuaded their GP and a young psychiatrist to sign on the dotted line. I later confirmed that the psychiatrist had attended university with his daughter-in-law.

"Why do they keep you in this hospital if there is nothing wrong with you?" I asked.

"Did you ever hear of one doctor contradicting another in this country? They say I am suffering from paranoid schizophrenia. To tell you the truth I never felt healthier in my life. My estate is worth £25 million and there are many people who would do worse things to get their hands on that amount of money. My daughter-in-law rules the roost in my son's home and now that she has her hands on my money she intends to keep it. If it is necessary to have me locked up for the rest of my life, so be it. She is a formidable young woman. She managed to convince people that my occasional eccentricity was enough for incarceration and so the first game goes to her." At this his eyes became troubled. He looked at me intensely and said, "Let us hope, Mr Chapman, that it is only the first game that she has won. Would you like to stay for tea?"

At first I refused and then after he had told me that I was the only visitor he had had, besides Jonathan, in the four months that he had been locked up there I detected that his invitation meant more to him than it did to me. He was a lonely man who had been shelved by people he loved and trusted and so after a little more conversation I changed my mind and decided I would stay for tea.

The dining room looked like the dining room of any top grade hotel. One wall consisted of brown tinted glass with etchings of decorative designs. As we walked down the corridor Mr Price informed me that most of the patients were alcoholics in for their annual dry-out. When we sat down at the table another man about forty five years of age and a young woman joined us. Mr Price insisted I call him Michael. The waiter came and he ordered.

"I'll have a salad – you know I like plenty of lettuce; a small helping of beetroot, a firm tomato, a boiled egg, some sweet corn and a sprinkling of diced cheese."

The middle aged chap introduced himself as Denis. "Are you a vegetarian?" he asked Michael.

"Yes," Mr Price answered.

"This is my daughter Cynthia." Denis introduced the young blonde at the table. She was about my own age.

"Why are you a vegetarian?" she asked.

"Because I don't approve of the killing of animals."

"Do you eat fish?" she asked.

"From time to time," Mr Price said.

"Eggs?"

"Of course," Michael said.

"They are the produce of animals. We are beef farmers from County Kildare."

At this Mr Price gave her a withering look up and down. "Indeed you are old girl," he said. "Indeed you are."

Tea arrived and everyone tucked in. All through the meal Cynthia disparaged Michael's vegetarian stance. Finally she came up with what seemed to be her best argument. "Scientists in America, using very sensitive equipment have discovered that every time you pluck a plant it screams. Surely that is no different from killing an animal for food?"

"It might be but it isn't. More than likely there's a strain of logic to what you say. If I fell in love with the sea would all the sunsets of the year go down in my heart? If the sky fell would we all be able to catch robins? No, my charming young lady, you are not going to seduce me to your devious ways. Let me put it in a way that a farm girl might understand: why don't you go and have a good crap and fall back into it?"

He said all this with such amused charm that when he finished we all laughed. We had a second cup of tea and before I left I promised Michael Price that I would see what I could do.

Over the next four weeks I did a lot of checking. I checked with business associates. I checked with Price's drinking companions at his local gold club. I checked with neighbours and with the few relatives I could trace. Slowly but surely I built up a picture of a wealthy man who lived a full life. When I thought the time was right I decided to pay a visit to Mr Price's old home, which was now occupied by his son Graham and his wife Martha.

They lived in Clontarf and that is one part of old Dublin that has a touch of class. As you know a public garden without walls or railings runs along the sea front. Palm trees look pleasantly out of place. Then the main road meets long gardens that lead to old fashioned houses. It was to one of these I went to meet Graham Price and his wife. When he opened the door and ushered me in I felt I knew who I was dealing with. Martha Price called from the kitchen, "Graham make sure Mr Chapman wipes his feet before stepping onto the carpet."

Graham visibly quaked before her shrill voice. The ignorance of the woman would be a great asset to any opponent in a court case. She came out of the kitchen drying her hands.

"I want to talk about your father-in-law Mrs Price."

"I don't see what business a daft old man would have with a criminal solicitor." Either she had done her own checking or my fame had travelled before me.

"That's what I would like to discuss with you." I noticed that the lounge we arrived in had many fine original paintings on the wall. If I'm not mistaken one was a Picasso and another a Miro. You could see a resemblance between Graham Price and his father but it was as if someone had taken out his backbone. He had a slight stoop and reminded me of a cornered snake – sly, afraid of being beaten to death but quite capable of making a stinging bite if the opportunity arose.

"I don't see what profit there is to gain by discussing my father-in-law's misfortune." His wife Martha was like a female version of Muhammad Ali.

"There is everything to profit or lose," I said. "Especially for you." I turned to Graham Price. "I believe you have taken over your father's estate since he was hospitalized."

"Yes we did," Martha answered. "What has any of this got to do with you?"

"I have been employed by certain people to find out a few things that will help to represent your father's point of view when the six monthly review of his case comes up."

"Six monthly review?" she said and she couldn't have looked more horrified.

"Yes," I said and decided to put the boot it. "You don't think the authorities in this country allow anyone to lock up a person forever based on the statements of a few people substantiated by old university friends?"

Graham Price looked more like the cornered snake. "My father showed all the classic symptoms of paranoid schizophrenia. He told us he was being followed by people from outer space. He befriended tramps he met in town, brought them home and gave them his own clothes and money. His behaviour became more bizarre all the time. Believe me, Mr Chapman, my father is a sick man."

"I am going to represent your father at the next review. I think he is one of the sanest men I have ever met in my life."

At that Martha Price smiled cynically. "Look, Mr Chapman, whatever fee our father has offered you to do this we'll double it. I'm sure you have gone through a lot of trouble to date on his behalf but you must know that he is in the best place at present."

"The best place for who Mrs Price? For himself or for you?" I asked.

"For everybody Mr Chapman."

"You are the one who ended up with all the money as a result of your father's convenient illness." There was no harm, I felt, in letting them know where I stood.

"You don't know what you're talking about. The man is as nutty as a fruitcake."

I decided there was no sense in going any further with this conversation. There was no way they were going to allow a peaceful resolution of the problem so I thought it best to keep my ammunition dry for the review.

The review itself lasted a lot longer than anyone thought. I called a few of Michael Price's drinking companions, business associates, and even a few cured alcoholic patients of Hillcrest Hospital to give evidence. The Hearing lasted a week and Mr and Mrs Price junior didn't know what hit them. I brought in psychiatrists to give counter opinions to the original psychiatrist with the information that he was a former university chum of the Prices junior and he visibly squirmed on the stand. In the heel of the hunt Michael Price was released from hospital and had his property returned to his control. We shook hands and he paid me my cheque.

"I'm going to celebrate tonight," he said. "And I must consult you about drawing up a new Will. That useless son of mine and that bitch he married won't get a penny. I'll leave it all to charity. Let's go for a drink."

It was late in the afternoon and as we sat and talked one drink led to a second. I was halfway down my second pint when Michael whispered to me conspiratorially. "I was talking to God last night," he began.

"There is nothing wrong with praying," I said. "They can't lock you up for it." I thought that was an appropriate pun considering all that had happened.

He then put his hand into his pocket and produced what appeared to be a map. I couldn't see what it was exactly since it was upside down. He still had that conspiratorial air about him. "I hope you aren't prejudiced against black people," he said.

"No," I said, becoming more perplexed.

I began to feel uncomfortable, but not half as uncomfortable as I felt after he said, "God told me I should give you a special gift for helping me so much – so I have decided to give you Africa." With that he turned the map towards me and it was indeed a map of the dark continent.

Best wishes,
Patrick

A Holy Clown

Dear Friend,

Ballyskerry District Courts were in full session. My favourite Justice, Mr Justice Goldberg, was in command.

The defendant was a young woman who explained that she was an alcoholic and a drug addict in recovery. She smiled a beatific grin, not unlike that worn by the Mona Lisa as she stated with calm:

'I'm completely clean now, Justice.'

'Do you intend keeping your nose clean in the future?' the Justice asked.

'Immaculately clean Justice.'

'I believe you,' said the Justice, smiling, and then as if it might be amusing he said, 'You have told me that the only reason you ever committed acts of theft was to feed your drug habit. I don't expect to ever see you in the dock here again. You have convictions for shoplifting, handbag snatching and pocket picking – tell me now, what was the funniest thing that ever happened to you in your former life of crime?'

'Well Justice, I went into a major department store in Dublin and went behind the counter when the staff were on their coffee break and took a handful of large plastic bags with the shop's logo. Then I went around the shop and filled the bags with three suits and fifteen sweaters – they were very easy to sell around the flats at bargain prices.

'The shop had a uniformed doorman – I suppose they call him a commissionaire or a hall porter Justice. I was weighed down with the bags Justice and as I tried to go out the door the porter rushed to my assistance and held the door open for me. Then seeing the load of bags of clothes I had he smiled and said, "Come back again," and I said, "I certainly will!"

We all laughed. The Justice wished her well and off she went.

One thing Justices dislike, given their middle class sensibilities, is when a crime involves violence. The next young man into the dock was convicted of a crime involving violence.

'I'm convicting you,' said the Justice. 'Now can you think of any reason why I shouldn't send you to jail?'

'Well, yes I can Justice. My wife has just had a baby.'

'Congratulations.'

'Thanks very much Justice.'

'And are they both well?'

'They are thank God Justice.'

'Right, well they don't need you.' Down came the gavel. 'Twenty eight days,' said the Justice. 'Take him down.'

That was funny in a cruel sort of way. Merriment was high on the solicitor's bench.

Next into the dock was Charlie Chaplin. There he stood dressed as the little tramp holding his bowler hat and cane in his hands. His moustache, bow tie, curly hair and suit were all in black. His face and shirt were white.

The Guard gave evidence that Charlie was flogging books of poetry in Grafton Street without a street trader's licence. He was arrested and charged. When asked if he wished to make a statement in the police station he said the following:

'Once upon a time a Rabbi went to the market place at Lapet. One day, much to his surprise, the prophet Elijah appeared to him there. After their greetings were exchanged they looked around at all the people, customers and businessmen, buying and selling there.

'The Rabbi asked Elijah:

"Is there anyone among all these people who will have a share in the World-To-Come?"

'Elijah answered:

"There is none."

'Later two men came to the marketplace and Elijah said to the Rabbi:

"Those two will have a share in the World-To-Come!"

'The Rabbi asked the newcomers:

"Gentlemen, what is your occupation?"

'They replied:

"We are clowns, sir. When we see someone who is sad, we cheer him up. When we see two people quarrelling we try to make peace between them".'

'That's a lovely statement,' said the Justice.

Charlie was representing himself so the Justice said:

'Would you like to ask the Guard any questions?'

'I would Justice,' said Charlie. 'Do you know the essence of the Old Testament Guard?'

'I don't,' said the Guard.

'Would it surprise you to know it is found in the Book of Micah, chapter 6 verse 10 and goes as follows:

"What does the Lord require of you but to do justly, to love goodness and to walk humbly with your God."?'

'Very good.'

'A rabbi once said, "This is the whole of the Law; all the rest is commentary." Did you know that Guard?'

'I didn't but I do now.'

'Do you know what the essence of the New Testament is Guard?'

'You're going to tell me.'

'I am. Love the Lord with all your heart and with all your mind and with all your strength and love your neighbour in the same way that you love yourself.'

'Fair enough.'

'Do you know what the first article of the Irish Constitution is?'

'I don't.'

'The Irish Nation hereby affirms its inalienable, indefeasible and sovereign right to choose its own form of government, to determine its relations with other nations and to develop its life, political, economic and cultural, in accordance with its own genius and tradition.'

'That's more than I ever learned in school.'

'Are you aware officer that the Irish Constitution bestows on all of us, as citizens, the right to earn our living, the right to our good name, the inviolability of the home, the right to free expression of our opinions, the right to form associations and unions, the right to personal liberty, the right to freedom of religion and the right to private property?'

'I knew that.'

'Justice my right to earn a living is a constitutional right and since I submit the Street Trader's Licence Act is a nullity because Dublin Corporation does not have the power to extract a fee from me for a licence to do something that I already have a constitutional right to do. I rest my case.'

The Justice was nonplussed. There was a pause while Charlie's statement sunk in.

'You could be right,' he finally said. 'It would take a very learned constitutional lawyer to contradict you. Since I am not one of them you have raised a reasonable doubt in my mind and I am dismissing the charge.'

'Did I make sense there Justice?'

'No but you were very consistent.'

'God bless Justice.'

'God bless son.'

Charlie shuffled out of court but not before landing a flicking arse-kick to the next defendant into the dock.

Outside the court Charlie opened his briefcase and began selling his books of poems. I bought one and bought it down to the basement restaurant of the Four Courts. I had a smoke and a cup of coffee.

One of Charlie's Poems:

If you think you are beaten – you are.
If you think you dare not – you don't.
If you'd like to win but think you can't
It's almost a cinch you won't.
Life's battles don't always go
To the stronger or faster man
But sooner or later the man who wins
Is the one who thinks he can.

The End.

Drugs

Dear Friend,

The abuse of drugs is a dreadful menace to every young person in our society.

Do you know how the term 'cold turkey' and 'kicking the habit' first arose? Allow me to tell you.

The addict, like the mentally ill, often come before the courts. In between their first appearance in court and their trial it is good legal strategy to have them treated, quite apart from human and medical considerations.

Patrick Hamilton was a young man who came to me charged with possession and distributing 'controlled substances'. He was an addict and pusher of a line of illicit drugs. When I met him I noted he had the weasel face and scrawny body of a malnourished addict. He had long, blond hair and a wispy bear. I managed to persuade the court to release him on his own bail and he agreed, after a little persuasion to come with me to a drug treatment centre. I drove him in my car to the centre and he made a pathetic plea that I should stay with him for a while. He imagined he would get some methadone to help him in his withdrawal phase, but the centre I brought him to believes in 'tough love'. I stayed with him as requested.

Twelve hours after his last injection of heroin he began to grow restless and paced up and down his small room. A male nurse wrestled him back to bed every time he made a lunge at the door. He grew weak and began to yawn and shiver and sweat. A watery discharge poured from his nose and eyes. Then he fell into a restless sleep. The male nurse and I chatted while my namesake went through this phase of his private hell. When he awoke he yawned so violently that he dislocated his jaw. Mucous poured from his nose and tears from his eyes. The hair on his skin stood up and his skin became cold. Gooseflesh covered every area of his body and this is where the phrase 'cold turkey' came from.

I went home and came back the following day. It was now thirty six hours after his last infection. He was an awful sight. His bowels had reacted with extraordinary violence and he had passed fifty large watery stools. The contractions of a pregnant woman in labour are mild compared to the contractions of an addict's stomach, going through withdrawal. The pain was severe and his stomach looked as if a colony of snakes were involved in a civil war beneath his skin. His whole body shook and twitched and his legs kicked involuntarily. This phase of withdrawal has led to the phrase 'kicking the habit'.

Pat Hamilton spent many months experiencing the tough love of the recovery centre and still faced a future of many years in jail. However, unlike every other addict and pusher I have represented, his is a story with a heartening ending. After a few months of keeping in touch and chatting with him he asked me had I ever heard of the Full Gospel Businessmen's Fellowship International? I told him that not only had I heard of it but I was a member in good standing of the Dublin West Chapter. He said, "That's great. Will you bring me to a meeting?"

I discussed the matter with the therapy centre's Board and when the time came to take a gamble on allowing Pat out under supervision, I brought him to a meeting in the West County Hotel.

We sat in the back of the room and enjoyed a meal of chicken and peas and chips, dessert and coffee. The tables were laid out in the E shape with the committee members at the top table. Out of deference to recovering alcoholics nobody drinks alcohol at the meetings. Pat and I were on Seven-up.

After a meal a few speakers gave their testimony as to how Jesus Christ had positively changed their lives. The main speaker was a Methodist minister who had been an alcoholic – a completed down-and-out. He became a Christian and with help recovered to such an extent that he was allowed to train as a Minister of Religion. I looked at Pat a few times during the speaker's testimony. He was totally absorbed. At the end of the testimony when the minister asked if any non-Christian would like to accept the friendship of the living Jesus Christ, Pat's hand shot up in the air. The minister led the meeting in a short prayer and made a bee-line for Pat. He gave him some Christian literature, laid his hands on Pat's head and said a prayer of healing. He told Pat that his new life had just begun and that all the promises of the Bible were now meant for the new Pat Hamilton.

I told the minister Pat's story. He promised to visit the new bright-eyed young man at the therapy centre and to help him through his difficulties. "What's impossible with men is quite possible with God," he said.

Pat's new Christian friends visited him regularly over the next couple of months. He became a changed man. He got his hair cut, shaved off his wispy beard, put on weight and exercised regularly. He located a job and eventually went into court with me, praising Jesus for his new life and faith.

I felt nervous. I felt certain he was going to jail for a long time. We sat in the court before a crusty old judge who was notorious for dishing out large dollops of porridge to drug pushers.

We waited our turn – Pat, the minister, and a few Full Gospel Businessmen. Two cases of possession of hard drugs preceded Pat's case. The defendants tried to pull the wool over the Judge's eyes by pleading not guilty. They were convicted and given long prison sentences. There was a mumble 0f prayer from the minister. "Lord you promised in Roman 8:28 that all things would work together for good for those who love you. Please work out the truth of your Word for Pat right now." the minister held Jesus to his Word and expected the best.

"How do you plead?" the Judge asked Pat with a hint of malice in his voice.

"Guilty, my Lord," said Pat. The Judge nearly toppled over.

"Guilty?" he asked, astonished. "Do you want to give up your right to be tried by a Judge and jury?"

"Yes, my Lord," said Pat. "You see I know I am guilty and I prefer to take whatever medicine you care to dish out."

The minister went into a high speed prayer of thanks for the life of the accused and the businessmen and I praised the Lord. The Judge was shaken by Pat's honesty. This was a new experience for him. He read the charge sheets laid before him and now and again shot questions at Pat.

"Did you sell drugs to a member of the drugs squad?"

"I did, sir."

"Did your solicitor, Mr Chapman, tell you that if you threw yourself on the mercy of the Court that I would go easy on you?"

"No, sir. No one ever said any such thing."

The Judge got back his determination. "A good job," he said, "because I'm never lenient with drug pushers. You're going to get what I give to every pusher who comes before me."

Prayers of praise and thanksgiving continued unabated behind be back. The Judge turned his ire on me. "Well what have you got to say?" I opened by briefcase and took out my Bible – it is one of a few different translations I own.

"I've got something very important to tell you, my Lord," I began. "The young man who strands before you is not the same young man who sold the drugs to the Guard six months ago!"

The Judge looked lost. He said, "Come again. Are you saying that this is a case of mistaken identity?" Then he answered his own question. "That couldn't be, the young man has pleaded guilty." He was baffled.

"What I mean, my Lord, is that a few months ago this young man became a Christian and the old drug pusher Pat Hamilton is dead. What you see before you is a new man in Christ." The Judge nearly fainted but I pressed on. I opened my Bible at second Corinthians, Chapter Five, verse seventeen and told the Judge what quotation I was reading. "If anyone is in Christ, he is a new creation; the old has gone, the new has come!"

Boy, did that blow the Judge's mind. In all his years on the bench no one had ever tried this one on him before.

Pat spoke up from the dock. "My Lord, three months ago I died to this world and gained an eternal life in Jesus Christ by becoming one of His friends. I am a completely new man!"

Did we freak out that Judge? He didn't know what to say.

"The old Pat is dead my Lord," I said. "The Pat Hamilton you see before you is a new creature in Christ. He has been born again. The

Word of God confirms it." We blew that unfortunate Judge's mind. He decided it was time to change the subject.

"Have you got a job by any chance?"

"Yes, my Lord. I'm a brick layer. We are building an extension to the drug rehabilitation centre I lived in before I became a new man."

"He is doing hard manual word," the Judge spoke to himself. We were reaching him where he lived, as the saying goes. A buzz of praise and gratitude was going on behind me. "If I was to suspend your sentence, you'd have to promise me never to go near that pub again."

It was in a pub that Pat had been arrested.

"My Lord," said Pat. "I'm afraid I would have great difficulty keeping to that undertaking. You see since I became filled with the Spirit I want to tell everyone about the wonderful chance that is available to them by becoming a friend of Jesus Christ. Only a few nights ago I was in that same pub and I met a young couple who were friends in my old addict days. They were so sick of the life they had, stealing to feed their habits, trying to find a vein to inject, hiding from the police, that they decided to end it all. I gave them my testimony about the love of Jesus and although they had told me that they were so miserable that they had entered into a suicide pact, they changed their minds. They so envied me my new life that they didn't commit suicide, they accepted Jesus Christ as their personal saviour and Lord of their lives. Today, they are on their way to maturity as Christians."

"Praise the Lord!" said one of the Full Gospel Businessmen. "Praise the Holy Name of Jesus!"

"That is wonderful," said the, by now, much subdued Judge. "You could be a blessing to many – case dismissed." The Judge blew his nose into a large white handkerchief. The minister, Christian businessmen, Pat and I gave thanks.

Best wishes,
Patrick

Rape Cases

Dear Friend,

When I was a student just finished secondary school I wasn't sure what to do with my life. I was employed temporarily as a labourer in a local factory for the summer. The hiring and firing policy was a straight forward one of first in, first out. So, in mid-August, I found myself unemployed again. I decided, since my Leaving Certificate results would be out shortly, to investigate a few careers that I suspected might suit me.

One day I made my way to Court No. 15, Chancery Place. Then, as now, that Court was the Circuit Criminal Court. I sat down at the back of the Court and watched the drama that unfolded.

It was 11am and the jury had all been sworn in. The prosecution barrister began his case by calling a Garda Sergeant. The Sergeant outlined what had happened on a specific recent evening. He had been in the police station when a young woman of 18 years of age had come in and complained of having been raped. He took her statement and called the local doctor. The statement he took from the girl was extraordinarily graphic. It wasn't until a few years later that I learned that this is how these things are conducted. The only other place I have come across a similar sort of graphic statement was in a pornographic novel.

Next on the list of witnesses came the doctor who took a vaginal swab and confirmed that intercourse had taken place. He also gave evidence of bruising on the girl's thighs. After the doctor, the raped girl entered the witness box and gave her side of the story. It was typical of such cases. She worked as a barmaid in a pub three miles from her home out in the country. She finished worked late one night and her boss who usually gave her a lift home was sick with flu. So she headed home on foot and hitched a lift from a local man who had been in the pub earlier. Seemingly, halfway home the man pulled the car over and tried to kiss her. She tolerated this as she thought it was the price she had to pay for her lift home and she didn't want to risk the violent response by making too strident a protest. The man then placed his hand inside her blouse, unhooked her bra and tired to feel her breasts. Her job entailed wearing a white blouse and a black skirt. Like me, she had just finished school and the barmaid job was a temporary summer one. The man then placed his hand up her skirt, tore off her pants and proceeded to rape her.

All the time she and the other prosecution witnesses gave their evidence the accused sat quietly in the dock. The Judge took notes and made the occasional comment or asked a clarifying question. But the real focus of people's attention, beside the witness, was the defence solicitor. Although it is usual for people to have a barrister in the Circuit Court, a solicitor has equal right of audience. Possibly because of lack of funds, or because of his faith in his solicitor, the man, whose name was Reynolds, didn't have a barrister. The solicitor was well into his sixties and, although I didn't know it at the time, he was known as Archie the Actor. His modus operandi was to sit at his bench and make assorted noises clearing his nose and throat, folding and unfolding his legs, thumping the floor with the soles of his shoes and finally fiddling with his hearing aid so that it made a whistling noise. Whenever a statement of a fairly damning nature was being made old Archie turned up the whistle on his hearing aid full blast. This distracted the jury and made it almost impossible to hear what was going on. The Judge himself was an elderly man and occasionally gave daggers looks to the defence solicitor, but since it appeared as though he was merely trying to fix his hearing aid so that he could hear with it, the Judge said nothing.

In addition to this trick Archie the Actor was a sight to behold. He wore a three piece black suit with a watch chain across the front. Although going towards pension age, it was obvious he took great pride in his appearance. He cross-examined the Sergeant, the doctor and the raped woman with great élan, playing to the gallery and the jury box all the time. But he really came into his own when the accused took the stand. He asked his client, "Are you a married man, sir?"

"Yes," replied Reynolds.

"Is your wife standing by you through this grotesque ordeal?"

"Yes, she is."

"Is she in Court at the moment?"

"I think so," said the accused, squinting out into the body of the Court. "Yes, she is," he confirmed when he had spotted her.

"Will you point in the general direction your wife is sitting?"

He pointed. Naturally enough the wife had been placed close to the jury box where they could all see her.

"Please ask her to stand up."

"Stand up Jessica," said Reynolds. Jessica stood up and for the first time those of us sitting at the back of the Court could see he was holding a baby in her arms. She was a pretty woman in her mid thirties with light blonde hair. The child was the sort of cute child they use in nappy advertisements. The women on the jury were misty eyed with admiration.

"That's your wife standing there holding the infant is it?" asked Archie.

"Yes," replied the accused.

You could see the prosecution was barely holding himself in check. None of this evidence had anything to do with the case, but he didn't want to risk alienating the jury by bluntly objecting.

Then came the prosecution's chance to cross-examine. Archie sat down and produced a bottle of pills. He rattled them and shook them before taking off the lid. He cleared his throat and blew his nose. Then to his later cost he began fiddling with his hearing aid until he had it whistling noisily. He didn't want anyone to hear anything that the cross-examination delivered. He juggled his silk handkerchief and proceeded to blow his nose again. All the time the young prosecution barrister tried to cross-examine to the best of his ability. Despite Archie's antics the prosecution struck gold and began to mine it.

He asked the defendant, "How many times a week do you and your wife make love?"

The defendant swallowed hard and looked frightened as he replied, "We don't ..... ever."

"Why is that?"

The defendant blushed and stammered, "Because we've separated."

"How long have you been separated?"

"Two years."

"That baby your wife has in her arms. Are you the father?"

"No," said the defendant. "But just in case anybody thinks my wife is a loose living woman I have to say that it's not her baby. My solicitor told her it would help my case if she brought a baby to Court. So despite our differences in the past we have a chance of coming back together after this case is over .... if everything goes all right."

The prosecutor looked at the jury to see if they had taken in the bit about the baby. The foreman of the jury was shaking his head in amazement and was smiling broadly. Meanwhile, Archie the Actor was still fiddling with his whistling hearing aid in his hands and wasn't hearing a word of this fatal testimony.

The prosecutor decided to underline the vital evidence. "Your solicitor told your wife to bring the baby to Court?"

"Yes. He must have thought it would have helped."

"Is your wife employed?"

"Oh yes. She has a good job. She is a librarian."

"Do you have any children?"

"Yes, one. She is twelve years old and I give my wife some money every month for her support."

"But your wife has a good job and is able to support herself?"

"Correct."

There was some more testimony from the defendant. He admitted he made love to the girl, but claimed it was with her consent. When asked to explain how her underwear was torn, he coughed and blushed and stammered that he didn't know; he couldn't remember.

After the defendant stepped down from the witness box the Judge invited the prosecutor and the defence to make their closing arguments. For this Archie the Actor put his hearing aid back in and the prosecutor, to everybody's surprise, didn't say anything about the baby. All he did was wink at the jury foreman as he was finishing up and said, "I hope sentimentality about babies won't cloud your judgement concerning the facts of the case."

It was time for Archie to make his summing up speech. I noticed some more people came in to Court to listen to him so he must have been famous. He began off with a quotation, "My Lord, ladies and gentlemen of the jury, in 1884 a man named Robert C Ingersoll write 'Justice should remove the bandage from her eyes long enough to distinguish between the vicious and the unfortunate'," it was unfortunate for his client that he had been seduced by a young Jezebel who then decided to shout rape. It was unfortunate that his client faced the prospect of hearing the clang of prison gates behind his back. It was unfortunate that in the heat of passion motives were sometimes misunderstood. It was unfortunate that women sometimes uttered a feeble no when what they meant was a resounding yes.

Then he began praising the sacredness of family life and we were really off to the races. "Who among us has the heart to cloud this little baby's life with the knowledge that her father was a convicted criminal and missed the occasion of her first tooth, her first step and her first words because he was languishing in some draughty prison cell?"

This sweep of oratory was met by wide smiles, nudges and glances by members of the jury. Archie wasn't looking at them and didn't notice. Terrific ham that he was.

Then he went over to the defendant's wife, took the baby out of her hands, held it up for the jury to survey and asked, "Who among us has the right to blight this baby's life?" For the next ten minutes it was corny sentimentality and Archie never once noticed the fun her was provoking in the jury box. On and on he went in a flight of gooey rhetoric. At one point he removed his hankie from his top pocket and brushed away an imaginary tear. The defendant squirmed in the dock as he listened to his freedom slipping away but even he seemed to be hypnotised by the booming voice and theatrical antics of his solicitor. A break seemed to develop in his voice as he finished up his speech. Cyril Cusack couldn't have done it better. Here was a master actor giving of his best but it was all to no avail.

The jury were out for half an hour and the defendant missed the child's first tooth, first step and first words just as surely a he would have were he not sentenced to 8 years in Mountjoy jail. You should have seen the look on Archie's face when the verdict was brought in. It registered disbelief and shock. "Where did I go wrong?" he seemed to be asking and no doubt his client told him in colourful terms later when he visited him in the cells beneath the Court to say goodbye.

Best wishes,
Patrick

P.S. This case was one of those that brought me to the belief that a life invested in the law was one that brought with it the promise of intellectual stimulation along with a bit of occasionally indecent entertainment – an intoxicating mixture. I'm sure that listening to Archie the Actor trying to make a few bricks out of straw brought home to me how important a job a good solicitor or barrister can make of attempting to prevent a client from being banged up with his own chamber pot in a cell with two psychopaths. It amazed me to think how people generally don't ascribe life-saving qualities to lawyers. Yet that is precisely what Archie was trying to do. If Reynolds had been acquitted there was a possibility that he might have been reconciled with his wife and kept his lively paws and prick to himself for ever after. However, that was not to be the case. As the Judge said, before he passed sentence, Reynolds would have to live for a few years by the knowledge of his misdeeds underlined to him by the nature of his address, whereas his victim would have to live with the memories and nightmares of her victimisation for the rest of her life.

I remain your friend,
Patrick

Dear Friend,

I have just gone through a case that could have been disturbing to me if I had let the soft side of my nature show. But I didn't. I remained hard as nails throughout the whole proceedings.

Harry Carling is a twenty two year old client who was accused of rape. Although he is a university student from a respectable family and has all the appearances of a wholesome, clean-cut, middle class boy, there was something about him that I didn't like right from the start.

You know the saying, 'he is too sweet to be wholesome'? Well that is the phrase that came to mind as I wrote up the brief for the barrister.

Harry Carling is a spoiled boy. It could be said that university students, except for farmers, are the most subsidised members of our society. There is a common consensus among the establishment that we need a skilled middle class in order to maintain the status quo in society, so we subsidise the education of all the bright young things.

Harry Carling was given a new car by his parents for his twenty first birthday. It was in this car that the alleged offence took place. One night last summer Harry got a touch of the hots and drove to a pub in a rough and tumble working class district of Dublin. He chatted up one of the waitresses and offered her a lift home. On the way home he drove down a back laneway and said, none too seductively, "Are you going to take your knickers off or am I?"

When the seventeen year old girl to whom he said this told him to go to hell and tried to get out of the car he punched her in the face and broke her jaw. The second time he asked her to strip off the unfortunate girl did so, in fear of her life. The girl was a virgin and despite Harry's best efforts of pushing and shoving he was unable to penetrate her. He drove her near her home and sped away. However, the young girl got his registration plate number. The girl made it to her home on wobbly legs and received assistance from her family.

Some weeks later, after her jaw had been wired up and healed a good deal, the girl managed to tell the police her story. They arrested young Mr Carling and charged him with assault and battery and rape. Mr Carling's defence was that the girl consented. She had wanted to make love. How had her jaw been broken? Easy to answer by a resourceful Mr Carling. "She must have fallen when he was getting out of the car. You see she was very drunk." Young Mr Carling had been raised with the idea that the middle class were never wrong when it comes to dealing with the lower orders. He was so much more intelligent be believed, and that was the rock on which he perished.

The prosecution had the young girl tell her story and it went flown well with the jury. Her employer had testified that she had not had any alcohol to drink that fateful night. The doctor who examined her at the hospital gave evidence of bruising and tearing in the genital region although the girl was still a virgin. He also confirmed that the girl had not smelled of alcohol. I had informed Mr Carling that if he was found guilty his 'not guilty' plea would not go down well with the Judge. He protested his innocence and expressed his determination to plead not guilty. I had tried to warn him but to no avail.

There comes a point in every court case where the defendant is on his own. Either he finds favour with the Judge and jury or he sinks in their estimation. Harry Carling took the witness stand all smiles and cocky confidence. He was led through his story by his own barrister and he told quite a different tale to the young girl. Some of the jury softened towards him. Then came cross-examination by the prosecution.

The prosecution began by making a joke. "It is said by some that many older Americans come to Ireland each summer looking for their roots. It is also said that younger Americans come looking for their nuts."

The jury smiled.

"That's what you were out looking for that night Mr Carling wasn't it? Weren't you out to get your nuts?"

"No, I wasn't."

"Weren't you out to get your rocks off and it didn't matter to you whether this young woman co-operated or not?"

"It did matter to me, I seduced her. I didn't rape her."

"Breaking a girl's jaw with a punch is your idea of seduction?"

"I didn't punch her, she fell, she was drunk."

At this the prosecutor went closer to the witness box.

"Have you ever got away with it before Harry? Ever got your dad to pay off some working class family and persuaded them by cheque book not to prosecute?"

"Objection," said Mr Carling's barrister.

"You know better than that," said the Judge to the prosecutor.

"Sorry, my Lord," said the prosecutor. Then he took another tack, "You're a good looking boy, aren't you Harry?"

Harry smiled and said, "I have been told that before once or twice."

"You're a wholesome, clean-cut boy. Aren't you Harry?"

"I like to think I am." He was all self deprecating modesty.

"You like girls don't you Harry?"

"Yes, I do." A sheepish smile again. "And they like me too."

"Did you ever see this girl before the night of the incident?"

"No, I did not."

"Pretty fast worker aren't you Harry?"

"Yes, I am."

"Did you use a Johnny the night you seduced her?"

"A what?"

"A prophylactic? A Frenchie? What we might call a rubber or a johnny?"

"Yes, I did, but it worked it's way off."

"Do you usually carry a packet around with you?"

"No, that was the first night I ever carried them."

He was confident and sparring well but his overweening confidence was to be his undoing.

"Why did you have a packet of johnnies with you that night?"

"Because I didn't want to catch a venereal disease from any fast-living girl."

"Like the plaintiff for instance?"

"Yes, like her."

The prosecution was feeding him enough rope to hang himself.

"Tell me Harry, why did you drive up the darkened laneway?"

"She told me to. She said she wanted me to kiss her."

"Was she any good at kissing?"

"Yes, except she smelled of alcohol."

He was trying to regain ground when the prosecutor released more rope.

"Who was the first to drop the hand?"

"I believe it was the girl. Yes, it was. Yes I remember now, it was the girl."

"Did either of you say anything?"

"Yes, she said, 'I want you to be my lover'!"

This was so phoney. The jury members began to look at each other. The prosecuting barrister walked over to the jury and faced Harry Carling.

"Let us recap. She asked you to drive down the laneway. She started the kissing. She dropped the hand first. She practically forced you to have sex with her, didn't she?"

"Yes."

The prosecutor saw the jury's faces harden but he pushed ahead.

"If there was any justice in the world she should be on trial here today instead of you, shouldn't she?"

"Yes" the egotistical little bastard had just gone too far.

"Did you hear the doctor telling the ladies and gentlemen of the jury that the young girl was a virgin?"

"I heard that."

"Did you hear the doctor telling us about the tearing and bruising?"

"Yes, but it was her own fault. She was the one who was rough."

He was desperate and letting his mouth say the first thing that came into his head. The prosecutor had young Mr Carling just where he wanted him.

"Would you mind telling my Lord, and the jury why this seventeen year old, respectable girl should choose you to give away her virginity to?"

Heatedly, "I don't bloody well know!" He clenched his fists and looked as if he would love to do violence to the prosecution.

"She is a real slut in your opinion, isn't she?"

"Yes."

The revulsion and hardening of the jury's attitudes was palpable. Harry Carling's goose was well and truly cooked. His massive egotism was his downfall. No jury in their right mind could let him off.

In the fullness of time the jury returned to the jury box and handed down a verdict of guilty. It didn't surprise me and there was no sense in appealing to the High Court.

Harry Carling's address for the next 7 years is Mountjoy Jail. He has shown no ounce of remorse or contrition but he has plenty of time to regret his actions.

Best wishes,
Patrick

Burglars

Dear Friend,

I have just had a triumph down in Ballyskerry Courts that you wouldn't believe. As you know, my life is normally spent making useless mitigation's on behalf of the guilty, or trying to make bricks out of a straw-filled alibi or trying to convince some scruff to wash himself and wear his Sunday suit to court. If it wasn't for the money and the fact that I don't know how to do anything else I swear I would never again be seen near the grey grained buildings of Chancery Place.

Sometimes I sit back in my office and fantasize. I ask myself, what would I really like to do with my life? Over the years the answer has changed and become more realistic.

One fantasy is that I am the owner of a substantial commercial property. I own a block of apartments, filled with good tenants who don't wreck the place or whine about the plumbing, and live the good life on the income. I always think property owners have it both ways. It is like having your cake and eating it too. On the one hand, they have the income popping through the letter box once a month and on the other hand they always continue to own the property.

However, enough of fantasy for the time being, and back to the smelly old courts. My client was a 40 year old man named John West. He had a fatalistic defeatist attitude to his plight. Although he told me a story that was hard to believe, because he didn't try hard to convince me, I was certain of his innocence. Unfortunately he had some form – as we in legal circles call previous convictions – and they were all for robbery, which is what he present charge was also. The man actually wanted to plead guilty and get it over with, until I convinced him we had a chance. Usually it is the other way round, with me trying to convince some hopeless chancer that he would be better off taking the medicine than brazening it out against the Guards and witnesses. But this guy was such a negative thinker that I had to invent past successes of a similar nature in order to pep talk him around to a 'not guilty' plea. He allowed me to convince him and so we were off to the races.

The Clerk called out in the crowded court, "Guard John Finnegan versus John West."

The Justice decided it was joke time.

"I hope this is not the John West of tinned salmon fame." The Guards, always certain of 91 convictions out of 100, laughed and thumped each other on the shoulder. Mr Justice Blocker was encouraged. "There are some left wing politicians who say that a working class man voting for a Conservative politician is like a fish voting for John West or a chicken voting for Colonel Saunders." He received his response from his audience and even I had to admit it wasn't the worse kind of comment to be heard from the bench.

"Right Mr West, how do you plead?" asked the Justice.

"Not guilty," replied my client.

"Right," repeated the Justice and stamped the form in front of him. His expression seemed to say, 'We'll see about this!'.

The Guard swore on the Bible, got up on the witness stand and proceeded to give his evidence.

"I was patrolling a back lane to a row of shops in Stillorgan at 12 midnight on Thursday 30th October when I noticed the defendant coming out of the back entrance of one shop with a pair of leather suitcases in his hands. The defendant stopped dead in the lights of the patrol car. When challenged he made no statement Justice. The suitcases were found to be full of goods which the shop owner later identified to be his, in addition to identifying the suitcases. The contents consisted of shirts, trousers, sweaters and clock radios. I arrested the defendant, advised him of his right and transported him and the stolen goods to the station."

That was the essence of the policeman's statement. It may not be word perfect, but it was there or thereabouts. The Justice asked me would I like to cross-examine. "If it please the Justice, not right now," I said, "but perhaps later on, after my client has given evidence the Guard might be recalled for a few questions."

"Very well," said the Justice agreeably. Next it was the defendant's turn to tell his side of the story and, after being sword, he told the following tale.

"Justice my name is John West, I am 40 years of age and I live with my wife and 4 children at 250 Glen Parade, Stillorgan. When I was younger I got into trouble with the police for stealing cigarettes from a vending machine in a local pool hall. I was also convicted for importing pornographic magazines one time even though the quantity was small and they were for my own use only. So, as you can see, the police and I have not had a good relationship in the past.

"The evening I was arrested I went down the lane behind the shopping centre to relieve myself. I have a weak bladder Justice. After I zipped myself up I noticed two men piling stuff into a station wagon from the back door of the shop in question. I shouted at them, "What are you fellows doing there?" and in response the two of them shouted obscenities at me, jumped into the station wagon and drove off.

I saw that they had left two suitcases outside the laneway so I thought to myself if I leave them there somebody is going to pinch them. I picked them up and was just about to bring them back into the shop when I was challenged by the Guard."

He stopped. The court waited for him to continue but there was no more to the story. The Judge looked the defendant up and down as if to say, that's the hairiest one I've heard in a long time.

"I didn't tell the police the story because I knew they wouldn't believe me," Me West added.

The Judge turned to me and asked, "Well Mr Chapman, what magic are you going to perform to make this story stick?"

I smiled, like a lickarse, and said, "No magic at all Justice but perhaps, with your assistance, a tragic miscarriage of justice could be averted here today. I would now like to cross examine Guard Finnegan."

Guard Finnegan went back to the witness box, after my client had returned to the dock. The Guard looked at me with mistrust and caution. There was no way he was going to be tricked out of a solid conviction that might help his promotion prospects.

"I'm sorry to ask you to come back to the witness stand Guard, but there is just one small point I would like to clear up. You say when you first saw my client he was stopped dead in your headlights?"

"That's correct," said the Guard, "but he was coming out of the shop, not going in."

"How do you know that Guard?"

"I know that because he was facing outwards and not inwards." The Guard was adamant. He felt himself to be on sure ground.

Just then Sharon, my secretary, came into court carrying a heavy suitcase. She tripped the light fantastic out the swing doors to the court and came back in carrying a second suitcase. She placed both in front of the Guard. The suspicion grew in his eyes while the rest of the court looked on with interest.

"I'm sorry to trouble you again Guard," I said, "but perhaps you would show the court the way things were that night. I would be grateful Justice, if the Guard would take these two suitcases out to the adjoining hallway and bring them back into court to demonstrate the way things were that night behind the shop in Stillorgan."

"The Guard can do so if he likes but he needn't feel compelled," the Justice said. It seemed to me he was anxious to bang his gavel, convict and sentence. The Guard decided there was nothing to be lost so he came down the steps of the witness stand and took up the two suitcases. "I would be grateful if no one assisted the Guard in this task," I said, raising my voice to make sure the Guards lined up on the bench beside the door stayed in their places and didn't spoil the experiment.

There is one thing you should know about Ballyskerry District Courts in order to appreciate what I am going to tell you and that is that the doors are swing doors that open in and out both ways, while closing by themselves very swiftly.

The Guard, laden down with the two suitcases, ready to return them to the hallway, walked over to the doors. He put one of the suitcases down and opened the door. It swung closed. He picked up the two suitcases and tried to walk through the doors using his head as a battering ram to open the doors. It didn't work. Finally he decided to kick open the doors and swing around in full circle to use his bum to stop the doors closing. As he did so, I shouted at him, "Stop Guard!" He did so, very surprised and huffed that anyone should shout at him, a member of the police force on his own stamping ground. I turned to the Justice and said, "Justice just because Guard Finnegan is facing in doesn't mean he is coming in. In the same way just because my client was facing out doesn't mean that he was coming out on the night in question. I suggest to the Justice that Guard Finnegan's behaviour must raise a reasonable doubt and I plead with you Justice that that doubt be given in favour of my client."

I sat down with some satisfaction. T he experiment had worked. The Justice had to agree and so my client regained that freedom which had been at risk.

The unfortunate Guard stood with his bum to the door for a long time before Sharon and I took the suitcases from him.

Best wishes for now,
Patrick

Courtroom Dramas:
General Cases

Dear Friend,

Let me start by saying, I believe in the Probation Service. It gives first time offenders a chance they mostly deserve and need. It provides and alternative to incarceration or a fine and allows a judge to take extenuating circumstances into account and to use his discretion. After all, there is a whale of a difference between some middle class university students committing crimes out of a sense of high spirits and some unfortunate working class man with an eviction order hanging over his head or some poor housewife out of her reason with worry over the impossible challenge of meeting an electricity bill or putting food on the table for her family. A probation officer can help an offender to get a grip on life. He or she can help the person to organise and put some meaningful structure on to their everyday existence.

However, one probation defaulter turned up on my doorstep recently. The probation officer had some rather esoteric notions about the effectiveness of psychodrama. His probationers were organised in a circle sitting on chairs and told to act out various roles. Martin, my 26 year old client, felt embarrassed and unable to cope with some of the improvisations suggested. I was a bit surprised at the things he told me and decided a dollop of humour was the best defence when we went to court. District Justices take a very dim view of probationers defaulting on the terms of their probation, so Martin feared he was gone for porridge. I was taking a risk in the way I decided to address the court but, I hoped it would work out for the best.

The probation officer got up on the witness stand and told the Justice how Martin had failed to turn up for sessions of social therapy at his day centre and consequently had broken the terms of probation. I got up and addressed the following speech to the Justice.

"Justice, my client was required to participate in some questionable form of psychodrama. He was told to pretend that he was different pieces of fruit. Firstly, he was told to experience himself as an orange, rind, skin, juice, pulp, pips and all. Then he was told someone had been given permission to bite, cut, suck or eat him up. Now Justice, this sort of thing might appeal to some budding student of drama but it embarrassed my client, who is an unsuccessful burglar, not a drama student.

"The whole matter came to a head when he was told to experience himself as an apple. He thought the probation officer had said chapel so he churchsteepled his fingers over his head. The other probationers laughed at him and he was acutely embarrassed. Justice, my client doesn't mean to blow a raspberry at the terms of his probation but the fruit therapy made him feel a right lemon. The apple incident was the core of the problem. It left his ego bruised and his enthusiasm on the orchard floor. He is no Granny Smith and the experience was not all Golden Delicious. He had some difficulty in understand the role-playing exercise he was asked to perform. He found the sessions difficult to cope with. I hope my pleas won't be met by sour grapes, Justice."

I sat down and hoped for the best. The Justice smiled at my play on words. He said, "Right, it is something of a windfall that this young man found you for an advocate. I won't be an old crab. I'll commute his sentence to 120 hours of community service."

It was a great outcome to what could have been a bad day for Martin.

Best wises,
Patrick

Dear Friend,

I have a client who has a hobby which has led to unfortunate results. His hobby is to get well tanked up on beer in his local pub and then go out on the prowl looking for the nearest Guard to beat the living crap out of. He has done this quite often and I have seen him off to Mountjoy on more than a few occasions.

I have heard boxers once described as poets devoid of a verbal capacity to articulate their feelings and so they do their talking with their fists. This was certainly true of Andy. I lined up psychologists and psychiatrists to try to examine and explain away his tendency, but all to no avail. District Justices are allergic to those who assault Guards. They get a sudden rush of blood to the head and instead of breaking out in spots they double the amount of porridge a reasonable man would expect them to dish out.

The last time Andy attacked a Guard he excelled himself. Not only that, but in addition, he claimed he couldn't remember the assault. This left me up the proverbial shit creek without a paddle or a sail.

"I don't know what it is," he told me, "but I can't help beating the shit out of them." A cop posing for the admiration of the general female populace was enough to bring on a literal attack.

Another feature of Andy's hobby is that he is always caught. He sometimes gives his cases to other solicitors because he is ashamed to come to me too often. I received an SOS from him to visit him in Mountjoy. Despite the fact that I did not act for him in his most recent attack, he asked for me because of the trust he had in me. Although I am no push-over, since I didn't have anything else to do, I visited him.

"Thanks very much for coming to see me Mr Chapman," he said. "I want you to do a favour for me."

"As long as it's legal I'll listen anyway," I said.

"Oh its' dead legal," he said. "I'm sorry I didn't look for you instead of the solicitor I hired this time. The favour I need done is that someone should visit my father and check that it's alright for me to go home when I'm released in a month's time. You see I need to know if it's alright for me to stay at home while I'm looking for a job. If you could do that I'd be ever so grateful."

I promised Andy that I would see what I could do. Before visiting his home I rang up his most recent choice of solicitor, one Tom Clancy, a college mate of mine, and asked him if there was anything I should know before visiting Andy's father.

"I don't remember the case in all its details," Tom told me, "but one thing I do remember is the Guard he assaulted with the knife. He talked kind of funny on account of the fact that Andy sliced him down the face and across the mouth."

"That's nice."

"It gets better. You should have seen the sewing job those surgeons did on him. If they had taken him out to Howth to the fishermen mending their nets by the quay they would have done a better job. It was really awful."

I didn't think this had any relevance so I phoned Andy's father. "I'd like to talk to you about your son," I said.

"I'm not sure I want to hear anything more about him," Mr Molloy said.

"I have a message from him that I would like to deliver in person," I said, hoping for a break.

"Right then deliver it," Mr Molloy said.

"I'll call around to your house on Saturday afternoon if that is convenient."

"Makes no difference," said Andy's father before putting down the phone without saying goodbye.

On Saturday afternoon I made my way to the address Andy had given me. It was in a working class estate – my old hunting ground – and the particular house didn't look any different from many others in any working class area. Part of the garden had been cemented over to make a driveway for the car that now stood in it. I noticed a pair of navy blue trousered legs sticking out from under the old Morris Minor parked in the driveway.

I addressed myself to the navy blue legs that protruded from the car.

"Hello Mr Molloy," I said as I introduced myself. "I'm Patrick Chapman, the solicitor you spoke to on the phone the other day."

"Yes I remember. What have you got to say?"

"Well, you see it's like this Mr Molloy, your son has asked me to speak to you."

"Has he indeed?" The sarcasm was dripping from the voice beneath the car.

"Yes he has," I said and added, "He is anxious about coming home from jail."

"So he bloody well should be ," came the comment. It was obvious he was servicing the car and had the sump valve out. He was waiting for all the oil to drain out into the waiting basin so that he might put the sump valve back in and fill the car up with new oil.

"Andy is basically a decent chap," I said.

"Is he really?" came the paternal reply. "He hasn't struck me as such."

"I think he has a lot of good in him," I carried on relentlessly.

"It's funny I never noticed it."

"He's coming out in less than a month."

"Too bad for all decent living people."

"I think he has learned his lesson."

"About bloody time for him."

"He wants to get a job and be a gainfully employed member of society."

"So do a lot of people and they don't have criminal records."

"He has paid his debt to society and his past should not be held against him."

"Like hell it shouldn't."

"His record has not been all that bad!" It was like I was pleading mitigation for a client before a judge. "His crimes could be considered as no more than youthful indiscretions."

"There's nothing minor about attacking a Guard with fists or a knife."

"That is very true Mr Molloy," I said and I almost added that his background was against him but I caught myself on before the words were out of my mouth.

"But there again we must try and see this from Andy's point of view. It is obvious that there is something in his past which makes it difficult for him to respond to the average Guard."

"You can say that again. As a matter of fact if you had a tune you could sing it."

I felt I was banging my head against a stone wall. I thought I would give it one last try before giving up. "The Guards know what Andy is like and in my opinion they were waiting outside the pub in a provocative mood."

"What did you say your name was?" came the voice from beneath the car.

"Chapman," I said. It was obvious I was getting nowhere.

"Right Mr Chapman. Are you aware that this spell in jail is his third time there following his seventh assault on Guards?"

"Yes," I said, "but if he could be treated by a psychiatrist he might never do it again."

"Trick cyclists are only human Mr Chapman. They are not magicians. You didn't handle Andrew's most recent case, did you Mr Chapman?"

"No I didn't," I said.

"Let me fill you in on a few details," said the voice from under the car. "First of all the Guard he attacked was one he sought out with malice in his heart. It was not his usual random assault on the nearest Guard available. He went on the prowl looking for this Guard and when he found him he attacked him from behind. He gave him two black eyes, a broken nose and then for his finale he slashed the Guard's face and mouth with a fisherman's knife."

"That was a particularly vicious thing to do," I said.

"I'm glad you concede that much," said the voice from under the car. Then Andy's father wriggled out. His face was splashed with oil. He took out his handkerchief and began to wipe it away.

"There's just one last thing I'd like to say to you before you go. I was the Guard in question."

I was dumfounded. As the handkerchief cleaned his face I could see the clear furrow the knife scar had left on his phisog. I thanked him for his time and walking backwards in confusion, I made a hasty exit.

Best wishes,
Patrick

Dear Friend,

You should have been there. You should have seen it for yourself. It was enough to gladden any emotional anarchist's heart. It was pure magic and of course it ended up with a hearing in Ballyskerry District Courts. It was a Saturday morning and the drunks came up charged with drunk and disorderly and the usual petty nonsense. They were fined and dismissed in the summary manner. A couple of apprentice hardmen then came before the Court. With nauseating regularity they were the unemployed who turned to petty crime out of frustration with their plight. One was given the benefit of the Probation of Offenders Act, the other was given six months jail. Their offences slip my memory, but doubtless it was the ordinary small time manifestation of evil that comes before our Petty Sessions.

The sight that you should have seen was the fifteen old age pensioners – three of them in wheelchairs, one with an aluminium walker, that told the tale of his stroke, all appearing before the Court charged with conduct likely to lead to a breach of the peace. These were people who don't belong to the Third World victims who normally find themselves in the District Courts.

The first into the witness box was the Guard. If he had any respect for old age he would have been ashamed of himself to have been prosecuting fifteen pensioners.

However, enough of my prejudice, even through it is founded on reality.

The Guard explained that he had been called on his walkie-talkie to the Schiller Hotel in the city centre. When he arrived there, there was a disturbance which he diagnosed was the fault of the Old Civil Rights Association. He arrested the accused – he listed the fifteen names and the old timers all looked on with amused interest. Next in the case for the prosecution was the hotel manager. He looked as clean cut as a Mormon; bright young face, conservative dress and spoke with an educated accent. He explained that the contretemps – his word – had developed after he had requested the Old Civil Rights Association to vacate the room they had originally been assigned. He had made a mistake and it was meant to be used by the monthly meeting of the Junior Chamber of Commerce.

The first member of the defence was an old timer who looked as if he had all his wits about him. None of the fifteen were pleading guilty. Joy to my heart from the very beginning.

"Are the accused represented?" asked the District Justice.

"I'm here to speak up for all of us," replied the first member. He gave his name as Larry Higgins.

"I would like to make a statement from the dock," he said. This meant that he couldn't be cross-examined. It is seldom that people who decide to defend themselves know this or know enough of the law or their own rights to do the job properly, but this old boy seemed to have picked up a few tips on the law over the years.

"You have something to say?" prompted the Justice.

"I have plenty to say," said Mr Higgins. "Have you got the patience to hear me out?"

The Justice was obviously taken aback to have this question put to him. "I'll hear you out," he promised.

"Right then," began Higgins. "This story goes back to the time of the Civil War. I mean the Civil War that began in Northern Ireland in 1969. Before that began the Catholic Nationalist minority thought there was a chance that they could copy the blacks in America and achieve a few civil rights. The blacks are clever people. Far more clever than a lot of people give them credit. And, of course, with a genius like Martin Luther King leading them, how could they not obtain what they set out to achieve?

"We, in North and South, read of their success and how they obtained it, so we decided that a bit of peaceful protest might manage to get us a bit of what we were after: So we all joined in.

"I don't need to explain to you Justice, about the discrimination in housing, education and jobs that existed in Northern Ireland since partition was enacted. A high percentage of the mentally aware founded the Civil Rights Movement, including the gang of old lefties you see before you this morning."

"Watch who you're calling a leftie," came the cry from one old man in a wheelchair."As I was saying, we founded the Civil Rights Movement, but we were not looking for the reunification of Ireland. All we were looking for was to be treated as equal British Citizens as the Protestant Loyalist majority. Now I know the problem of Northern Ireland is a conundrum of two minorities. The Loyalists see themselves as a minority on the island of Ireland whilst the Nationalists see themselves as a minority within the Six Counties. However that's not the problem we're going to solve here this morning.

"My co-defendants and I used to take part in many a march for Civil Rights. Needless to say that was before August 1969 when the Troubles began. You'll remember the murders of four Catholics started the game off. We used to go on all the marches behind Bernadette Devlin, Gerry Fitt and John Hume. And those of us who were on in years discovered that we had quite a few things in common – not the least of which was that we filled the nearest pub at the end of a march.

"So anyway, years later, 3000 plus lives lost, we decided a reunion would be a good idea. 'Let's make it neutral ground,' I said. 'Dublin,' Bradshaw said. 'Done,' I said. Now you see Bradshaw is our treasurer. Can't stand the sight of money. Who better to put in charge of it? He organised the Schiller Hotel for our reunion.

"First of all we had a meal in the room which was booked and paid for in advance by Bradshaw."

"I've still got the receipt," shouted Bradshaw from a bench in the Court.

"Quite so," said Higgins. "So we were all ensconced in our seats halfway through our meal when Mr Bright Eyes – the hotel manager comes striding in. 'Terribly sorry,' says he. 'You'll have to vacate this room,' says he. 'One of our junior staff made the mistake,' says he. It seemed that the Junior Chamber of Commerce had booked the same room as us and, or course, Mr Bright Eyes decides that he can bully a bunch of old fogies."

"What happened?" said the Justice, genuinely interested.

"'Sorry to disturb your reunion,' says he. 'There's nothing for it but to move,' says he. 'Piss off,' says Bradshaw."

"That's true Justice," said Bradshaw from the body of the Court. "I said that." He was quite proud of himself.

Higgins tried to take up the narrative again. "'No way,' I said. 'It's completely out of the question. We paid good money in cash for this room. You entered a verbal contract and we're going to make sure you stick to it'. 'We have a nice room to move you to,' says the

Manager. 'We've already got a nice room. We don't need another', Boxer Thompson says.

"At this point everybody had surrounded the Manager. Fifty old time Civil Rights Protesters. The smile began to slip from his face.

"'They must be paying by cheque, so you're afraid they'll cancel it', says Bradshaw. 'Either that or they've slipped you a little bribe to get rid of us?' The Manager smiles his condescending smile. 'Nothing like that at all I can assure you,' he says. 'It's just that we've got to keep everybody happy'.

"'Keep us happy by taking a run and jump into the river,' says Thompson. 'Well,' says the Manager, 'If you people can't find a way to oblige and co-operate, I'll have to call in the police to help you change your minds'. It shot through the room like an electric shock. 'He's going to call in the police,' said Mick Carroll, knuckles going white on the arms of his wheelchair. 'Everybody lie on the floor. Make them carry us out'.

"The Manager turned on his heel, elbowed his way through us and went off in search of the police. We got all the chairs and the tables and stacked them against the door. It was our room. We had paid for it. Besides, we were the Old Civil Rights Association. Who could teach us anything about protesting? When the Manager and his two cops returned we were all lying on the floor singing 'We shall overcome'. They shot us in the streets of Belfast, Derry and battered us at Burntollet. We don't give up our rights easily!."

"I see," said the Justice after a pregnant pause. "It seems to me that this whole incident was sparked off by the incompetence of the hotel manager and his staff. Case dismissed." The smiles were broad and genuine.

Dear Friend,

A solicitor, like a barrister, has a tradition of representation in certain courts although, in theory, all have the right to audience in all courts. The solicitor usually represents clients in the District and Circuit Courts while the barrister has a special tradition of representation in the higher courts. Even that is not true to say, since barristers can and often do represent accused persons in the lower courts also.

The difference between the two is defined by education and tradition. The solicitor has to pass examinations in book-keeping and office management, whereas the barrister must steep his head in the law books and be an expert on a higher legal plane.

Sometimes the law can be a cruel bastard and it is easy to believe in the old saying that the law is a blunt instrument. Other times it can be a pleasant surprise to see a Judge exercising compassion. It is good to see a young fellow being given the benefit of the Probation of Offenders Act or to see a young guy being let off after making restitution. The case I want to tell you about in this letter concerns a young couple who should never have been in court at all. The defendant was a twenty year old young man who had fallen in love with a ripe fifteen year old girl. Their youthful passion had overflowed with the result that the girl had become pregnant. She had reached her sixteenth birthday by the time the case had come to court. This meant that she had reached the age of consent, so that it didn't look as bad as it could have for her young Romeo.

Juliet entered the witness box, blushing with modesty but unable to conceal that she was heavily pregnant. The prosecuting barrister, who had a badly hidden sneer in this voice, asked, "What did you do when you first discovered that you were pregnant?"

"I went to church," said Juliet, "and said a prayer to St. Jude, the patron saint of hopeless cases."

"Very good," said the barrister, "but what else did you do?"

"I blessed my stomach with the holy water and placed my child under the protection of the Blessed Virgin."

At this a few smiles appeared in Court.

"I see," said the barrister, "and what did you do then?"

"I took courage in my hands and told my mother. She, in turn, told my father and then the Guards became involved."

"My Lord, at this point," said the barrister, "I would like to read a few extracts of letters sent by this young Romeo to his Juliet."

"No objection," said the defence barrister.

"My dearest friend, at night when I have cycled home, I look up at the moon and think that you may see it and so we are joined together although the world's ways deny us the togetherness we need to share our love.

"I love you more than I ever thought I would ever love anyone. I never knew such sweetness would lie in my grasp. I long for the day when instead of a few hours snatched from life, we may share all of it."

The barrister droned on. It was obvious by his rendition that he was a man who lacked a romantic sense and had a surfeit of cynicism. I watched the Judge as the extracts continued and noticed his Adam's apple bob up and down as he swallowed back some feelings. After a further few extracts the Judge took out his handkerchief and blew his nose. It was obvious that he was affected.

"Hold on there a minute Mr Cooper," said the Judge. "There appears to be a great deal of feeling between these two young people. Can't something be salvaged before it's too late?"

"What does your Lordship mean?" asked Cooper.

"I mean couldn't they get married if I give this young man a suspended sentence?"

"It takes money to get married," said Cooper.

The defendant piped up, "I have enough money to put down a deposit on a sited mobile home."

"There we are," said the Judge. "There is a good start."

Turning to the girl in the witness box he asked her, "Have you any strong feelings towards this boy?"

"I have, my Honour. I love him very much," the girl said, stealing a nervous glance at her father.

"Will you marry him then?"

"I will if he asks me."

"Did you hear that young man? The ball is in your court."

"Will you marry me then?" asked the prisoner.

"Don't you know I will! It's what I've been praying for, for many a sleepless night."

"Right," said the Judge. "I can't remember a better day's work in many a long year. I would like to see the parents of both these youngsters in my room right away."

I don't know if those two young people worked everything out but at least they began with flying colours.

Dear Friend,

If is often the case that when the hurly-burly of a trial is over and the jury come back in with a guilty verdict, the Judge puts off sentencing for a week so that he can review all the reports and case notes. He settles in his mind on an appropriate sentence and delivers it in the cold light of a new day. This same procedure is also followed in the Circuit Court when a defendant pleads not guilty.

People who visit court to sit in the public gallery seldom bother to attend sentencing sittings. There is no high drama. There is no cross examination. In short, there is usually no entertainment to be had. It is often a time of tears.

The families of the defendants sit in small huddled islands of desperation. They wonder whether they are going to hear the good news of a probationary term or the bad news of a jail sentence. The electricity of expectation that hums throughout the court comes to a halt when the Judge enters from his chambers. The court clerk barks "Be upstanding!" and the room rises as one. When the Judge subsides into his seat, everyone else sits also.

The Judge and the court clerk have similar lists of names. A state prosecution barrister goes through an ancient formula of words which begins, "May it please my Lord …." And the ritual has begun. First time offenders whose crimes did not involve violence or any grave threat to society are usually given a probationary sentence. They are told to be on good behaviour for one, two or three years and to refrain from their previous nefarious activity. The Judge usually tells them why they are there, what they have been convicted of and then gives the convict a homely warning such as, "If you appear before me again, you had better bring your toothbrush because they don't hand them out free in Mountjoy Jail!" Usually with that threat hanging over his head the defendant keeps his nose clean and disappears back to whatever normality is for him.

However, there is another side to these rituals which doesn't end in the defendant receiving hugs, kisses and back slaps from his relatives and friends. Where a defendant has 'form' (Previous convictions) or his crime was considered grave, he can be certain of sharing large bowls of porridge for the foreseeable future. Usually before this sort of sentence the Judge will ask the defendant, "Have you anything to say before sentence is pronounced?"

In almost a hundred percent of cases the defendant realises what is coming next, so he just shakes his head or mutters "no". They have nothing to say. Everything is low-key. Friends and relatives hold their breath. Sentence is pronounced and off the convict goes to jail.

I have before me the transcript of one extraordinary case when a convict who had pleaded guilty to the crime of embezzlement actually did have something to say before sentence was pronounced. It was a moving ordeal to witness. I have dreamt about the young man and his statement and often wondered what became of him. "Have you anything to say before ......" the Judge asked the convicted embezzler.

"Yes my Lord, I do."

The defendant was an intelligent looking man who had seem the passing of thirty five summers and winters. He looked like ever mother's idea of conformity. His black hair was neatly trimmed and beginning to thin. His brown eyes held a look of resolve and diffidence. He had a Roman nose and a dimpled chin. He wore the middle class uniform of a blue blazer, grey slacks, blue shirt and red tie. His black shoes were neatly polished. He began to tell his life story. He had come from one of the large working class estates which Dublin Corporation built in the forties and fifties. He had won a scholarship to secondary school and managed to sustain a Leaving Certificate level by doing well in his yearly examinations. He won a scholarship to University but could not go.

"I wanted to but my father died in a road traffic accident the same day I received notification from the University. I felt I had to help my widowed mother and my younger brothers and sisters to keep the family together, so I got a job. In addition to those pressing obligations I met a girl from the same neighbourhood and we fell in love.

"I wanted desperately to go to University but fate or destiny or God or what have your determined that I would not be the first in my family to attend University. My father's death set the seal on my future. All through my years in secondary school I had written poems and short stories. I could have eventually papered this courtroom with rejection slips but I was over the moon to land a job in a publishers. The company from which I have now confessed to stealing money.

"I worked hard for that company as an account's assistant. I took care of the money which bookshops sent the publishers and I continued writing poems and stories in my spare time.

"I kept my girlfriend tagging along, hoping that I would eventually be promoted and get a decent wage to set up home and still help my mother. But what happened? I worked for five years and got my first increment. I also got a gold star to place beside my name on the list of employees near the clock-in machine. I begged by girlfriend to wait for me. I told her that time and diligence on my part were bound to lead to a promotion. We got engaged and controlled our passion.

Another five years passed and I got another small increment and another gold star. After twelve years of hard work I got my lucky break in the back-handed way these things happen. One of the accounts managers died suddenly. I had been his apprentice for many years and a mixture of emotions roared through me – sorry for my old boss's departure without his having enjoyed any retirement, and happiness that at long last my chance for betterment had arrived.

"The job I deserved was given to one of the directors' sons. He didn't know the difference between a royalty and a hole in the ground. But he had the family connections to come into the company over my head. I don't blame him for what happened but I ended up doing most of his work as well as my own. I became cynical and bitter. I told my girlfriend that I had gotten a raise. I began to steal from my employer; I felt my career was over. I lost confidence in myself and bolstered my failing self esteem by writing more and more unpublished stories and poems. I told my fiancée that we could marry soon. I didn't have the spirit to quit my job and start a new career at the age of thirty."

His voice began to shake with emotion as he confessed.

"I'm a thief. But I'm not the only thief in that publishing house. I stole a lot of money over the following three years and I covered my tracks so well that when I was caught by the auditors I was cynically amused to discover that I was accused of taking less than I had actually taken.

"I am not sorry for my crime. I feel I was only taking what I was due. I poured the virility of my youth into that company and other people got the rewards that I deserved. I confessed. I was prosecuted and now I'm going to jail. My girlfriend says she will wait for me. I hope she will but I won't blame her if she doesn't.

"Before I finish up there is something else I want to add. I'm bright enough to know that I'm finished. My only hope when I get out of jail is to get some small number of my booklets of stories printed and to hawk them door to door. My employers couldn't even encourage my little bit of compensatory talent. I confided in the personnel manager that I hoped to one day be published. He asked me to show him some of my stories."

He reached into his inside pocket and produced a small manuscript. "This is the booklet of stories I showed him. It contains only ten short stories. He maliciously and, as it turned out, falsely told me I should be in the best seller lists.

"I was always the first into work every morning. One morning I came in and discovered that my calculator's batteries were dead. I went to the personnel division to help myself to new batteries and I found my personnel file on the personnel officer's desk. He had filed a copy of this booklet of stories on my personnel file with the following ten comments preceding each of the stories:

<u>One:</u> He may embarrass the MD with his trashy tales. I will try to elicit more of his yarns from him so that we can be pre-warned on any damage limitation exercise we may have to undertake should we be so unfortunate that he gets some of his rubbish published.

<u>Two:</u> I don't think he should put more fire into his stories but I do think he should put more of his stories into the fire.

<u>Three:</u> I told him his tales were like something written by an angel who has fallen from the skies. I didn't add that I thought it a pity that he landed on his face!

Note to the Personnel Officer

Dear Sean,
There are two things I like about you ...... your face!
TF

<u>Four:</u> I wish I had a lower IQ so that I could enjoy his yarns.

<u>Five</u>: He is a man of rare talent – it's rare when he shows any.

<u>Six</u>: What do you think of his latest excursion into literature? I suppose we can't all be mentally sound.

<u>Seven</u>: There is no sense in challenging him directly. After all what is the use in having a battle of wits with an unarmed man?

<u>Eight</u>: He spends half his day trying to be witty. You might say he's a half-wit.

<u>Nine</u>: The only reason I invite him into my office to recite and read his drivel, is to remind myself that mental illness strikes every 60 seconds!

<u>Ten</u>: Is comment really necessary?

"Thank you Lord for the opportunity to get all this off my chest."

The Judge was moved but still had to do his duty.

"Young man, it is seldom that a defendant takes up the offer I made to you to say a few words before sentence is passed. I have certain sympathy with you and gratitude to you for sharing your life story. However, I must be ruled by my head as well as my heart. I sentence you with a heavy heart and the hope that someone as articulate as you will find a new niche in society when your debt is paid. I sentence you to 12 months imprisonment."

The Evangelist

He came into my office, wide eyed behind his spectacles. He was a man about the sixty mark with silver hair, a slim face and a sober business suit.

"They arrested me for telling the people of Ireland about Jesus!" he exclaimed. "I was handing out my book 'LIFE ENHANCERS' when a pagan Garda pushed me into the paddy wagon. Please ready this!"

He pushed a copy of his book towards me.

"Will it calm you down?" I asked.

"It will," he replied.

As a solicitor specialising in criminal defence he was unusual as a client. The Incorporated Law Society carried out a scientific survey, some time ago, and discovered that 85 percent of defendants before the District Courts are unemployed. There is a 91 percent conviction rate. Losing your good name in the District Courts is easier than falling off a log. In so far as this client was able to pay my fee and not depend on Legal Aid, he was off to a better start than most.

I turned the cover of his book over and began reading Life Enhancers.

The Rabbi's Answer

The rich American man got off the train in the poor Polish town. He had come on a pilgrimage to see Rabbi Singer. He thought, since adolescence, that the Rabbi was the world's greatest short story writer.

A maelstrom of emotions careered through the American's heart as he knocked on the door of the Rabbi's dilapidated house.

The Rabbi welcomed the American into his one-roomed home. The floor was made of hardened earth and a log fire blazed in the hearth. Two chairs that had seen long service and better years waited by the fireside. A small table, kitchen press and made-up bed constituted the only other furniture.

The American gushed praise and bonhomie and the Rabbi smiled. The visitor told of the benign influence of the short stories on his life. Finally, the guest ran out of verbal steam. He wanted to say, "You have a beautiful home here," but the shock of the poor state of the room stopped him. His curiosity got the better of him.

"Rabbi," he began, "where is your furniture?"

The Rabbi raised an eyebrow and asked, "Where is yours?"

The American blurted out the obvious answer after shrugging his shoulders. "I'm only passing through!"

The Rabbi smiled, took down his Hebrew Bible from the shelf above the fire and said, "So am I!"

*   *   *

The Wise Old Irishman

Once upon a time there was a wise old Irishman. He lived in a small, peasant, rural community and was considered rich by his neighbours because he owned a horse. All his wealth was contained in that one horse.

Then one morning he woke up and his only son told him that the horse had escaped during the night, from the paddock.

"I'm sorry dad," said the son. "This is really a bit of bad luck." The wise old Irishman stroked his beard and asked, "How do you know it is bad luck?"

The horse had run away up to the mountains, among the wild horses. The following morning the horse returned with ten wild horses to the paddock. The son closed the gate of the paddock and ran to tell his father. "Dad, our horse returned and brought ten wild horses with him. What a bit of good luck!"

The wise old Irishman stroked his beard and said, "How do you know it's good luck?"

Later that day the wise man's son tried to tame one of the wild horses and the horses kicked him in the leg, breaking it in several places. The wise man brought his son to the local bone setter but the bone setter said he was a hopeless case. He would be semi-crippled for the rest of his life. The son cried on his father's shoulder, "What bad luck!" The wise old Irishman said, "How do you know it's bad luck?"

The son hobbled about the farm, trying to help out as much as he could, and then the local Chieftain called to the village. He told the villagers that he needed ever able-bodied young man to fight for him but the crippled boy would be no good as a warrior. All the young men went to war, on the Chieftain's behalf, and they were all killed.

The neighbours gathered in the wise old man's house and congratulated him. "Your son is the only young man left alive in our village. What a bit of good luck!"

The wise old Irishman stroked his beard and said, "How do you know it is good luck?"

And all the village laughed. And the wise old Irishman laughed loudest and longest.

*   *   *

The Price of a Field

The year was 1960. Ireland stood on the brink of its first industrial revolution. International businessmen visited the towns and cities, ferreting out suitable locales for factories. Seamus and Paudgeen sipped pints of Guinness in their local pub, as they discussed their dilemma.

"He wants four hundred pounds for the field," said Seamus.

"Begob that's enough money in pound notes to choke a horse," said Paudgeen.

"Pardon me, gentlemen," said the Japanese businessman. "Perhaps you could tell me where I could best to go hunt brown bears?"

Seamus began to inform the son of Nippon that there were no brown bears to be found in Ballyskerry woods, when he received a kick in the shins beneath the table.

"Begob now sir, there was a time when brown bears were very plentiful in these parts," said Paudgeen. "As a matter of fact, you couldn't put your hand out at night without one of them falling over your foot. But it would cost four hundred pounds to hire two men to locate a brown bear these days."

"Honourable Japanese businessman would be willing to pay five hundred pounds for the pleasure of shooting an Irish bear."

"Five hundred pounds!" Seamus nearly choked on his beer.

"Could you meet us back in here at this time tomorrow?"

"Sure, even if its' Sunday itself, we might be able to help you along for the sake of the national tourist industry!"

The arrangement was made.

*   *   *

The following morning the parish priest was cycling home from Mass, congratulating himself on his homily. "There would be no abortion clinics in Ireland ever," he had told his congregation. "There will be no euthanasia and no corruption in business and politics as long as the Church is given its rightful place." Father Mac Donald was a very forward looking priest.

As he cycled towards Ballyskerry woods, Father Mac Donald wondered if Satan would send a demon to stop the continued veneration of God and His Holy Church.

Meanwhile, Seamus and Paudgeen had bought a brown bear, aged and redundant, from a circus which was in a nearby town. They hunted it into Ballyskerry woods and tethered it to a tree. They parted the Jap with his five hundred pounds and Seamus pointed him in the direction of the bear. When Paudgeen saw Seamus and the Nip approach he let the bear loose. The bear stood stock still and eyed the forest curiously.

Just then, with the threat of demons in his head, Father Mac Donald came cycling into the woods. He knew a messenger of Satan when he saw one and on spying the bear, he fell off his bicycle shouting, "I rebuke you in the name of Jesus!" He ran back to town and into local legend.

Meanwhile, the circus bear did what he had been trained to do all his life – he mounted the bicycle and cycled towards the hunter. The Jap, confronted with the cycling bear shot himself in the foot and that evening was mollified by tales of fairies whispering devilment into brown bears' ears, by Seamus and Paudgeen.

*   *   *

A Soldier's Story

I was a soldier in Romania while our dear old dictator was alive. In those days it was a criminal offence to be a Christian. Many Christians spent miserable years in our jails. Pastors, priests and other leaders of Christian groups were given specially long sentences.

Pastor Richard Wurmbrand spent fourteen years in jail – many in solitary confinement. He was only one of thousands.

It was my job as a soldier of the Special Branch to root out Christians and bring them before the courts. The effect of these Christians going off peacefully and quietly to jail had a profound effect on me. Why didn't they fight back? Why did they claim to have eternal life when they were subject to the same death that finishes us all? Why did they wish me well and promised to pray for me and my family to their mythical Jesus Christ?

On one occasion, a few years before the revolution that was to topple our dictator, I received news that a group of Christians were meeting in the basement of a restaurant in a prosperous part of the city. I decided to get my machine gun and pay them a visit. Through informers I learned that the password for men to get into the restaurant was, 'I would like to visit the new Adam'. The password for women was, 'I would like to visit the new Eve'.

I arrived at the restaurant with my machine gun carefully concealed beneath my bulky raincoat. I gave the password and was allowed in. I walked down the stone steps towards the room the Christians occupied. They were expecting persecution. Their grapevine was rife with stories of betrayal and incarceration, and still they met to pray and read the book they called the Holy Bible!

I took out my machine gun and lifted the latch. I could hear them singing one of their songs which they call hymns. I kicked open the door and pointed my gun at them. They were a sorry looking lot. Their singing had dwindled into silence. I looked at them – perhaps only a dozen all together – and said, "Any of you who do not believe in Jesus Christ, get out while you have the chance."

The Pastor began reciting a prayer which they called 'The Lord's Prayer'. I looked at them menacingly and about half of them left. Gradually one by one they chose to leave or to join the Pastor in his prayer. There is a saying in Romania – 'When push comes to shove, you know where you stand with everyone'.

The half dozen who remained looked at me with fearful eyes. Their moment of truth had come. They did not know what was going to happen next. The last of the deserters had left.

I closed the door behind me and resumed my position in front of the Christians. I put down my machine gun, smiled and said, "I believe in Jesus Christ too. We're much better off without those that left. I have the gift of a Holy Bible for you and would like to join you in prayers and praise for our Saviour!"

*   *   *

Mad Priest

The priest walked down the busy city street and began talking aloud. "The world is topsy-turvy Lord," he said. He addressed the words to the sky and people gave him a wide berth on the footpath.

"Do you remember, Lord, creating the anchovy? A wonderful little fish. Well, as you probably know, the seas around South America are teeming with protein-rich anchovy. The poor people of South American need all that protein – especially the children. And do you know what happens to the anchovies? They are sold to American and Canadian companies to be turned into cat and dog food. Ridiculous!

"People are starving to death all over Africa and Asia while surplus food mountains rot in Europe and America. What are you doing about it, Lord?"

Across the street men came reeling out of a pub. One vomited and fell into the gutter with a loud wallop. Having fallen down, he stayed down and blood trickled form his head. People passed by but the mad priest crossed the road and took a handkerchief out of his pocket. He wiped the face of the now comatose drunk and stemmed the flow of blood from his head.

The priest looked up at the sky and asked aloud, "What are you doing about this fellow, Lord?"

To the mad priest's surprise the Lord answered, "I have already done something about him."

"What is that Lord?" asked the mad priest.

"I have brought him to your attention," answered the Lord.

*   *   *

The Long Silence

At the end of time, billions of people were scattered on a great plain before God's throne. Most shrank back from the brilliant light before them. But some groups near the front talked heatedly – not with cringing shame but with belligerence.

"Can God judge us?"

"How can He know about suffering?" snapped a pert young brunette. She ripped open a sleeve to reveal a tattooed number from a Nazi concentration camp. "We endured terror .... beating .... torture .... death!"

In another group a Negro boy lowered his collar. "What about this?" he demanded, showing an ugly rope burn. "Lynched for no crime but being black!"

In another crowd, a pregnant school girl with sullen eyes. "Why should I suffer?" she murmured. "It wasn't my fault."

Far across the plain were hundreds of such groups. Each had a complaint against God for the evil and suffering He permitted in His world. How lucky God was to live in Heaven where all was sweetness and light, where there was no weeping or fear, no hunger or hatred. What did God know of all that men had been forced to endure in this world? For God leads a pretty sheltered life, they said.

So each of these groups sent forth their leader, chosen because he had suffered the most. A Jew, a Negro, a person from Hiroshima, a horrible deformed arthritic, a thalidomide child. In the centre of the plain they consulted with each other. At last they were ready to present their case. It was rather clever. Before God could be qualified to be their judge, He must endure what they had endured. Their verdict was the God should be sentenced to live on earth – as a man! Let him be born a Jew. Give Him a work so difficult that even His family will think Him out of His mind when He tries to do it. Let Him be betrayed by His closest friends. Let Him face false charges, be tried by a prejudiced jury and convicted by a cowardly judge. Let Him be tortured. At last, let Him see what it means to be terribly alone. Then let Him die. Let there be a whole host of witnesses to verify it.

As each leader announced his portion of the sentence, loud murmurs of approval went up from the throng of people assembled. When the last had finished pronouncing sentence there was a long silence. No one uttered another word. No one moved. For suddenly all knew that God had already served His sentence.

*   *   *

The Comeback

Once upon a time there was a King who had a beautiful diamond. He was so impressed by the diamond that he boasted about it all the time. The diamond was the biggest, most beautiful diamond in the world, he thought. He was so proud of it that he had a line drawing of the diamond incorporated into the country's flag. Kings, Queens, Princes and Princesses came from all the surrounding countries to see and admire the King's diamond. Experts came from Amsterdam and South Africa and were unable to place a value on the diamond such was its rarity. They all concluded it was by far the most valuable diamond in the world.

One day the diamond-keeper rushed to the King to tell him that someone had attacked the diamond and made a big long scratch down the face of the diamond. The King rushed to see his prize in its greatly devalued state. He called on restorers from all over the world to see if it could be restored to its former glory. The experts came, shook their heads and concluded there was nothing they could do. The King never lost hope and one day an eccentric little diamond restorer arrived at the door of the palace. "I might be able to do something about the diamond," he said. "But you would have to trust me completely."

The Kind conceded and the restorer set about his work. One week passed and the restorer continued his work. Two weeks passed and the restorer had no news for the King. Finally after four weeks the restorer announced that his work was finished. The King rushed to see his previous diamond. At the top of the face of the diamond the restorer had sculpted a flowering rose and the scratch now looked like the stem of the rose.

Experts came from far and wide and proclaimed the diamond to be worth more than it was originally. The King was delighted and he rewarded the restorer handsomely.

Sometimes people are able to make great comebacks too.

*   *   *

(By Sister Mary de Monfort Bray)

'Out of the mouths of babes'

I look after the Babies.
I'm looking after the babies for nearly thirty years.
I have had all sorts of babies ....
big babies, small babies, high babies, low babies, babies who were boys and babies who were girls, town babies, country babies, babies who were bright, and babies who were not so bright ....
I teach the babies
I introduce them to A B and C
and to 1, 2, 3.
Maria, one of my babies was promised a present for her birthday,
from her Granddad.
During the Irish lesson, which is known to all in Primary School as the Buntus,
the interruption came

"Sister, Granddad is buying me a Shetland pony!"
In the middle of a mathematical conundrum
and I at my wits end trying to impart the important
knowledge
that 4 is greater than 3
"Sister, Granddad is buying me a Shetland pony!"
Right at the opportune moment when paint landed
all over my dress onto the floor
and all over the place
I heard
"Sister, Granddad is buying me a Shetland pony!"
That was the limit of my endurance
I quickly retorted
"I don't want to hear any more about that Shetland pony."
Quiet was eventually restored, the paint was cleared up, the storm had
abated.
Maria came up, put her arms around me neck and said, "Sister, I'll bring
you for a ride on my Shetland pony."
I was figuratively at the other end of the rostrum. Maria hadn't the
chalk, she hadn't the blackboard, she hadn't the teacher's diploma
....
She was one of the babies,
But she taught me that
"Love is always patient and kind, it is never jealous. Love is never
boastful or conceited, it is never rude 0r selfish and it is not resentful."
It took Maria, my four year old baby to remind me that to know a lot is
less important than to love a lot. Children are great reminders.
Why not listen to them?

                    *   *   *

                 I Appreciate Life

    Although I now have a degree in Biblical Studies there was a time
when I felt very depressed about my academic chances. When I was
18 I passed 4 subjects in the leaving certificate examination. I needed
5 passes in order to obtain the certificate so I had to attend night

school the following year to prepare to sit the examination again. I achieved the necessary extra pass and one Honour the next year. I was temporarily unemployed during that year and I invested the time in studying at the local library. Along with most students I had prayed that I would pass my examinations and felt bitterly disappointed when I failed at the first try. I was bitterly disappointed with myself, with the system that would label a young man a failure on the threshold of adult life. I was also bitterly disappointed in God.

One day in the library in order to take a break from my studies I turned around in my chair and picked a book from the nearest shelf. It was a book of poetry. I imagined it would be about the birds and the bees and the flowers and the trees and would be good for a cynical laugh. Sure enough when I opened the book I discovered many of the poems were in praise of a life in which I felt so disappointed. However, just as I was about to laugh at the naivety of the poems I noticed that they were written by a concentration camp victim named Robert Desnos.

He was a French poet who had been active in the Resistance and had been a prisoner of war in many concentration camps. He died shortly after the end of the war in a hospital near the camp in which he endured his final incarceration. I thought the poems found in his breast pocket by a Polish student who visited him during his final illness, were wonderful. It inspired me to think that despite being a prisoner in a concentration camp he was still able to find something to praise about life.

I told all my friends about this brilliant man and I especially told them about one poem he had written entitled 'I Appreciate Life'. I went around to all my friend, sharing my discovery and quoting lines from the poems. Many years later my son and I were watching a war film. I told him of my experience as I have just outlined above and told him that I had regarded the book as so important that I bought it from the library. I went to my bookcase and found the volume. I looked up the poems by Robert Desnos and found there was no poem written entitled 'I Appreciate Life'. I couldn't understand this. After all I distinctly remembered reading it, memorising many of the lines and of relating it to my friends. I looked everywhere in the book for it in order to share it with my son. It was nowhere to be found. The miracle of Robert's positive thinking poem remains a mystery to me to this day. The only consolation I had is that I still remember many of the lines of the poem and I reproduce them here for you now:

I Appreciate Life

I sit here in this concentration camp,
my back to the wall, out in
the open air and I have escaped today.
I have escaped the confines of
this camp.
I have flown over the barbed wire
fence with God's little swallow.
They have reduced me,
a fully grown man of forty five years,
to a six stones skeleton.
But I still appreciate life:
the blue of the sky,
the green of the grass,
the fresh air and
memories of my wife and friends.
I appreciate life
and today my spirit has
flown over the fence with
a little bird to victory.
I appreciate the gift of life
God has given me.

*   *   *

The Litmus Test of Grief

As a clergyman you get to hear a number of testimonies of people, in quiet conversations, that challenge or consolidate your beliefs.

It was a bright summer's day in Ballyskerry. The sea gulls cried overhead and the wind freshened the air at an outdoor garden party. I had just come from officiating at a funeral and so I wore my clerical grey and dog-collar. The newly mown grass threatened to bring on my hay fever as I stood on the edge of the party, sipping a cool glass of wine. A man of about 40 years of age came up to me and introduced himself. We shook hands. He had a bright cheerful face, sandy hair flecked with grey and wore a green striped shirt, open at the neck. His green summer slacks were an avocado shade and as we made our initial male bonding chit-chat, his eyes clouded over. It was obvious he wanted to get something off his chest.

"When I was little more than a toddler my mother had a miscarriage – God how I hate that euphemism! It sounds more real to call it an abortion even if you prefix the word with 'spontaneous'.

"When I was twenty eight years of age my wife had an abortion induced by stress. I intended to sue the people who had caused the stress but my wife's gynaecologist counselled against that course of action. He informed us that one in every four or five pregnancies result in abortion. A court case against the people who induced our abortion would have failed on the ground of balance of probability.

"We called out child Kim. We don't know if it was a boy or a girl. Every twelfth of February finds me blinking back the tears, wishing Kim had lived and writing 'Happy Birthday Kim' in my diary. Why do I believe that Kim is alive and maturing in the presence of Christ?

"When my wife went into hospital to have her appendix out and on another occasion, her gall bladder out – I was worried. I went to church to pray for a successful outcome. But I didn't grieve.

"For me the litmus test of grief was the deciding factor in coming round to the belief that a child had died.

"I don't agree with the Pope or other fundamentalist Christians about much, but when they defend the right to life of the unborn, I have to agree with them out of experience.

"The day or night I arrive in heaven I am going to meet a son or daughter and a brother or sister. What a celebration will ensue that day!"

I thanked him for his testimony and reflected, as he merged back into the party, how good it is to hear the truth.

*   *   *

The Dizzy Nun

Sister Mary looked at the convent she hoped to build. The architect's plans were perfectly in keeping with her dream. The stream of novices who hoped to dedicate their lives to helping the sick and homeless were already waiting to be admitted. But where was the money to build to come from?

The year was 1940 and war raged in Europe. Mr De Valera had, so far, managed to keep Ireland out of the conflict. The cost of the proposed building was a whopping one hundred thousand pounds. "Who will give it to us, Lord?" asked Sister Mary. As usual the generosity of the poor could be relied on. The rich had their own agendas which did not include the sick and the homeless.

Today, Sister Mary expected the arrival of a multimillionaire whose ancestral home was now occupied by the nuns. Even now Sister Mary could hear the big black chauffeur driven car crunching to a halt on the gravel outside. Sister Mary hurried out to greet her visitor.

"Mr Dunne," she gushed, "how wonderful that you could come!"

"Pleased to meet you, Sister," said Mr Dunne pulling his black winter overcoat around him as protection from the elements.

Sister Mary brought Mr Dunne on a tour of the house, warmed him up with hot whiskeys and allowed him to speak of his childhood in the house before introducing him to the architect's plans. She explained how much the proposed development would cost and hinted at the hope that Mr Dunne would make a donation.

"I have buckets of quotations from the Holy Bible in my head but I can't remember chapters and verses. I believe it is Second Chronicles, chapter sixteen, verse nine that says, 'The eyes of the Lord roam throughout the earth to strengthen those whose hearts are totally committed to Him'."

Mr Dunne was lost in thought. He imagined a donation would be requested but how much to give? Sister Mary interrupted his thoughts with more quotations:

"There is somewhere in the New Testament that says the Lord will reward those who are generous to Him with full measure, pressed down, shaken together and still overflowing. I wish I could remember the book, chapter and verse so that you could look it up for yourself." Sister Mary rushed on. "I think it is the Book of Malachi, chapter three, verse ten that says, 'Bring all the tithes into my storehouse so that there may be good in my house, and prove me now in this,' said the Lord of hosts, 'if I will not open for you the windows of Heaven and pour out for you such blessing that there will not be room enough to receive it'. And it says in the Book of Proverbs that those who give to the poor are really lending to the Lord! I wish I could remember the chapter and verse.

"The whole development will cost one hundred thousand pounds and we were hoping that you could start the ball rolling by making a little donation."

Mr Dunne smiled and the nun waited for him to speak. "I'll tell you what Sister; I'll give you ten thousand pounds."

"Oh Mr Dunne!" Sister Mary's dreams were coming true. "You're a wonderful man! We'll tell all the newspapers and may your many businesses always prosper!"

*   *   *

The following morning the national newspapers vied with each other to commend the extraordinary generosity of Mr Benedict Dunne. 'Dunne gives £100,000 to Convent' ran one of the many headlines. All spoke of his donation being one hundred thousand pounds. When Mr Dunne read the headlines he was alarmed. "Get me that nun on the telephone!" he barked at his secretary and when she did, he asked Sister Mary if she had seen the headlines.

"I did indeed Mr Dunne. Isn't it a shocking mistake?"

"It certainly is Sister. I promised only ten thousand pounds."

"You're not to worry Mr Dunne, I'll contact all my friends in the national newspapers and get them to correct the matter giving the proper sum equal prominence. Tomorrow morning's headlines will read "Mr Dunne only gives convent ten thousand pounds'. I'll insist on banner headlines Mr Dunne."

"Hold on a minute Sister," said Dunne, looking at the sheaf of congratulatory telegrams strewn over his desk. He made his mind up quickly. "I don't want that headline. You've got your hundred thousand pounds."

Sister Mary sang loud hosannas in praise of Mr Dunne and after the convent was built she insisted on a plaque being placed on the new building. She did not remember the book, chapter or verse but she knew the quotation she wanted on the plaque:

This extension to our lovely convent was built thanks to the extraordinary generosity of Mr Benedict Dunne: 'He visited us and we took him in!'

*   *   *

Jesus Was Born In Dublin

It was the event of the year in the convent – the nativity play. Five, six and seven year old boys and girls dressed in flowing robes filled the school hall stage.

Sister Mary had arranged a special treat for the parents. Joseph and Mary came on stage on the back of a real donkey. With some difficulty Joseph got down and approached the innkeeper.

'We have come a long way,' said little Joseph. 'Is there any room at the inn?'

'Certainly,' said the innkeeper. 'We'll find a room for yourself and the missus, all right. We couldn't have a woman in that state sleeping in a shop doorway or a stable. Even if I have to give you my own room, we'll find a place for you and the missus.'

'My wife is with child,' said Joseph.

'I know the story,' said the innkeeper with all the wisdom of a seven year old. 'Sure amn't I a married man myself?'

The parents in the audience fell around the place laughing. Sister Mary was gratified but a little uneasy at the improvisation on the stage.

In just under an hour the play was over; Jesus had been born in Dublin in the luxury of a hotel room; parents were proud and amused; children tucked into chocolate biscuits and lemonade. Sister Mary couldn't contain herself asking the innkeeper why he had strayed from the script.

'You were supposed to say, "There is no room at the inn".'

'Ah God I couldn't say that Sister. I'd be murdered when I got home. The boy playing the part of Joseph is my cousin.'

*   *   *

I Don't Understand Why Everybody Isn't Happy

We sat sucking our pints around the open fire of the Ballyskerry Boozer. A casual glance from a tourist might have led him to believe that we were a typical group of Irishmen enjoying a quiet pint.

In actual fact we were an alternative world government. Our Minister for World Minorities was in very good form. We had already requisitioned fleets of tankers to ship Canada's and America's grain surpluses to Africa and Asia; Europe's wine lake, butter and beef mountains were also on their way accompanied by Delia Smith's cookery course translated into 500 languages.

'Now lads,' said the Minister for Minorities. 'Before we go home tonight I think we should solve the refugee problem. Why is there a problem? After all – this is the way I see it. There is nothing Irish people enjoy as much as looking down on other people; the rich enjoy looking down on the middle class; the middle class like looking down on the working class; the working class like looking down on the travellers and now – hallelujah! – the travellers have someone to look down on – the refugees. I don't understand why everybody isn't happy!

'As a matter of fact I would like to thank the refugees for coming to this country because they have helped working class people like me to take one step up the social ladder.'

We all laughed.

'What does it matter whether they are black, brown, yellow or purple with pink polka dots – aren't they all god's children?'

We ordered another round of pints, satisfied with a good day's work done and the world put to rights and thank you very much for asking.

*   *   *

The Theology of Chocolate

I was converted to accepting Jesus Christ as my personal Saviour and Lord of my life at the age of thirty five. I had been fervently pursuing a business career but receiving Jesus as Saviour of my soul changed my life completely.

I now had, not a miserable little life of three or four score, but an eternal life. I felt, in my heart, that there was nothing more important than introducing unbelievers to my best friend – Jesus Christ.

I sold my business and invested the proceeds in an income-producing account. I paid off my mortgage and decided that I was best suited to evangelising other businessmen. My formula was simple. I walked into a business premises, asked to speak to the top man and went into a spiel about a famous evangelist named Robert Laidlaw.

Robert Laidlaw was a New Zealand businessman who made a resounding success of his life. He began a mail order business at the age of twenty three and by the end of his earthly life he employed two thousand, seven hundred men and women. Queen Elizabeth the second awarded him a Companion of the British Empire medal and title. Robert wrote a small book entitled 'The Reason Why'. The substance of this work encapsulated his Christian answer to the question, 'Why am I alive?'

I told my businessmen targets about Robert Laidlaw's business success. I followed this up be relating my own tale of success. Finally, I gave them a gift of 'The Reason Why' and told them that if they needed any further information about Jesus Christ or becoming a Christian, they should phone me or drop me a line. I stuck my business card to the inside back cover of the book.

One Easter Monday I told a Muslim businessman my story and Robert's story. Just before I was about to present him with the gift of 'The Reason Why' he interrupted my spiel.

"If you are going to discuss religion," he began. "You must allow me to go next door and get the Rabbi."

He told me he wouldn't be a moment as he skipped out of his grocery shop to fetch his friend. I was fearful he wouldn't accept and read Robert Laidlaw's book. He returned shortly with a grey-bearded, black-suited, liberal Jewish Rabbi.

The Muslim man told me that as representatives of the three great monotheistic religions of the world – Christianity, Islam and Judaism – we had much in common. "Perhaps," he said diplomatically, "all roads lead to God."

I countered this by saying that Jesus was the Way, the Truth and the Life. The Rabbi smiled and stroked his beard. A bemused silence was his only contribution. The Muslim shopkeeper was a natural nurturer. He saw how eager and sincere I was and did not want to burst my bubble.

"Jesus was a very great prophet. All three of us have Abraham/ Ibrahim as our ancestor. In May – next month – I am going on the hajj – the pilgrimage to Mecca. It will be a great event in my life. I was taught as a child that just as the prophet Jonah spent three days in the belly of the whale, so Jesus spent three days in the belly of the Earth," said my new Muslim friend.

I began to talk. Then I began to speak faster. I spouted scripture from the New Testament and threw around Sacred quotations like confetti at a wedding. The two men smiled benignly at me as I practically went into a spasm of hyperventilation.

Finally my rippling torrent of words came to an end. I asked both men if they would do me the kindness of accepting a copy each of 'The Reason Why'. They accepted graciously.

"You must accept a gift from me," said the Rabbi, speaking for the first time. The Muslim man's children were behind the counter of his shop. The Rabbi went over to the counter and asked for the last three Easter eggs, sitting forlornly on a shelf. He bought them and then presented one to the Muslim, one to a nervous Christian Evangelist (me) and tucked the third under his arm. "Now, my friends," he said, smiling broadly. "The three great monotheistic religions of the world are joined together by the theology of chocolate!"

We all laughed and a somewhat chastened Christian Evangelist thanked his older brother in God.

*   *   *

Two Little Boys

It was the year 3,771 in the Jewish calendar. Israel was occupied by the Roman Army. The sun blazed down on the compound, as it always does at midday in that part of the world.

Two little ten year old boys were sent on an errand. One, in that land of fine Roman noses, had a particularly fine proboscis. It was hooked at the end and earned him the nickname 'Hooky'. His friend, who was always studying the Hebrew Bible and other holy books in the Temple had the nickname 'Booky'. Booky's father was a carpenter, much in demand by the upper echelons of the Roman Army. He had a talent for turning out pieces of furniture which found favour with the occupying forces. Today, he was working on furniture which he constructed in situ, in the compound.

He had brought his son to work, in the hope that the boy might develop as much affection for working with wood as he showed for the Holy Books. It would be no shame to the family if Booky turned out to be a Rabbi, but, even still, his father believed a bit of an appreciation for his own trade would be no hardship to carry through life.

Booky's father wondered if his high-minded son was really a suitable candidate for his trade. Still, it was good to have the boy with him to fetch water in the midday sun and to assist at the work.

"I want you to go into the village and buy me a portion of figs," said Booky's father, placing a coin in his son's hand. "Yes father," said Booky and together with Hooky, set off for the gates of the compound.

The guard of the gate did not see the boys coming. He was outside the gate, snoozing in the sun, his helmet providing an adequate shelter from the always clement weather,

Hooky and Booky stepped through the hole in the gate and noticed the sleeping guard. Booky suddenly had an idea. He answered Hooky's question, "Where are you going?" by placing a finger to his lips in a request for silence. To Hooky's amazement, Booky took off the sleeping guard's helmet and placed it on the ground quietly. Hooky stifled a snigger.

"His brains will boil."

"Not at all," said Booky. "The sun will just give him a nice tan."

The road to the village was wide enough to take a chariot. The dusty red earth was dry and allowed the invader a smooth journey. Soon the two boys reached the little white houses of the village and, within minutes, the marketplace. Booky gave the silver coin, with the bust of Caesar, to a stall holder in return for a portion of figs. The stall holder wanted to give him change in kind. He suggested a pomegranate. When Booky declined, the merchant suggested a portion of dates, raisins and some fresh fish, caught that very morning in the local lake.

Booky finally received his change and with Hooky in tow, headed back along the dusty road to the compound.

When they reached the compound a new guard was at the gate.

"Where is the other guard?" asked Hooky, with the spirit of devilment that was characteristic of him.

"He had to go to the apothecary," said the young Roman soldier. "He fell asleep in the sun and when he woke up he had a headache. It seems his helmet fell off halfway through his watch."

"Tell him I will pray for him," said Booky.

For the second time that day Hooky stifled a snigger. "Don't worry," he said to Booky, as they approached the house his father was working in. "I'd never betray you."

"I know you mean that sincerely, right now, Judas," said Jesus looking over the walls of the compound, to the hills around Nazareth, as if he was looking into the future.

*   *   *

I finished and said, "That's very interesting. I don't see anything illegal in there."

"They said I was in breach of the peace and trading without a hawker's licence. I wasn't trading. I was giving copies of my book away."

"Then you haven't anything to worry about."

I tried to reassure him.

The following morning, in court the Guard said the defendant was causing a breach of the peace. The Justice said to his Clerk that the defendant was a respectable looking man.

"What is your background?" asked the Justice.

The evangelist quoted from the Book of Psalms.

"My father owns the cattle that live on a thousand hills."

"A farming background," mused the Justice and added, as if to himself, "...... prone to exaggeration. Well I'll let you off with a warning – try to keep the peace. Probation Act."

"Thank you Jesus!" said the evangelist.

And so say all of us!

Both Sides of A Honeymoon

Dear Friend,

First of all I must tell you of a new development in my life. I think I'm falling in love with my secretary, Sharon. I see her every day and I cherish the morning and afternoon tea breaks when we talk to each other about everything. I have never opened up to a woman as much as I have with Sharon. She has a lovely sense of humour and a good heart – not to mention a voluptuous figure which would tempt the Pope or as a client of mine once put it, referring to a sexy singing star – she would put a horn on a snowman.

I haven't taken to writing poetry to her as yet, but we have had dinner together at my favourite Chinese restaurant. The afterglow of a couple of bottles of wine can even ward off the worst of our winter weather. I once read somewhere that people in love tend to live longer and enjoy better health. I must say that my own experience supports that.

Will the eternal bachelor follow up and snare himself on a delicious female trap? Will he step back and allow the old hormones to cool down? Watch this space for further news.

Best wishes,
Patrick

Dear Friend,

It has finally happened. The Great Bachelor has finally fallen head over heels in love. Between the lines of the letters I have been writing you over the past while you may have picked up a sign that the relationship between Sharon and I has been more than employer/employee. Out of our different needs an affection has grown which we both have been unsure of until lately.

The decisive night occurred last Saturday in Hefners Hotel. As you know this white wedding cake of a building attracts a young up-market clientele at weekends because of its location and basement discothèque. When you go into the main foyer you have a choice of two lounge bars, the ABS on the right and the XYZ on the left. Before arriving there last Saturday night I put away quite a few pints. I was gliding along on alcohol induced euphoria when I looked into the ABC lounge and spotted Sharon. She was by herself and I felt a pang of jealousy at the thought that she might be waiting for another fellow.

I walked down the corridor and made my way to the reading room. There were a couple of residents having a leisurely read. I bid them a polite good evening, sat down at a bureau, took out some hotel notepaper and wrote:

Dear Miss Thomas,

I have been watching you for some time now and I would like you to know that I fancy everything you are. I am considering you for the position of mistress/wife, presently vacant, and I wonder if you would care to apply?

Please forward applications together with any references you may have recommending you for the above position at your earliest convenience.

Yours Sensually,
Patrick

I put the note in an envelope, addressed it and went out to the foyer. I gave it to the porter, told him who it was for and gave him a generous top for delivering it. I was taking a risk by spelling out my love for her. She could easily take offence.

Five minutes later a bewildered porter brought me in a letter. "How many maids and butlers have you people worn out?" he asked as he walked away shaking his head. I opened the envelope and her reply read as follows:

Dear Patrick,

I refer to yours of ten minutes ago. I would like to be considered for the position as advertised. You will find that I have had a lot of on-the-job training and I believe I am suited to any position mentioned in the Kama Sutra and a few more besides.

I am afraid I don't have any references from my former lovers. I always left them too exhausted to write.

Yours Sexually,
Sharon.

I put away her letter and walked into the ABC lounge grinning as wide as a slice of melon. I found her and bought us both a drink. We clinked glasses and offered each other "cheers"! I felt like the cat who had got the cream. The future would never again be the same as the past.

Back in her flat that night we made love for the first time. I wish I was a poet so that I could let her know in an exotic fashion all that she meant to me. We hope to marry shortly. I want it to be a day no one will ever forget.

Best wishes,
Patrick

Dear Friend,

Sharon and I are now married! For starters we made the decision to get married at Christmas time. So in a few short months we managed to get all the necessary things done in time for an April wedding. We had to find out when a hotel would be able to cater for the list of guests we had drawn up. There is a tradition that the bride's father pays for the wedding breakfast and Sharon's father footed the bill in a gesture of generosity that is typical of him.

A girl with whom I worked offered to sing in the church during the wedding ceremony, so that was one task taken care of. We spoke to the priest as one of our first priorities. There were flowers to be ordered, clothes to be bought, a photographer to be lined up, an organist to accompany the singer, place cards and wedding invitations to be printed, posted and R.S.V.Peed.

The day comes back to be in moments caught in the camera of memory. In the chapel at the altar Sharon looked lovely with her hair twirled in ringlets. When I gave her the gold ring and silver coin, tokens of all I possessed, my best man looked at the fifty pence piece and said, "You're getting a bargain for that."

We ran through a number of possible ceremonies with the priest and finally settled for the following:

Bridegroom:	Do you consent to be my wife?
Bride:	I do. Do you consent to be my husband?
Bridegroom:	I do. I take you as my wife and I give myself to you as your husband.
Bride:	I take you as my husband and I give myself to you as your wife.

(At this point in the ceremony we joined hands and said together:)

To love each other truly
for better, for worse
for richer, for poorer,
in sickness and in health
all the days of our life.

Then the priest then said:

> What God joins together
> Man must not separate.
> May the Lord confirm the consent
> that you have given and enrich
> you with his blessing.

Outside the chapel our two families and all our friends posed for photographs. The full wedding party posed for the group photograph and the photographer was helped out by Sharon's uncle Dan. He couldn't get everybody to say "cheese" or smile at the same time so Dan said, "Some people say cheese and more say knickers." The photographer took advantage of the ensuing laughter.

Sharon and I got into a black Mercedes limousine with white bunting, to go to the hotel. Cars pulled over en route, tooted their horns and waved us good luck. It was a special day.

The meal began with our priest saying Grace. We had a starter of grapefruit cocktails, turkey and ham with mint peas, golden carrots, roast potatoes and a choice of red or white wine. To follow we had dessert and coffee and although it was all first class I did not taste a bit of the meal. My nerves had my stomach churning. Although I had meticulously prepared my speech I was as nervous as a kitten about delivering it. Here follows my wedding speech:-

Ladies and Gentlemen,

I knew the minute I clapped eyes on my beautiful bride that she wasn't just another one-night-stand-drop-the-hand-and-see-how-far-you-can-get-with-sort-of-girl. We met in a pub and one of the first things she said to me was, 'When I smoke I get passionate'. So I said, 'Come here, sit down on my lap and have a cigar!' I walked her home and said to her at the gate, 'Would you like to come out with me tomorrow night?' She said, 'I never go out with perfect strangers'. I said, 'So who's perfect?'

I said, 'Is it OK to kiss you goodnight?' She said, 'No. I'm sorry. I've got scruples'. I said, 'That's all right, I've been vaccinated'. Yes, some girls shrink from lovemaking and others get bigger and bigger. Here we are at last: Sharon is all in white and I'm white and all in.

> Very much unlike the young fellow from Lyme
> who lived with three wives at a time.
> When asked 'Why the third?
> He replied 'One's absurd,
> And bigamy, sir, is a crime!

Popping the question can be a dicey business. My grandfather once proposed to a woman with the words, 'How would you like to hang your knickers on the end of my bed every night? Begob and I wouldn't mind swapping my hot water bottle for you!' Naturally the woman declined. But a man not easily defeated, he shouted at her, 'If you don't marry me I'll die.' And sure enough 54 years later the man died. When a woman finally accepted his proposal he was 80 years of age, and he went to the doctor's for a check-up. He said, 'Doctor, my thingy fell off and I'm getting married next month. I have it in my pocket'. He took a little brown yoke out of his pocket and the doctor said, 'This is a bit of a cigar'. And granddad said, 'Jaysus, Mary and Joseph I musta smoked my thingy'. The doctor said, 'What age is your girlfriend?' Granddad said, 'She's 22'. The doctor said, 'Good God man! Don't you realise this could be fatal?' Granddad said, 'Ah well. Sure if she dies, she dies!' The doctor said knowingly, 'I think you ought to get in a lodger to keep your wife company. Someone young and about her own vintage'. Granddad said, 'That's a good idea!'

What a day we had at the wedding! Her family threw confetti and our lot threw pep pills. The priest was cross-eyed. He married the best man to the bridegroom, kissed the money congratulations and put the bride in his pocket.

Six months later Granddad met the doctor. After the usual greetings the doctor said, 'How is your wife?' Granddad said, 'Great .... she's pregnant!' The doctor smiled cynically and said, 'And ...... eh ...... how is the lodger?' Even better,' said Granddad. 'She's pregnant too!' What a great man!

It was so sad the way he died. He fell off a platform and he would have broken both legs if it wasn't for the rope around his neck. I sympathised with his young widow. I said to her, 'How exactly did he die?' She sniffed and said tearfully, 'We used to make love every Sunday morning in rhythm with the gentle chimes of the church bells and on the morning he died a fire-engine went racing up the road.'

Popping the question for me was a dicey business too. I said to Sharon one evening very bluntly, 'Will you marry me?' And just then her father burst through the door and said, 'We have your name, address and phone number. We know how much money you earn a week and if no one better qualified for the job turns up – we'll be in touch!'

To tell you the truth the night I proposed to Sharon she got such a surprise she nearly fell out of the bed,

No! Even that is a lie! To tell you the truth it was a leap year and:

> This joyful girl who has just eaten
> This beauty with the white dress on
> Said, 'Marry me dear
> And you'll find that my rere
> is a nice place to warm your cold feet on!'

Unfortunately love is not all wine and roses. Sharon and I have had many rainbow kisses – they're the sort you have after a storm. One row we had blew up because after I'd shown her a picture of myself as a little boy, sitting on my father's knee she said, 'The ventriloquist looks nice but I don't think much of the dummy'. I got my own back later on that night as we sat on the sofa having a session. Sharon said, 'Say those three little words that will leave me walking on air'.

And I said very romantically, 'Go (kiss) hang (kiss) yourself (kiss)'. Another time I stood up on a weighing machine, put in a penny and out popped a card. I said, 'Hey Sharon look at this. It says here I'm good looking, rugged and virile, a born leader and irresistible to the opposite sex'. She said, 'Gimme a look at that. Yes, just as I thought, it's got your weight wrong too'. One night, after a row, I grabbed my coat and was rushing out of the house when I bumped into Sharon's little brother. I said to him, 'I think your sister is rotten!' And he said, 'Ah no she's not rotten. That's just the smell of the perfume she wears'.

I said to Sharon one time, 'Do you know what I like about you most?' She said, 'My hair?' I said, 'No!' She said, 'My face and figure?' I said, 'No!' She said, 'My brains and talents?' I said, 'No!' She said, 'Ah I give in!' I said, 'That's what I like about you most!'

You know there are lots of funny definitions of marriage floating around these days:

Marriage, they say, is a three ring circus, engagement ring, wedding ring, childering.

Marriage, they say, is that state where a man gives away half of his dinner in order to have the other half cooked. Love is blind and marriage is an eye-opener. Love is a sweet dream and marriage is the alarm clock. Love is the wine of life and marriage is the hangover.

Since we're on the subject of definitions, if men were really honest with themselves, I'd say their ideal woman would not be the Hollywood, dolly bird type but most men's ideal woman would be a deaf and dumb nymphomaniac who owns a pub. My brand new wife – straight from the cellophane pack – has just told me to invite you all to the child's christening, which is next Saturday week.

I have written a special poem for Sharon for today and this is it:

> In the next few weeks we'll share
> Great fun, good times and plenty of loving.
> You'll be like a Summer chicken salad!
> Fresh, tender and with little dressing.
>
> Wedding days are first class
> with friends and relatives
> and double meaning telegrams
> such as:
>
> Take a tip from one who knows
> Tie your nightie to your toes!
> If an apple a day keeps the doctor away
> What would a pear do tonight?
>
> You were shy last night
> And the night before

But after tonight
You'll be shy no more

May your wedding night
be like the coffee table
- all legs and no drawers!

Wedding days lead to help from Christ,
nice presents, big eats and jokes about sex.
Our wedding cake is a whitewashed scone
with a superiority complex.

Take your time about having our first baby.
I'm sure he'll be small, loveable and weak.
And the first time I take him in my arms.
He'll more than likely spring a leak!

Love for us has never been a word,
to be scoffed at or regarded as naïve.
Love is like a winning goal scored.
And places us in a whole new league.

All totted up that makes a good sum.
So let's have a lively party.
I hope you'll stay for many years to come.
As happy as you are today!

We went to Spain on our honeymoon. Even through it was only
April the weather was exceptionally good. A funny thing I remember
was the fact that in the town there was a pub which had originally
been called the Duke of Wellington. Some jazzy loving vandal had
removed certain letters so that the pub's name was changed to the Duke
Ellington.

We lay in the sun. We swam in the sea and in the hotel's swimming
pool and we made love at all times of the night and day. We went to
the organised barbecue and laid into great hunks of chicken and pork,
light green lettuce and beef tomatoes. We went to a nightclub – free

champagne all night was included in the admission price. Flamenco dancers – all frills and ruffles – trousers they had been poured into, glittery lurex tops, brightly coloured skirts – rapped their heels to guitar tunes.

I sent an oversized postcard home which I still have. It reads:

Hi folks!
Having a great time. The weather is beautiful, sunny and warm. Booze is cheap and hangovers are common. The shops are swamped with souvenirs. On the first day's sunbathing we looked like a pair of milk bottles. Now we hope out sunburn will turn into a tan. The sun has shone all the time except for a few hours on Wednesday when it was wet and windy – like a baby with colic.

We are both discovering places where previously the hand of man has not set foot.

Best wishes,
Patrick and Sharon.

Dear Friend,

Something has happened in my life that has taken us by surprise – Sharon is pregnant.

We had hoped to postpone baby-making for a few years and live the young upwardly mobile life without the patter of tiny feet. However, nature and bad planning have gazumped us in that respect. We are slowly resigning ourselves to the reality. Sharon is determined to be a most fashionable expectant mother and the clothes brochures have already arrived.

Thank God we are financially secure. I'm glad I made my name before this occurrence. I don't mean to weigh you down with my problems but you are a man who has already been in this situation? So, have you any advice for me? Any old poems I can give Sharon to bring her round to the idea that this is one of the best things that could ever happen to us? To tell you the truth I'm a bit half-hearted in the belief that it is one of the best things.

I really had other plans for our first years of marriage. After every year of expansion you need a year of consolidation. Progress first, then relax and enjoy the progress and get used to it. We performed this trick sooner than planned. Help!

Best wishes
Patrick

Dear Friend,

I'm a Dad! Sharon had a baby boy in the Rotunda Hospital yesterday. I was present for the birth but what an ordeal poor Sharon had. Her labour lasted 36 hours. She was overdue so the gynaecologist induced her. However, when God cursed woman-kind with hardship in their labour, He really did a good job of it.

The gyny gave Sharon some hormone tablets to get the show on the road and she had a bad reaction to them. I took her into hospital two days ago and it was the afternoon that her inducement began. When she had an adverse reaction to the hormones the gyny stopped treatment and let Sharon have a rest. I went home and came back the following day. Before I was allowed into her room I had to put on a gown and mask. I was all ready to make with the Dr. Kildare jokes but when I saw Sharon I got a shock. She was tied up to a number of drips and she looked exhausted.

Eventually her waters broke, contractions began, an epidural was given, labour pains diminished and at 9pm Larry Pio Chapman came sliding down the vaginal canal and made his entry into the world with the help of forceps.

I'm a right bastard! I have kept a secret from you for a long time. When Sharon went in for her scan in the early part of her pregnancy the doctor discovered not one but two heartbeats. Melissa Ashling Chapman came sliding down the vaginal canal two minutes after her brother. I am the father of twins! How about that? We are the parents of two little miracles!

In recent years a gyny discovered that the sound of music in the delivery room aids the mother. So there was a speaker playing music in Sharon's room. Just after Melissa was born Stevie Wonder sang out of the speaker 'Isn't she lovely!' We all concurred with Stevie and were amused at how appropriate the song was.

Poor old Sharon was delighted that all her labour was so rewarded. It was no joke toting the two of them around for nine months and now we have our family.

I made phone calls. I handed out cigars and I got merry if not drunk. I brought champagne into the hospital and Sharon and I drank a toast to our lovely children and ourselves.

Best wishes,
Patrick

Dear Friend,

I'm exhausted! Revelations are coming fast and furious. I never knew women get so weepy after giving birth. Boy did poor Sharon weep a river! And then, of course the kids joined in!

Sharon didn't get the hand of breast-feeding so we put the two tykes on bottles. How taxing night feeds are! Sharon woke up one night recently, totally bushed, and got out of bed to a fanfare of the twins squealing. She said, "I'm knackered. I'm so tired. There babies are a blessing, you know?" I laughed. "Yes, a gift from God," continued Sharon. "Come up here gifts until I clean your shitty bums!"

Another early morning the two tykes were crying for their bottles and again it was Sharon's turn to feed them. With all the caterwauling I was awake. Sharon gave me a kiss and asked, "Is it too late to have an abortion?"

I am slowly getting used to baby crap. The first few days made my stomach heave and I shot out of the room like a hot snot.

Best wishes,
Patrick

Dear Friend.

The twins are a month old and thriving. Sharon is a wonderful mother but how naïve we were! We thought we could cope with anything and that it would not take a gig out of us. Life has a way of putting us straight. Sharon and I had a good heart-to-heart. We realised things will never be the same again. We also admitted that we need help.

Sharon confided in me that she wanted to continue being my right hand man in work. Obviously she could not do everything so we have employed an au pair to help out with the twins. She is a lovely French girl named Anne-Marie. She has blonde hair, blue eyes and if I wasn't cracked about Sharon I would be sorely tempted. She has a soothing effect on the terrible twins and they have become used to her.

Sharon was traumatised by the long labour she had to endure having the babies. She goes out walking each evening and is getting back her figure. Like the repentant, hung-over drunk, she swears 'never again' when I jokingly tell her I'd like more children. We now have our 'gentleman's family' and I think one of us will be putting a knot in it.

Best wishes,
Patrick

Dear Friend,

Preparation for parenthood is not just a matter of reading books and decorating the nursery. Here are some simple tests for expectant/aspiring parents to take to prepare themselves for the real life experiences of being a mother or father.

1   Women: to prepare for maternity, put on a dressing down and stick a beanbag down the front. Leave it there for nine months. After nine months take out 10% of the beans. Men: to prepare for paternity, go to the local chemist, tip the contents of your wallet on the counter and tell the pharmacist to help himself. Then got to the supermarket, arrange to have your salary paid directly to their head office. Go home pick up the paper. Read it for the last time.

2   Before you finally go ahead and have children find a couple who are already parents and berate them about their method of discipline, lack of patience, appallingly low tolerance levels and how they have allowed their children to run riot. Suggest ways in which they might improve their children's sleeping habits, toilet training, table manners and overall behaviour. Enjoy it – it'll be the last time in your life you will have all the answers.

3   T0 discover how the nights will feel – walk around the living room from 5pm to 10pm carrying a wet bag weighing approximately 8-12lbs. At 10pm put the bag down; set the alarm for midnight and go to sleep. Get up at midnight and walk around the living room again with the wet bag until 1am. Put on the alarm for 3am. As you can't get back to sleep get up at 2am and make a drink. Get up again at 3am when the alarm goes off. Sing songs in the dark until 4am. Put the alarm on for 5am. Get up. Make breakfast. Keep this up for 5 years. Look cheerful.

4   Can you stand the mess children make? To find out first smear Marmite into the sofa and jam onto the curtains. Hide a fish finger behind the stereo and leave it there all summer. Stick your fingers in the flower bed and then rub them on the clean walls. Cover the stains with crayons. How does that look?

5   Dressing small children is not as easy as it seems. First buy an octopus and a string bag. Attempt to put the octopus into the

string bag so that none of the arms hang out. Time allowed for this – all day.

6   Take an egg carton. Using a pair of scissors and a pot of paint turn it into an alligator. Now take a toilet roll. Using only Sellotape and a piece of foil turn it into a Christmas cracker. Last, take a milk container, a ping pong ball, and an empty packet of Coco Pops and make an exact replica of the Eiffel Tower. Congratulations, you have just qualified for a place on the playgroup committee.

7   Forget the Peugeot 205 and buy a Sierra. And don't think you can leave it out in the driveway spotless and shining. Family cars don't look like that. Buy a choc-ice and put it in the glove compartment – leave it there. Get a 20p piece. Stick it in the cassette player. Take a family size packet of chocolate biscuits. Mash them down the back seats. Run a garden rake along both sides of the car. There. Perfect.

8   Get ready to go out. Wait outside the toilet for half an hour. Go out the front door. Come in again. Walk down the front path. Walk back up it. Walk down it again. Walk very slowly down the road for 5 minutes. Stop to inspect minutely every cigarette and piece of chewing gum, dirty tissue and dead insect along the way. Retrace your steps. Scream that you have had as much as you can stand until the neighbours come out and stare at you. Give up and go back into the house. You are now just about ready to take a small child for a walk.

9   always repeat everything you say at least five times.

10 Go to the local supermarket. Take with you the nearest thing you can find to a preschool child; a fully grown goat is excellent. If you intend to have more than one child take more than one goat. Buy your week's groceries without letting the goat out of your sight. Pay for everything the goats destroy. Unless you can easily accomplish this do not even contemplate having children.

11 Hollow out a melon. Make a small hole in the side. Suspend it from the ceiling and swing it from side to side. How get a bowl of soggy Wheatabix and spoon it into the swaying melon by pretending to be an aeroplane. Continue until half the Wheatabix is gone. Tip the other half into your lap, making sure a lot of it falls on the floor. You are now ready to feed a twelve month old baby.

12 Learn the names of every character from Postman Pat, Fireman Sam and Teenage Mutant Ninja Turtles. When you find yourself singing the theme from Postman Pat at work, you are finally ready to qualify as a parent.

Best wishes,
Patrick

P.S. There will be times when it will seem like you haven't got a prayer. So I enclose one.

Because God Loves Me
I Cor. 13:4-8

Because God loves me He is slow to lose patience with me.

Because God loves me He takes the circumstances of my life and uses them in a constructive way for my growth.

Because God loves me He does not treat me as an object to be possessed and manipulated.

Because God loves me He has no need to impress me with how great and powerful He is because *He is God* nor does he belittle me as His child in order to show me how important He is.

Because God loves me He is for me. He wants to see me mature and develop in His love.

Because God loves me He does not send down His wrath on every little mistake I make of which there are many.

Because God loves me He does not keep score of all my sins and then beat me over the head with them whenever He gets the chance.

Because God loves me He is deeply grieved when I do not walk in the ways that please Him because He sees this as evidence that I don't trust Him and love Him as I should.

Because God loves me He rejoices when I experience His power and strength and stand up under the pressures of life for His Name's sake.

Because God loves me He keeps on working patiently with me even when I feel like giving up and can't see why He doesn't give up with me, too.

Because God loves me He keeps on trusting me when at times I don't even trust myself.

Because God loves me He never says there is no hope for you, rather, he patiently works with me, loves me and disciplines me in such a way that it is hard for me to understand the depth of His concern for me.

Because God loves me He never forsakes me even thought many of my friends might.

Because God loves me He stands with me when I have reached the rock bottom of despair, when I see myself in a distorted mirror and compare that with his righteousness, holiness, beauty and love. It is at a moment like this that I can really believe that God loves me.

Yes, the greatest of all gifts is God's perfect love!

Scallywag Love

The house in which fourteen year old Scallywag O'Connor lived was regarded as the height of opulent splendour during the reign of King William IV. With Queen Victoria it went steadily downward from respectability to shabbiness with lace curtains, to shabbiness without lace curtains and finally gave up all pretension to number one of the almost six thousand tenements, housing ninety thousand Dubliners in the second city of King Edward VII's Empire. Scallywag contributed to putting bread on the table of his mother's third floor two-pair back, but selling newspapers to 'the quality' who lived in Fitzwilliam Square.

On a dismal February evening with rain cascading down like stair rods the 'quality' were drenched as they alighted from trams and buses. It was a well known fact, at the time, that a good wetting could carry a soul off to heaven before he or she had grown old enough to have a decent walk around the city centre.

Scallywag did not fear the wet bareness of his beat. His shoulders were protected by a hessian sack and although he had a touch of a cold, which lingering winter did not help, he found shelter in the doorway of Parnell's public house. Every now and again Scallywag let out a raucous roar that assaulted the heart as well as the ears of passers-by. "Herrel or Mayel! Herrel or Mayel!"

All at once his grimy face lit up with a smile and he ran across the asphalt, his bare feet leaving fountains of rain water behind. His Princess had just alighted from a tram and was waiting for him on the steps of her home with full confidence in the weather defying quality of her Selfridge's bonnet. Scallywag had many favourite customers, from Mr Flitterman, the pawnbroker to the Reverend gentleman who pastored the Peppercanister Church but the elegant and graceful Mrs Connolly was Scallywag's Princess. Scallywag loved her. The young wife of a well-to-do medical doctor, Mrs Connolly's custom of her suppler of the Late-Extra Evening Mail had blossomed into friendship on her part and infatuated heroine workshop on his. To Scallywag Mrs Connolly was as near to the fanciful ecstasy of a wax lady in Clery's window coming to life as he could hope. Her clothes were always graceful and elegant. Not only that but she favoured him with a wink and a generous tip on Christmas Eve. She was a good sport and all that a lady should be.

"Good evening, Scallywag," she greeted him.

"Good evening, Miss."

"You really should be wearing shoes in weather like this."

Scallywag was touched by her concern but who ever heard of a newspaper boy wearing shoes? The thought was as ridiculous as it was kind.

"Here," said Mrs Connolly, handing him a half crown. "Go and buy yourself something to cover those feet. It's bad enough that I have a cold without you getting one too."

"Thanks very much, Miss."

Scallywag was in seventh heaven with the coin jingling in his good pocket.

The next day was as dismal weather-wise as the average Irish winter evening. Although it was officially spring, no one seemed to have told the rain. Mrs Connolly did not appear for her Evening Mail. This was not unusual when another day and a third went by without any sign of her, Scallywag began to worry. He watched her hall door carefully and hoped against hope.

On the fourth evening a car arrived at the door and a gentleman carrying a black bag went into the house. He was inside for about half an hour and then Scallywag saw the boy from H.C.R. chemists ride up on his bicycle and deliver a parcel. Scallywag ran across and questioned him. "Hey!" he said. "Who's sick?"

"The lady inside," said the messenger boy. "She's dyin' – pewmoaneeya."

Scallywag was shocked to his core. He turned on his heel and made for a hidey-hole he sometimes retreated to, down the lane at the back of Baggot Street. He climbed over the wall and dropped down into a stable. He sat down on a bale of straw and felt in his jacket pocket for the butt of a cigarette, lit it and drew a few puffs with melancholy satisfaction. It was then that Scallywag's agony dissolved into the healing solution of tears.

Why her? Why her? Why the Princess? His grieving heart admitted no consolation except tobacco. It wasn't right. It wasn't fair. Why should she be dying? Now himself, out in all weathers, it would be understandable if he was the one for the long jump. But the lady – why her?

Scallywag could not make sense of life or the world. Please God, don't' let her die, he prayed in his mind. I'll be a good boy. I'll even give up the smokes. He was at the bargaining stage of bereavement. I won't mitch from school either, he promised.

As he strolled home, that evening. Scallywag was a pitiable object and a sorry spectacle. In the main room of the tenement flat his mother sat in front of a roaring fire with her feet up on the low set mantelpiece. She was allowing the heat of the fire to warm her nether regions.

His Da came in looking very sombre, morose and sullen.

"Did that landlord call today?" his father asked his mother, totally ignoring Scallywag.

"He did," she answered shortly.

"Did you pay the rent?"

"Well, you know the story – it's the rent or a ride."

"Did you pay it?"

His mother smiled, her feel still on the mantelpiece, the warmth of the fire swirling up her skirt.

"Do you not see me drying the receipt?" she asked and both Scallywag's Ma and Da laughed. He didn't know why they were so happy but he was glad.

Early next morning Scallywag ran to Fitzwilliam Square to find out the news. The curtains were closed and from his vantage point later that morning he saw a maid, her eyes red with crying, come out and fix a ribbon of crepe on the door-knocker. Scallywag's heart sank and it seemed to him that the whole street was draped in black, the wind whistled venomously up from Merrion Square and Scallywag's sensitive conscience impelled him to run all the way to Clery's department store where he handed over his half-crown for a new pair of black boots. He paid no attention to the weather. It had worked its worst on the slender, graceful lady whom he had worshipped.

The funeral was the following morning at Westland Row church – a great temple built, like most of the cathedrals of Europe, by the pennies of the poor. The group of black-clothed mourners in the big church was very small. One mourner, however, went unnoticed; a small ragged boy with new black boots, prayed an Our Father, a Hail Mary and a Glory Be for his Princess. When Mass was over he slipped out of the chapel and set off at a trot down Pearse Street, across Butt Bridge and up Gardiner Street, heading for Glasnevin Cemetery – the dead centre of Dublin. He was not at all afraid that the funeral would arrive there before him. If you have to run every evening from the Herald van in College Green to Fitzwilliam Square, in order to get a good sale for your papers, you find it an easy matter to compete with even the least staid of funeral coaches.

When Scallywag trotted to the main gate of the cemetery he congratulated himself on getting there in time. The coffin was carried in with Dr Connolly, pale and stern, behind it. As the coffin, on the shoulders of men in frock coats and silk hats, officially sad, wended its way to the graveside, Scallywag stayed about a hundred yards away. Dr Connolly stood at the head of the grave with a grey, stunned look on his face.

The light spring breeze bore down to Scallywag the voice of the priest as he intoned the prayers. Scallywag pulled off his ragged cap and made the Sign of the Cross. It was not long before the grave diggers filled in the grave and Dr Connolly and the other mourners walked to the gate. As he did so Dr Connolly looked back to see the small ragged boy walk to his wife's grave and place a beautiful red rose on it. Even from the distance Dr Connolly recognised that, like the Widow's Mite, this tribute was more costly than the four wreaths of expensive hothouse flowers pile upon the grave. Dr Connolly experienced a blinding flash of the obvious. That little ragamuffin loved her too, he thought.

The same evening Scallywag took up his post outside Parnell's public house and let out his roar: "Herrel or Mayel" Herrel or Mayel!" He didn't see Dr Connolly approaching with a coin in his hand. Scallywag blushed and thought he should say something.

"I'm very sorry sir – about your wife – the lady."

"Yes, I know you are," said Dr Connolly. He smiled in sympathetic fellowship.

"Tell me what would you do if someone gave you a pound?"

"Gosh sir – I don't know. I suppose I would buy a shovel for my Da – a man can always get a day's work if he owns his own shovel."

"What would you do with the rest of it?"

Scallywag thought for a while. "I'd buy a big Bewley's cake for my Ma."

"And what would you buy for yourself?"

"I don't know, sir – a packet of woodbines I think."

"I'm going away to the Isle of Man to recover from the initial shock of my wife's demise."

Scallywag took this in and thought: imagine going on a holiday; not only that but going on a boat on a holiday. It was how the quality lived and he didn't begrudge Dr Connolly an ounce of it.

Dr Connolly took out his wallet and handed a bewildered Scallywag a pound note.

"Thank you very much, sir," he gasped.

"What would you like to work at when you are a man?" asked the doctor.

"I s'pose I'll go on the buildings like my Da."

"Is your father a labourer?"

"Yes sir, he's a labouring man when he can get work."

"When I come back from my break I will help you begin as an apprentice bricklayer. A man can have a better life if he has a trade."

"Thank you very much, sir."

Dr Connolly turned to walk away but then he realised he had something else to say.

"Scallywag," he began. "God loves you and so do I. In this world you have to love yourself before you can love other people. If you have faith that there is a reason behind life, you have to love yourself and be kind to yourself as well as others. Be proud of yourself no matter what because there is great goodness in you."

"Thank you sir," answered Scallywag. No one had ever spoken to him like that before. His life was going to be a valid adventure.

After Dr Connolly had left, Scallywag completed his sales for the evening occasionally feeling the pound note in his good pocket. It called for a celebratory smoke. He trotted down the lane, scarpered over the wall and ensconced himself on a bale of straw in the stable. He felt in his pocket for his packet of cigarettes and pulled one out. He felt more tears coming but stopped them by wiping his eyes and nose with the back of his hand. He lit up and smiled. He was going to have a great life – the life of Riley. Here, at last, was peace.

How To Survive Practically Anything

I came into work one morning to find on my desk a formal notice of early retirement. I cleaned out my desk and wandered the streets in a bewildered state of mind. How could they do this to me, I asked myself. I had done nothing wrong but still the hammer had fallen.

I found myself at the top of Grafton Street in Ballyskerry. I spotted a new friend, Peter O' Brien, standing on the corner shouting out his wares. He was selling a small booklet for a pound. "Read all about it! Buy a book of poems for charity!"

Unlike most street sellers he was well dressed in a blue blazer, grey slacks, blue striped shirt and red tie. I approached him, gave him a pound and told him my tale of woe.

"There is a better life waiting for you," he said. "Don't give up on the brink of a miracle. At least you'll have a pension to underpin your income and you'll get another hike from the dividends on your gratuity."

I thanked him and we made an appointment to meet later for a sandwich and drink. I strolled to the Grand Hotel, ordered a pot of tea and settled down on a sofa in the foyer to read the booklet Peter had sold me. I thought that, at all costs, I must distract myself from the dismal thoughts I felt.

Peter arrived a short time later. "These are the gifts you need to give yourself in order to survive practically anything," he said.

"The give of determination.

The gift of creative problem solving.

127

The gift of self-awareness.
The gift of spiritual recommitment.
The gift of tolerating ambivalence.
The gift of patience.
The gift of calmness and self-control.
The gift of being non-judgemental.
The gift of meaning.
The gift of relationship.
The gift of decisiveness and action.
The gift of gratitude.
The gift of your mother
or father's way of handling this problem,
The gift of tolerance.
The gift of forgiveness.
The gift of self-love.
The gift of a clear conscience.
The gift of faith.
The gift of hope.
The gift of handling this
problem like a cultured
gentleman and not
like a guttersnipe.
The gift of the promises of the Holy Bible."

I counted them. They amounted to twenty one in all.

"I could certainly do with some of them," I agreed.

"I was unemployed when I was a young man for six years. I sent out hundreds of C.V.'s and answered hundreds of job ads. But still I couldn't get a job.

"I was enjoying a smoke and a cup of tea one morning, listening to classical music and reading a book of poems when my mother said to me, 'Why aren't you out looking for a job?' I said, 'if God wants me to have a job, He'll send me one.' 'Oh god is it – I'll get the parish priest for you,' she said. 'We'll see if the parish priest can't put the smile on the other side of your face.'

"She went off and came back with the parish priest in tow. 'Hello Peter,' says he. 'I believe you've been unemployed for six years – that's a long time.'

"'Not to worry father," says I. 'If God wants me to have a job – He'll send me one.'

"'Ah now Peter – God helps those who help themselves. Do you look for work every day?'

"'I don't, father. I've given up that game. If God wants me to work – He'll send me a job.'

"'Ah well now Peter, as I said before – god helps those who help themselves.'

"'The difference between you and me is this father – I have faith!' There was nothing he could say to that so he scarpered."

"I don't know what I'm going to do," I said. "I'm too young to retire and too old to get another job."

"Where there's life there's hope. Plant a seed of hope in your heart, tend it and watch it grow. Hope is the beginning of rebuilding. Don't look back at what you have lost – instead use what you have left as the foundation for a new life. Look at me. I was pensioned off from my job for being mad."

I smiled and asked, "Are you mad?"

He smiled, winked and said, "Not only am I mad but I have the papers and the pension to prove it! Did you notice the religious vein running through my book of limericks?"

"I did," I said.

"Yes indeed. I see myself as an evangelist. I got a form from the Revenue Commissioners and where they asked Employer's name, I write down: God. Further down the form they said, Name two people at your place of Employment who can verify your financial details. So I wrote down, Jesus and The Holy Spirit!"

I laughed.

"Yes indeed. They wrote back and asked, Are you serious? I send them back a quotation from St. Cyprian, 'This seems a cheerful world when I view it from this fair garden, under the shadow of these vines. But if I climbed from a great mountain and looked out over the wide lands, you know very well what I would see. Brigands on the high roads, pirates on the seas, in the amphitheatres men murdered to please the applauding crowds, under all roofs misery and selfishness. It really is a bad world, an incredibly bad world. Yet in the midst of it I have found a quiet and holy people. They have discovered a joy which is a thousand times better than any pleasure of this sinful life. They are despised and persecuted, but they care not. They have overcome the world. These people are the Christians ...... and I am one of them.'

"That shut them up" When I became an evangelist my wife Mary and her mother came to see me.

"'Mary and I think you need help.' My mother-in-law said.

"I raised my eyes heavenward and said 'I'm getting all the help I need.'

"'We mean a different kind of help – from a doctor.'

"They pleaded with me so I agreed to visit the doctor. They had already made an appointment for the next day. What they hadn't told me was that the doctor was a psychiatrist! I walked into his office next day and sat down in a chair in front of his desk.

"'How are you Mr O' Brien?' he asked.

"'I'm saved.'

"He nodded, looking at me doubtfully. 'What's your address? I need it for the file.'

"'Which one? My heavenly home or my earthly home?'

"'You'd better give me the one down here.' I gave him the address; then he asked, 'Where were you born?'

"'Which time?'

"'You mean you've been born more than once?'

"'Yes. I've been born twice.'

"'How many times do you expect to die?'

"'Once – when you've' been born twice, you only die once. But when you've been born only once, you die twice.'

"'You do need help Mr O' Brien,' he said in dead earnest.

"Then we talked for an hour. I explained to him how Christ had come into my life and changed me. Now I simply wanted to preach the good news of salvation by grace through faith. I remembered a verse from the Holy Bible – first Corinthians, Chapter five, verse seventeen: 'If any man is in Christ, he is a new creature, Old things pass away; all things become new'.

"After he heard me out I thought he was ready to diagnose me as a schizophrenic. Instead he stopped taking notes, came around to my side of the desk, dropped to his knees and said, 'Mr O' Brien would you ask Jesus to save me?' I got down on my knees beside him, said a prayer and delivered him to the Lord. I told my wife all about it when I came home. After that, Mary and her mother never mentioned psychiatry again.

"Do you believe in miracles?" he asked.

"I hope so," I said.

"The first prime minister of Israel in this century once said, 'A man who does not believe in miracles is not a realist'." He produced a news cutting from his wallet.

"Read this," he said.

The headline read, 'The legacy of prayer is now treasure on earth. A Spanish businessman and devout Roman Catholic who stopped to pray at a church during a trip to Stockholm ended up a millionaire.

'The church was empty except for a coffin containing remains of a man, so 35 year old Eduardo Sierra knelt down and prayed for the deceased for 20 minutes, counting off the beads on his rosary.

'Senor Sierra signed a condolence book placed by the coffin after he saw a note saying those who prayed for the dead man should enter their names and addresses. He noticed that he was the first one to sign.

'Several weeks later, Senor Sierra got a call from the Swedish capital informing him that he had inherited the fortune of the dead man, Jens Svenson, a 73 year old property dealer with no close relatives.

'Mr Svenson had specified in his will that 'whoever prays for my soul gets all my belongings','

"That's a nice story," I told Peter, "but how is it going to help me?"

"Give yourself the full list of gifts I recommend to you and you'll see – a miracle will come true for you. It might take patience and time but don't be anxious or impatient. Work at whatever talents you have and keep going."

I thanked him, paid for lunch and we went our ways having made an appointment to meet the next week. He had also given me another good idea. He told me to write down a list of every job I had done since I was a youth and to write down every skill I had and every seed of talent I possessed.

Over the next few months we met and had many talks. "You're a miracle," he told me many times. "If all else fails have a daydream about your future home – heaven. There the city is 1500 miles square. The streets are paved with jewels. Like Ballyskerry a river runs down the centre of it, down from the throne of Jesus. Along the banks of the river are trees full of fruit which renew and produce every month, not every year like down here."

Given that my pension and gratuity was bigger than Peter's I always wanted to pay for our meals in the Grand Hotel – but he wouldn't hear of it.

"It may be more blessed to give rather than receive but you've got to learn to be a gracious gift receiver as well," he admonished me.

Eventually I came up with an idea. It was a dice based board game. I remembered when my children were small how we enjoyed board games at Christmas. In the game I invented there were four characters. The Emperor of Hugs; The Prince of Pep Talk; The Sultan of Smiles and the King of Kisses. It was a family game and a game for little boys and girls.

When I told Peter that I was back in business he was delighted. He insisted on buying me dinner at the Grand Hotel and we had an excellent meal with wine. Coffee and cigars followed and Peter told me I must visit his home sometime. He gave me his business card and I stuffed it in my pocket without looking at it.

The following week he didn't show up for our weekly meeting. I decided to call to see him and remembered his business card. I took it out and it read:

Peter O' Brien
Encouragement Enterprises
Angel Avenue
Heaven.

Gujjala's Triumph

It was the beginning of December in our class full of boys and girls whose average age was twelve. We heard footsteps approach that morning and when the door swung open we all said in unison, "Good morning Sister Teresa."

"Good morning girls and boys," she said. Then announced, "Girls and boys, we have a new classmate for you all this morning. She is from India and her name is Gujjala Nagamani."

The girl nervously came in the door. It was the second time in my life I had been in school with a black girl. The first time was in kindergarten. I came home and told my mother, "Do you know what I noticed about Mahek?"

"No, what's that?"

"She's not pink like us!"

Gujjala's dark eyes were staring in astonished anticipation. Her skin was brown and her hair was a fuzzy black. Her uniform was far too large for her – obviously she was meant to grow into it. Her white socks were crumpled around her ankles and her shoes looked scuffed and second hand.

"Who will be Gujjala's special friend? How about you?"

I blushed to my roots and tried to think of an excuse. Finally I blurted out my compliance: "Yes, Sister."

Gujjala came and sat beside me. She smiled and forced me to shake hands with her. I hoped the earth would open and swallow me up.

When the lunch bell rang the rest of the pupils ran to the canteen. I brought Gujjala out to the playground. Even though it was cold, my main hope was that I wouldn't be seen with her. I opened my lunch box and began eating my strawberry jam sandwich and drinking my small bottle of milk. I had an apple for later. Gujjala opened hers and revealed a yellow meat in what appeared to be some sort of envelope with a fierce stink.

"What is that?" I asked, barely concealing my revulsion.

"Curried chicken in pitta bread. What is yours?"

I told her. She laughed. Then she tore her sandwich in two and gave me half. With great reluctance I did likewise.

Other students came out and joined us in the playground. My friend Gwen said, "It's Sister Teresa's birthday in 3 weeks time and my mother told me to ask your mother to bake the cake this year. Do you think she'll be able to do it?"

Before I could assure Gwen, Gujjala blurted out, "My mother will do it! She bakes cakes all the time."

"Are you sure?"

"Oh yes – my mother can cook or bake anything."

The class bully – Irene – came on the scene and began holding her nose in an exaggerated theatrical fashion, "What is the smell?" Then she answered herself, putting on a show for her friends who had joined us. "Foreign grub – yellow food for a yellow belly!" The other boys and girls took it up as a chant. Gujjala burst into tears and I ushered her inside. She cried and sniffled so hard when class resumed that Sister Teresa noticed. She rubbed her hand through Gujjala's hair and gave her a piece of marzipan sweet from the bag she always kept in her pocket. Sister Teresa loved marzipan almost as much as she loved Jesus.

My new friend was comforted and smiled at me again. She covered my hand with hers as a gesture of affection and, however ungracefully, I managed to bring myself to pat her hand reassuringly. Sister Teresa noticed and sent Gujjala to the toilet to clean up her sniffles, then she gave me some marzipan too. "I'm very proud of you. Remember what Our Lord said in the Holy Bible, 'Inasmuch as you have done it unto the least of my brethren, you have done it unto me'."

We began practising for the school Christmas concert. Irene and her cronies gave Gujjala a poke and a push every time she tried to join in the hymn. The boys and girls laughed as her voice cracked.

Walking home that evening I felt I ought to earn Sister Teresa's piece of marzipan by walking part of the way with Gujjala.

"Just wait till my mother bakes Sister Teresa her birthday cake — then everyone will see."

She continually repeated this in the following weeks. Finally the big day came — Sister Teresa's birthday and the day of the Christmas concert all rolled into one. Gujjala was anxious for midday to come. When it did there was a knock on the classroom door and her mother came in carrying a large box. We all sang 'Happy Birthday' and Sister Teresa dabbed her eyes with a linen hankie. Gujjala beamed with pride. The cake was unveiled and we looked at it astonished — it was yellow.

Irene — the bully — began to chant, "Yellow food for a yellow belly". Gujjala's tears splashed onto the floor. Sister Teresa didn't know what to say or do. Cakes were always finished with white icing — whoever heard of yellow icing? As the chant grew Sister Teresa raised her voice. "Enough of that!" I had to do something.

I poked my finger in the icing and tasted it. Instead of the curry taste I was expecting it turned out to be — marzipan! "It's marzipan!" I shouted. "Sister Teresa's favourite." The class fell silent.

One of the girls said, "Well done Gujjala — that was a great idea."

"Who wants some?" Sister Teresa asked.

"I do," "I do," "I do," said the class. Gujjala smiled as we all took a big slice each and told her to thank her mother.

That night at the Christmas concert Sister Teresa announced that we had a soloist in the school. To the amazement of the whole class Gujjala took to the stage wearing a beautiful white satin dress with a red silk ribbon tied around her waist. Her smile grew as she began to sing. Her voice was a pure soprano and it hushed the packed concert hall into silence. She sang:

I heard the bells on Christmas day
Their old familiar carols play
And wild and sweet the words repeat
Of peace on earth, good will to men.

She sang to her parents in the audience, then for the second verse she embraced Sister Teresa with her smile.

I thought how, as the day had come
The belfries of all Christendom
Had rolled along the unbroken song
Of peace on earth, good will to men.

She picked out Irene the Bully for the next verse. Her face scowled dramatically – Irene blushed.

And in despair I bowed my head;
"There is no peace on earth," I said.
"For hate is strong and mocks the song
Of peace on earth, good will to men."

With a confidence I had not noticed in her before she turned and smiled at me as she sang the last verse:

Then pealed the bells more loud and deep:
"God is not dead, nor doth he sleep;
The wrong shall fail, the right prevail.
With peace on earth, good will to men."

I felt very special. I had helped Gujjala to triumph.

Nicknames

Those of us who partake of the weeds are, these days, consigned to a smoking room reminiscent of the treatment of lepers in Biblical days. However, because the craic is ninety we attract non-smokers with a sense of fun.

One young woman, who eventually succumbed to smoking after much evangelism on the part of us older chimneys, told us a story last January. Her husband (Brendan) is a fire brigade man and, together with his working pals, he went out to celebrate Christmas. They all got drunk and had a great time. They called a taxi to go home and one by one the lads got out at their homes and struggled with keys and moving front doors. Brendan lived furthest away and was the last one left to journey home. The taxi man miscalculated his drunkenness and began hitting the "extras" meter with merry anticipation. When they reached Brendan's home the meter fare was twice what it should have been. Brendan put his foot down.

'I'm not paying that,' he said.

'If you don't pay it,' said the taxi man, 'I'm driving to the copshop!'

'Drive to the copshop,' Brendan challenged him.

He did so and they both got out of the taxi in silence and walked into the police station.

'How are you Brendan?' asked the Sergeant behind the desk.

'I'm grand thanks,' said Brendan. Naturally enough being a fire brigade man he knew all the local policemen including the Sergeant. 'I'm having a bit of trouble with this taxi man,' he complained.

'I'm a taxi man and I'm having trouble with this fare,' said the cab driver. 'I want him prosecuted if he doesn't pay what's on the clock.'

'Bugger off!' said the Sergeant to the taxi man. 'And if you don't I'll lock you up in the cell for the rest of the night and have you up in front of the Justice in Ballyskerry District Courts tomorrow morning charged with assaulting a Guard in the course of his duty!'

The taxi man tried to reason with the Sergeant who was having none of it and eventually the cab driver buggered off. Brendan was ferried home in the squad car.

Another fire brigade man got depressed and decided to top himself. He lay down in front of the fire tender and placed his head near the wheel. He thought that when the alarm went off the lads would run out and drive over him, ending all his troubles. The alarm went off; the lads ran out and jumped on the fire tender and then the driver instead of moving forward – reversed. Two of the lads got down off the truck and asked their depressed colleague what he was doing. He burst into tears and said, 'I can't even top myself!'

They put him in the ambulance and brought him to the psychiatric ward of the local hospital. The doctors kept him there for a month, gave him antidepressants and let him tell his tale of woe.

Early in the new year he came back to work feeling very much better.

'Happy new year Miwadi!' said one of the lads to him.

"Welcome back Miwadi!' said another.

He went to a senior officer and asked, 'Why are the lads calling me Miwadi?'

'That's your new nickname,' said the officer. 'Miwadi – you know – after the squash drink!'

One of our regular smokers had to go to a dinner being held by a Government Minister. After the dinner a man at the table lit up a cigarette.

The woman sitting beside my friend said 'That's a disgusting habit. This is a respectable company. He shouldn't smoke at the table – what a dirty habit. You don't smoke do you?'

'Well as a matter of fact I do,' said my friend. 'But if you find it so offensive I'll do out to the next room and have my coffee and smoke there. I smoke roll your own cigarettes – you know what that signifies don't you?'

'No,' said the highly strung woman. 'What?'

'It means you've either been in the army or in jail for a long time.'

'How long were you in the army?' she asked.

He gave her a menacing look and said, 'I wasn't!'

She gave out a little yelp and moved her chair away from him having received a lesson in good manners.

One of our regular smokers knew a man who had a complex similar to that alleged of Elvis Presley – he couldn't make love to a pregnant woman or a woman who already had children. These fell into the category of mothers and so were out of bounds.

On the fourth occasion he faced a paternity suit he came back to the factory and was asked, 'How did the court case go – Cornucopia?'

'I hope the judge didn't take too much of your wages, Cornucopia,' said another man.

He asked the foreman why the lads were calling him Cornucopia.

'That's your new nickname,' came the reply and the explanation; 'Cornucopia – the horn of plenty!'

The Telephone Operator

When I first came up to Dublin from the Country, I did the Department of Posts and Telegraphs' training course for telephone operators. I got on as well as anyone else and was assigned to operating duties, under supervision, within a short time. Boy, was my innocence in for a battering!

I was put on the night shift and after midnight, I discovered, was the time homosexual men like to call each other. They think, at that hour, that there is no chance of getting a crossed line or of anyone listening in. They're wrong, of course, because at that time, everyone is slack and there is nothing better to do than to listen in on a call.

I got a pair of them one night and you should have heard the romance of them! They were so passionate it nearly blew my circuits. One was quoting poetry and the other announced he had had his hair cut that day. The poetry fellow was furious. "Oh you didn't get your hair cut you bitch you! What am I going to run my fingers through now?" It was hilarious! I gave the nod to a few other lads and they wired into it as well. That was revelation number one.

Revelation number two concerned the larceny of telephone calls and a surprise culprit. There was a tradition that if a member of the public phoned from a private phone (as opposed to a call box), they could ask to make an A.D.C. (advised duration of charge) call to America or Australia and the operator had to put through the call without checking if the caller was actually at the number declared. Let me give you a 'for instance'.

When an operator asked a caller for his telephone number the caller might give him the number of some small hotel or some office block in town. The caller got his call to America scot free because when the operator called back to advise on the charge he would get no reply. He would then bill the small hotel or office block with the call and they might pay it or refuse and complain

Operators regularly used to receive sheaves of paper – complaints from people who never made long distance calls with which they were billed. There was nothing the Department could do. Operators replied to Personnel Division that since they were not allowed to check calls before putting them through, they had no way of checking whether the call was genuine or bogus. Operators always finished off the complaint sheet with the words, 'If you furnish operators with the means whereby we can check calls I will gladly comply with them and thus eliminate phoney phone calls'.

It used to drive Personnel Staff daft to read that phrase – 'phoney phone calls'. Everyone used it in reply to complaint sheets.

A few people were caught stealing long distance phone calls by this method. One operator, who was on the American line, put through a call to California. When he came back, after the tea break, the caller was still through to California, yapping away. The operator thought the call would cost £50. In actual fact it turned out to be a £65 call and this was at a time when average industrial wages were £20 a week. The operator contacted Investigation Branch and they got the engineers to check it out. The operator did not have to do this, but he was covering himself in case it came back as a complaint sheet.

The Engineers' Branch traced the call and the number given did not correspond with the actual number. The call was from a Garda's home number and the number given was an insurance company in the city centre. Before a recording device could be put in place the caller finished his conversation and rang off.

All operators were posted with the number of the insurance company and told to immediately inform their supervisor if a caller asked to be put through to California giving that number.

Sure enough, the gobshite tried the same game the very next evening. He was put through to America and recorded. When Investigation

Branch had enough tape they told the Guards to pounce and the dishonest caller was caught red-handed.

The Department tried to bring the case to court but since the tape recording could not be submitted as evidence in those days, the case was dismissed for lack of evidence. The Department's higher officials were determined to make an example and nail this guy to put off other would-be pirates. The only thing they could come up with, as a charge, was to accuse him of stealing electricity from the Department. The judge laughed the charge out of court. He instantly dismissed it. The Guard, who had been suspended from duty, was reinstated and paid in full for the term of his suspension.

My innocence was finally done for when I was put on the Overseas Line/American Division. One call, that I will remember until I die, jolted my simple innocence.

"Good evening Operator," said a woman's voice. "This is Sister Mary Concepta of the Little Sisters of the Burning Bush. Could you put me through to Father Patrick Murphy in New York?" She gave me the number and I put her through. The phone call went as follows:

"Hello, Pat – this is Mary here."

"Mary," gasp of breath. "Mary! This is wonderful. You don't know how hard my heart is hammering just listening to your voice. This is a blessed surprise! I wish you were here to put your hand on my chest and feel my heart thumping!"

"Pat! Pat! Sweetheart, it's so good to hear you, my love!"

They swapped affectionate tittle tattle for a while. Then Father Patrick said, "I'm so frustrated, Mary. I can't wait. Our plan demands too much. I'm leaving tomorrow. I'm taking a cab, first thing in the morning, out to Kennedy Airport. I'm catching the first flight to Ireland to be with you."

"No, no, Pat!" said Sister Mary. "We must be patient. We'll be in Australia in three weeks time, if we stick to our plan. Then we can get married and share the rest of our lives together."

"Fuck it Mary, I can't wait that long. Let's bail out together, this week, Goddamn it!"

"Now, now Pat, mind your language. Remember you have to say Mass in the morning!"

I had to unplug my earphones at that point, for fear the callers would hear my innocence sniggering away.

Thomas Edison (1847-1931) once asked and answered the following questions: What is a college? "An institute of learning." What is a business? "An institute of learning. Life, itself, is an institute of education."

How right he was! The Department of Posts and Telegraphs certainly turned out to be an institute of education for me.

The Facts of Life

I often wonder how come half of us grew up to be normal, decent human beings. When you think of our backgrounds and how we were educated, with the most savage corporal punishment inflicted, it amazes me that we ended up so well adjusted to society.

Our sex education was nothing of the sort, but I remember it so well and in retrospect it was funny.

Brother Fred was not our regular Christian knowledge teacher – he specialised in Latin and English literature – so it was a surprise one day when he walked into the classroom and announced that he was going to talk to us for a little while on the subject that would be important to us for the rest of our lives.

He told us all to be silent and then turned his back on us, to write a list of words on the blackboard in two columns. At the top of one column he wrote the word 'penis'. Underneath that he wrote a list of colloquial terms such as, 'Mickey', 'Willy', 'Roger', 'Prick' etc. At the top of the next column he wrote the word 'Testicles'. Underneath he wrote the word 'Balls'. I'll never forget the knowing grin he gave us then. He turned around with a swagger. He really fancied himself as a man of the world, although he was a celibate man who had taken a vow of chastity and, more than likely, he had never gone to bed with a woman in his life. Were our parents mad or just stupid to entrust this aspect of our education to a group of men as ignorant as the Christian Brothers?

"Now boys," Brother Fred began. "Some of you, I notice, have begun to grow hair on your faces and soon it will be time you began to shave. Doubtless you also have begun to grow hair around your penis and testicles – there is nothing sinful about that, so don't' be alarmed." He paused dramatically between sentences so that we would take in everything he said in a suitable attitude of gravity.

"You are becoming men," he repeated, "and that means you must take on board and reject the temptation of all that the female sex have to offer. Some of you won't win the battle and you will have to marry but, God forbid that any of you will ever give in to the temptation of women and remain unmarried. I pray, above all, that you will not fall foul at that hurdle.

"By all means be civil to women but that does not mean you have to give in to them." He paused and then continued. "Maybe I am getting ahead of myself. Your first battles in this area will not be with women but with yourself. I am talking of course about the most foul sin: masturbation." You could hear a pin drop in the classroom, we were so silent and intense.

"This sin, involving the spilling of your seed is a most reprehensible sin. It can lead to blindness and madness, for which there is no cure. The sexual desire you may feel as you grow older is something you must fight against all your life. Some men's occupations bring then into contact with women more frequently than others. Consequently they are in danger of sinning and breaking the sixth commandment more often. I am speaking now of jobs such as door-to-door salesmen."

At this the fellow next to me gave me a dart with his elbow and whispered, "That's the job for me!"

"Boys! If you ever put your hand at the top of a woman's legs you will feel the Devils' beard!" Someone down at the back of the classroom smothered a laugh with his handkerchief and pretended he was sneezing. Most of us listened in a respectful silence. My God, weren't we innocent!

"Fight your desires boys! Take a cold shower! Your body is a temple of the Holy Spirit. Resist temptation. Say no to Satan."

It is hard to believe that the perfectly healthy drive to fulfil our normal sexual role could be so mixed up with sin and guilt. All the good things the Christian Brothers taught us were lessened in value because of the negative emphasis they placed on normal sexual development. In reality they were the ones who were out of step and not us, god love them. Many of them were locked up in all-male environment from the age of twelve or fourteen and all they knew of the world came from that hothouse environment. Some of them were saints and others were completely bonkers.

It would have been about 1965 when one of my friends said to me that the Beatles were getting close to the knuckle with their song 'Ticket to Ride'. I agreed with him first, then realising that I didn't know what he meant I asked him to explain.

"Ticket to Ride," he said, "you know as in riding a woman." "What is that?" I asked. He sighed, exasperated with me. "A man rides a woman in order to get her pregnant. He puts his willy in her fanny."

"Surely not," I said. "Isn't that what doctors are for? Don't they make women pregnant?"

"There is a certain amount of pleasure involved in this sex business. In order to make children a man plants his seed in a woman's womb. If it was the doctor people wouldn't say, 'He looks like his father'."

It took a long time for this to sink in, but finally, having consulted a few books in Easons I had to concede the truth of the matter. I spoke to my wife one time about my 'sex education' – God bless the mark - and she told me she had heard it from the girls who played with her on the street. When they told her about boys putting their willies into girls' fannies, she said. "I'd never want a boy to do that to me." One of her friends said, "You will when you're married. You'll want to touch it and hold it in your hand!"

When she was about sixteen and ready to go on summer holidays from the convent, one of the nuns addressed her class in much the same fashion as Brother Fred had addressed us. "Girls, some of you may go on picnics with boys during this coming summer. Don't let them roll on top of you. Don't let them touch you in private places. If they try to remind them that they are Catholics and that Saint Joseph took a vow of chastity and slept in the same bed as Mary, the Mother of Jesus, all his life without ever fondling her in any way."

What an insult to Joseph and Mary that was! I have read the scriptures and have yet to find the Biblical evidence on which that piece of theory was based. The hatred and fear of sex was all they had to impart.

Some girls in Sharon's class were street-wise and knew that this sex talk was the last lesson they would ever hear from the nuns. They would be looking for jobs the following day and would not be going back to school after the holidays. It was their last chance to hit back. The nun finished up her sex talk by saying, "...... And girls, always remember an hour's pleasure is not worth a life time of shame." One cheeky little bitch down at the end of the classroom put up her hand and said, "Excuse me Sister, but how do you make it last for an hour?"

Snapshots From The Heart

Dear Monica,

I was there with you when our two children – Larry and Melissa were born. They are now teenagers and in getting them this far there have been many times when my heart sank and other times when my heart took a snapshot.

When Larry was 2 ½ we went to Tenerife on holiday. We met two young women from Belfast with whom we had friendly words. I said to Larry, "That girl's name is Sandra. What's that girl's name?" "Dancer!" he replied. "And that girl's name is iris. What's that girl's name?" "Arses", came the reply. My heart took a snapshot.

When Melissa was four she liked to drink coke. One Summer's day as she was drinking it she allowed some spittle back into the glass. "See? I'm magic", she said. "I'm changing coke into Guinness". My heart took a snapshot.

One day that same year you brought Melissa for a walk. It was winter and an old man was walking along the opposite footpath using a walking stick and well muffled up. Melissa said, "Do you see that old man there? He'll be going to Heaven soon, won't he?"

When Larry was four, you had the habit of giving him a bath in a little yellow plastic bath in front of the fire. One time he made a right performance of peeing in the bath. Then he announced, "My willy is going to grow up, up, up like an elephant's trunk!" My heart took a snapshot.

When he was a tiny little boy, he began calling me Jim instead of Dad. He came into the bedroom, one Sunday morning, and caught us making love. Although we were covered by the duvet, he studied us for a moment before asking; "Jim what are you doing up on top of that good woman? After all, her is not a horse!" My heart took a snapshot.

When Melissa was the same age she had a little wooden helicopter mobile hanging from the ceiling over her bed. You asked her, "Where did that come from?" She said, "My Daddy made that for me".
You said, "No he didn't. Where did you come from?"
"Where did I come from?" This was repeated as if it was the silliest question in the world. "Why, you knitted me, of course!" My heart took a snapshot.

Melissa was always a 'picky' eater. She eats slowly and needs to be coaxed. I was trying to persuade her to eat mashed poppies with gravy one Sunday. I fashioned a circumference of walls with her potato and poured gravy into the hole in the centre. I said, "Look at the swimming pool of gravy in your poppies". She was having none of my charm. She pushed her fork through it and let the gravy flow around the plate. Larry said, "I was going to put on my swimming togs and jump into that!" My heart took a snapshot.

One time Larry had worms and you said, "We'll have to stick a toothbrush up your bum, Larry". He said, "Will you?" You said, "Yeah". He said, "What colour toothbrush?"

Melissa told her first joke on the day her baby tooth fell out. She said, "I don't drink, I don't smoke and I don't use bad language". Pregnant pause. "Oh feck! I left my fags in the pub".

Following on from this she picked up every piece of vulgarity going. For a long time her favourite song was:

Mammy, mammy, mammy!
There's something in my nappy
It's big and brown
I can't sit down
If I do I'll squash it
Then I'll have to wash it
And that's no joke
- the washer's broke!

One Christmas after the festivities were over, as we were taking the tree down, the children insisted on shaking hands with all the branches and saying, "Bye, bye Mr Christmas Tree – thanks very much!"

First Holy Communion time came and Larry explained to me how he had finagled the Host up to the roof of his mouth, twirled up his tongue and swallowed it without it touching his teeth. I told him it was OK to bite it. He said, "Oh no it isn't. After all - you wouldn't want to bite Jesus would you?" My heart took a snapshot.

One Sunday, in church, Melissa threw a coin into the basket. She announced, "Money isn't everything". Then added, "Still and all – I'd like to have a lot of it!" You said to Larry, one time, "Wouldn't it be great if we were rich?" He said, "Yeah – we could have a swimming pool and Jim wouldn't have to go to work, he could stay at home and play with me all day …" And he went on to such an extent that you decided to rein him in by saying, "Still and all it wouldn't be any good to be rich if you were sick". "Oh yes it would", he insisted. "You could always sit up in bed and count your money!"

My heart took a snapshot and doubtless I'll need plenty of film in my heart for the charming incidents to come.

One of Larry's teachers asked him
"What do you think of God, Larry?"
"I don't think much of Him".

"Why don't you think much of him?"
"I wish he was a chef"
"Why do you wish God was a chef?"
"Because then he could feed everyone in the world".

Melissa declared her belief in the death penalty when she was four years old. Our next door neighbour's rabbit was being stalked by a cat. She shouted out the window: "Bold pussy! You kill bunny – I kill you".
Larry once knelt down beside his bed and said:
"First of all God let me tell you about the extenuating circumstances and mitigating factors …".

Will you ever forget the time Melissa developed sweat glands? She ran into the house shouting: "Smell me. Smell me. Smell me. I'm sweating; isn't it great!"

I used to read fairy stories to the kids at bedtime. As a change, one night coming up to Christmas, I told them the story of the baby Jesus. When I was finished Larry asked "When Jesus grew up. Did He marry a princess and live happy every after?" I said "Not exactly but that is a story for another night."

Love, Jim xxx.

Poetic Justice

Day 1

For years I thought that being the grown-up version of a good little boy would lead to success. I worked hard. I was respectful to my superior officers in Megabank Ireland – the state bank under the aegis of the Department of Finance and the civil service. The number of them who turned out to trip up the promotional ladder on the back of my work I couldn't count on all the fingers of my hands.

And the scandals hidden by the Official Secrets Act were numerous. The decent man who was bullied into a nervous breakdown by a Personnel Officer shouting and roaring and spitting into his face. He stayed seriously sick for ten weeks and his hapless medic put him on tranquilizers for the rest of his life. The kind, sensitive woman who suffered from leukaemia and sent in medical certificates attesting to that fact but still came into work until the day she died. The manager was a feminist who left Mary Anne lying dead in her bed for ten days before bothering to contact her next of kin. Her remains rotted in the summer sun and the smell of decay filled her small flat. I wept for two weeks. The great feminist went on to become a senior manager in the Department.

And what about the bewildered, mystified people like myself. The ones who got sick and didn't realise that that is the worst crime you can commit except for being poor. I downshifted into being an amenable, malleable gentleman.

I was tidying up the public section of Megabank Ireland – Ballyskerry branch – one evening coming up to Christmas when I picked up a crumpled withdrawal slip. For some reason best known to Fate, Destiny or God I unfolded the piece of paper and read the words:

I have a gun. Hand over all the money or I'll blow your head off.

The words were written in block capitals. I read it a couple of times. I was forty eight years of age and had sold my labour to the civil service for twenty seven years but this was a first. The 'g' in the word gun was a particularly childish attempt. Maybe it was some kid whiling away the time as his mother or father went to the counter. Maybe the security cameras were still on and it was a plant by one of the jokers in the bank to get another one over on Pete. Yes I was always good for a laugh. Old enough to be a bank manager and still sitting at the front office counter with seventeen years of same in front of me.

Like myself the bank manager, Sean Agnew, often stayed late. I decided to show him the piece of paper to see what he thought of it. I knocked on the door of his wood panelled office and let myself in. He had already gone home but I had often fantasised that, if things hadn't gone badly wrong for me, I too would have a nice office like this; I would be earning twice what I actually was earning and instead of four weeks holiday, I would have six weeks holiday.

I sat in his chair and daydreamed. I opened the top drawer of his desk and noticed a letter marked: Strictly Confidential. Curiosity got the better of me and I began to read:

Dear Sean,
As you know Megabank Ireland is due for privatisation shortly. The guys in the Department of Finance have for a number of years urged us to reorganise so as to be palatable to the market when this eventuality occurs.

We have already put in place a good commercial structure but there is one fly in the ointment before we finally launch. That is: geriatric staff at the lower levels time serving the clock and not suitable for promotion.

The guys in Finance want us to clear the decks and give them the push. Of course, with trade unions involved we will have to float the pretence that all retirements will be voluntary. The early retirement package will be the usual early retirement due to ill-health expanded in scope to encompass the grey haired brigade. We will be issuing a circular shortly. You are already familiar with the terms – a notional six point six six years will be added to actual service in the calculation of pension; one eightieth of salary for each year of total service with make up the pension and three eightieths for every year of service will constitute the gratuity or 'lump sum' as it is so gracelessly called.

All of the above you already know but here is the reason this letter is strictly confidential. Anyone who does not go voluntarily will have to be pushed. It will have to be done in an effective, none too subtle way but still adroit enough in method so that allegations of constructive dismissal will not stand up in court. We have put our heads together here in Head Office and come up with the plan of recommending that elderly staff be given a new job every three months without training. This should lead to health breakdowns and the sort of demoralisation which will lead the remainder to jump ship. We figure that this will frustrate even the most tenacious old bastard.

I hope the above will meet with your approval and support. Isn't it a good job we got our promotions when we did and kept a clean slate ever since? The boys in Finance would make Mussolini look like a bleeding heart liberal.

Looking forward to seeing you at the Head Office Christmas Party. When the season of goodwill is over we will strike.

Regards,
Paddy

I let out an expletive. I felt as if I had been kicked in the stomach. I was about to lose my sinecure. My job had always provided more than a modest pay packet; it had given structure to the week. Now it was to go. I was to go. Just so that my imagination did not play tricks on me I photocopied the letter. I wasn't gone yet. I was going to be allowed to enjoy Christmas in peace – probably the last Christmas I would be employed by the bank.

I stole a march on the next day by changing the number on the wall calendar. I looked out the window at the square. Car horns honked as the evening traffic jammed the streets. I placed the letter in my inside pocked and the now uncrumpled threatening note in my credit card wallet.

I stacked the waste paper baskets together to help the cleaning women. Then I put on my coat, turned off the lights and let myself out the back door. It was cold as I walked home. I could have taken the bus but I always found walking to be therapeutic when I had something on my mind. Christmas shopping had begun early and people passed me by with presents for the happy day. Headlights supplemented the street lamps. Shops sprinkled the square in which the bank stood. A large Christmas tree blinked on and off in the centre of the square. The bypass didn't seem to have lessened the traffic substantially. Whether I liked it or not my life was going to change. 'Change' – such a challenging word at my time of life and yet it was inevitable.

I let myself into my little house and put a microwave dinner on for myself. I had a few glasses of home-made wine, listened to some music and went to bed early. Just before I fell asleep. I saw once more in my mind's eye the childish 'g' for gun. I wondered why the mere thought of that note caused me to feel something that bore a striking resemblance to happiness.

Day 2

The following morning I went into the bank early. I filled my empty briefcase full of 500 Euro notes and placed it in the bottom drawer of my desk. I wondered when the criminal would come in and place the gun in my face. I wondered, as I saw Agnew, glad handling myself and my colleagues, just who the criminals were.

We were under strict instructions to press the floor buzzer that set off the alarm only when it was safe to do so. The thief came into the den of thieves later in the morning.

He wore a long black coat, black hat and sun glasses. He handed me a duplicate of the note I had found the previous evening. I was very nervous but managed to fill the bag he handed me with lower denomination notes. As he made a hasty exit I took my briefcase out of the bottom drawer and placed it in its usual place. I flicked the combination lock so that only I could open it. Then I pressed the foot buzzer.

All hell broke loose that day. Detectives and police arrived. Their questions were endless and very trying on the nerves. It was only with a couple of glasses of wine, a sleeping tablet and love with my wife that I managed to go off to sleep. I hid the briefcase in the attic.

Day 3

Christmas came and went in a pleasant celebration. I bought my wife and 3 teenage children modest presents. In Ireland Christmas tends to be a week long celebration so the new year came and I was due back into work. On my first day back Agnew called me into his office and showed me the early retirement circular.

"I'm sure," he began, "that sympathetic consideration would be given to your good self should you wish to avail of the offer."

I smiled agreeably and said, "It's certainly something to think about. I'll discuss it with my wife." As I left his office I'm sure my beatific grin would have given good competition to Mona Lisa.

I went home early that day and firstly showed my wife the photocopy of the letter I had made before Christmas. She was greatly distressed. Her reaction was refracted by her dependency. Then I told her about the circular and that day's conversation with Agnew.

"They're robbing you of your job!" she exclaimed. "Pete what are we going to do?"

Then I explained what I had already done. Like myself, my wife is a profoundly honest woman. When I showed her the briefcase full of money she laughed and then said, "We will have to seek spiritual advice about this."

She accompanied me to the priest's home. With my wife sitting beside me I began my confession. "Bless me father for I have sinned. It is 25 years since my last confession."

"Welcome back," said the priest.

"I have lived a life of sin and crime because I have sold my life's work to sinners and criminals."

"Did this life not make you sick to your stomach?"

"It did father but I took something for it."

"And what was that?"

"Money father."

I told him the full story. He scratched his chin and smiled.

"It strikes me that this problem is the theological equivalent of a good rugby game – in other words, you got in your retaliation first."

We all laughed.

"They decided to rob you of the next seventeen years of your career for ageism reasons and to save themselves some – a substantial sum – of money. You remind me of one of the sayings of Jesus in His sermon on the mount: 'Blessed are those who hunger and thirst for justice for they will be satisfied'. I'll give you absolution but I won't advise you to give the money back."

For my penance he told me to say an Our Father, a Hail Mary and a Glory Be. I reverently and gladly did so. God, my wife, the Priest and myself were satisfied.

I brought my wife out to dinner. I had barbary duck in a peppercorn and brandy sauce, a side salad and french fries after a starter of prawn cocktail. The apple pie, ice cream, coffee and cigar were especially satisfying. My wife had a nice meal also. We shared two bottles of wine.

We went home and made love.

"Perhaps we'll buy a little shop with some of the money," she said with a dreamy head on her pillow.

"If you like love," I said.

"And we can renew our marriage vows on a white sandy beach in the Seychelles with the turquoise sea and the exotic blossoms as a backdrop."

"If you like love."

"We can have afternoon tea in Raffles Hotel in Singapore and see Norman Rockwell's art gallery in Stockbridge, Massachusetts."

"Anything you like love," I whispered.

"You've always wanted to visit the Crystal Cathedral in California. I believe Disneyland is close by."

"Anything you like love."

The words echoed around my head as I dozed off. Anything you like love ….. anything you like.

How to Live on Fresh Air!

A few years ago, I was an inveterate cigarette smoker. I went through two twenty-packs a day and woke up every morning to the sound of my wheezing chest.

My wife began a litany of nagging as I gasped for air. "You've just got to stop smoking. Those cigarettes will be the death of you. Try acupuncture, nicotine patches or hypnotherapy. One of them will work for you."

I clambered out of bed to the bathroom and coughed my guts up. Finally, the message got through to me. There were posters all over town with the eye-catching headline: How to live on fresh air! This was followed by some verbiage urging the reader to stop smoking with the help of hypnotherapy. After one of my colleagues in work died of a heart attack because of smoking, I decided to give the hypnotist a chance.

I phoned up Peter French, hypnotherapist extraordinaire, and made an appointment for Saturday afternoon. I presented myself at his discreet, side-street office and after an initial introductory conversation, laid down on his couch.

Peter French was in his early fifties, and had a shaven head like Yul Brynner. He dressed all in black and charged a day's pay for his two hour session. He put a tape of soothing piano music on. He told me that music contained subliminal sound messages which would infiltrate into my subconscious and help me to stop smoking.

Over the nice piano music he began to speak softly and induce hypnosis. He explained that I wouldn't feel hypnotised, that there is no such thing as a hypnotised feeling, but I would feel extraordinarily relaxed.

For the first fifteen to twenty minutes of his monologue he induced a feeling of deeper and deeper relaxation. I was practically nodding off completely when he began the 'real meat' of the therapy.

"A man once climbed a snow covered mountain. At his foot he found a rattle snake. The snake spoke to him. It said. 'Put me under your sweater and take me down to where the earth is warm'. The man said, 'But you are a rattle snake and one bite from you and I will die!' The Snake said, 'I won't bite you'. So the man put the snake beneath his sweater and brought it down to where the land was warm. And the snake bit him!

"The man said, 'You promised not to bite me!' The snake said, 'You knew what I was before you picked me up'. After this talk, the video I am going to show you and the audio tape I am going to give you, you will know that you should have nothing to do with cigarettes from now on.

"If I were to ask you to play Russian Roulette with a loaded gun you would not do so. Yet by playing Russian Roulette with one bullet in six chambers of a revolver you would have one chance of six in dying. One in every four smokers die from smoking so it is a worse game to play than Russian Roulette."

He paused a lot and spoke quietly but insistently. He chided me for my stupidity in allowing the wealthy cancer-causing multinational tobacco companies to fool me. It all made perfect sense. Here follows much of what I remember him saying as I lay on the brink of the Land of Nod:

"You will be glad you stopped smoking. You are going to stop smoking because it will improve your overall health. You will take a pride and a pleasure in stopping to smoke and you will no longer suffer from nicotine stained teeth, bad breath, smelly hair or brown fingers. You will take a pride and pleasure in beating the demon nicotine.

"You will reap rewards and advantages from not sending your money up in smoke every day. You can look forward to a better holiday every year. You can deal with unexpected bills, all the easier, because you will have the money to deal with them now that you have ceased smoking.

"You will be glad you chose health over smoking. You will find that giving up smoking is well worth the effort and you will be surprised to find that there is very little effort involved. You will find your confidence and self assurance increasing noticeable now that you are no longer dependent on a smelly, burning tube of dried weeds. Your self-image will improve by leaps and bounds. You will find a great sense of relief immediately. You will find a sense of freedom now that you have decided to quit being a nicotine addict. You will find a feeling of early morning well-being that stays with you for the rest of the day. You will leave behind waking up to a mouth all furry and dry and unpleasant. When you wake up in the morning you will feel fresh and alert. You will come down to a breakfast you can actually taste. This will be a completely new experience and will be a cause of much rejoicing." And on he went, in this vein, for about 30 minutes.

After I came back to the land of the living, Peter French showed me a video, which lasted about an hour, showing testimonies of people suffering from cancer and other lung illnesses, which made for pretty riveting viewing.

He gave me an audio tape and told me to listen to it at least ten times in the following fourteen days. I paid him his hefty fee, shook hands with him and as he opened the door to let me out, he said. "Remember, anything that can be caused by suggestion can be cured by suggestion. Meditate on today's brainwashing and allow only fresh air into your lungs from now on!"

I was determined to give it a good try.

*   *   *

That precise day was my thirty-ninth birthday. My wife and I went out to a restaurant in town for dinner. We enjoyed a good meal together, shared a bottle of wine and I declined coffee since, prior to that day, I always smoked with coffee. My wife enjoyed her coffee and I sipped the last of the wine. There was a lull in our conversation as I gazed around the restaurant and took in the satisfied faces of the other diners.

Imagine my surprise when at the far end of the restaurant, in the smokers section, I spied Peter French enjoying coffee and a cigarette. I was furious! I got up from the table and walked towards him. He saw me coming and stubbed out his cigarette.

"It's too late for that," I said. "I saw it." I glared at him in anger. His eyes signalled fear.

"I'll be having my fee back now," I said as menacingly as possible.

"Yes, of course," he said. He was like a rabbit caught in headlights. He took out his wallet and gave me back my cheque.

Ironically, from that night on, I never did smoke another cigarette.

Hard Luck

A wise man once said that if you are idealistic in your teens and twenties, you will gather wood to build a bridge to the moon; and when you reach your sixties, you are satisfied to make a garden shed with it.

My idealism, as a young man in London, saw me joining a charity for homeless people. We delivered soup and sandwiches to alcoholics, drug addicts and prostitutes, late at night and in the early hours of the morning.

One night we found an eighteen years old young woman lying dead in a shop doorway. She had a syringe full of heroin sticking out of her arm. We called an ambulance and as we waited with her I noticed some paper in her jacket pocket. I hoped it contained her name and home address; but it didn't.

It was a poem which probably gave her solace and comfort.

I promised her that if ever I could, I would publish it.

And so I have:

They Say You've Gone To Heaven

They say you've gone to Heaven,
But I have heard them tell that before you went to Heaven, Lord,
You also went to hell.
So come down Lord from your Heaven,
For if you went to hell,
Come down into the clip joint, Lord
Come down to us as well.

Smoke rises in your churches
To praise your holiness,
Smoke rises from our reefers
To cloud our loneliness,
So come down from your Heaven,
To call, to heal, to bless.
You know that our smoke rings
Are signals of distress.

With publicans and sinners
They say you often dined,
They say a girl who was a tart,
With you found peace of mind.
So come down Lord from your Heaven,
For if you love our kind,
Come down to the strip club, Lord
Where only love is blind.

The sick – they need a doctor,
More than the healthy do,
They say you took a dying thief,
To paradise with you.
So come down from your Heaven,
If what they say is true,
Come down to the den of thieves,
Where thieves have need of you.

They say you were victorious,
Over hell and over death,
We know the hell of heroin,
The dying that is meth.
So come down from your Heaven,
You whom we can't confess,
And be the resurrection,
Of this our living death. Amen.

A Jolly Man

I met a lovely character in one of the pubs close to the Four Courts recently. He was a barrister who had studied anecdotes about the law, as much as the textbooks. He also had that gift, which my father has, of putting a good 'skin' on a story. Like myself, he had an excellent memory and some of the incidents which had passed before him in his thirty or more years at the bar he told with great relish.

(A) A young man came before the District Court charged with stealing from a chemist's shop. When asked why he had robbed the item he said, "I had a terrible pain in my head Justice and my father told me to go to the chemist's and take something."

"I understand that," said the Justice. "But I'm sure he didn't mean you to go and take an instamatic camera!"

(B) The vast majority of Justices are promoted from the ranks of solicitors, in the same way as the vast majority of Judges are elevated from the ranks of barristers. One of the most nauseating spectacles to behold is the sight of a man who was in the side of the defence all his life, turning into an ogre at the first chance he gets on the bench of a criminal court. Judges, in their new finery, like to show their new peers that they are as tough as the next when it comes to dishing out the porridge. However, one particular Judge had the following exchange with a prisoner who happened to be his first client:

"I don't understand why you committed the petty theft to which you plead guilty but you can think it over for the next twelve months in Mountjoy Jail."

The prisoner tired to ingratiate himself into the Judge's good graces, "Ah now my Lord that is really going a bit far. After all, the thing I stole was only a little yoke."

The Judge, whose good nature got the better of him, said, "OK. Do you think you deserve six months?"

"Six months is awful long time to be away from your family, my Lord. Sure, the children would not recognise me when I get out."

At this the Judge began to agonise. "I suppose I must take into account the fact that you pleaded guilty and didn't waste the time of the Court or the witnesses."

"Yes, indeed, my Lord," said the prisoner.

"Would four months be all right?" asked the Judge.

"Three would be better," answered the prisoner.

"Right," said the Judge. "Three months it is." Then realising that he was excepted to act the hardman, the Judge said, "If I ever see you in Court again I'll send you away for ...... well, it'll all depend on the circumstances."

(C) The man in the dock looked the picture of genteel poverty. He had a winning smile and the air of one who is eager and happy to please. He was had up for begging and generally making a nuisance of himself. The Justice asked him, "How do you get by?"

"Very well thank you Justice," he replied. "Meat, two veg and poppies for dinner and I have been known on occasions to stray into a chicken curry."

"I don't mean what do you have for dinner. I mean, where do you get your bread?"

"I beg your pardon Justice. I get by bread at the bakery shop usually but if they are out of yesterday's bread, I trot along to the supermarket."

Clouds of impending anger crossed the Justice's face. "Don't try to make a jackass out of me, my man. I want to know where do you get your money from?"

"Sometimes at the Post Office and other times at the bank."

The music hall repartee didn't end there. The Justice shouted, "How do you make out?"

"Quite well thank you Justice. I keep taking the pills for the arthritis and I sincerely hope you never suffer from it."

(D) The prisoner was wearing a quasi-religious garb and the police told the Justice that he claimed to be a Minister of the Church of Redistribution. He wore a Roman Collar and a charcoal grey suit. Unfortunately for him the Guards had unearthed his 'form' – his list of previous convictions. The Justice – so used to unemployed denim clad toughs coming before him – looked perplexed that this soft faced respectable looking man had pleaded guilty to a burglary and had the record of a hardened criminal.

"You stole a lot of money from the plaintiff and not only that but you took a number of works of art with you also. Have you any explanation?"

The prisoner coughed and shuffled around a little bit before answering, "A man of my calling knows from the Bible that money, by itself, does not bring happiness!"

(E) Charles Dickens, the famous novelist, had a son, Sir Henry Dickens, who became a Judge. One time when he was about to sentence an old character, the prisoner shouted at him, "You're nothing compared to your father."

"I quite agree," said the Judge good naturedly. "What do you know about my father?"

"I've read most of his books."

"Have you indeed? Where did you read them?"

"I read some in prison."

Sir Henry smiled amiable and said, "Good for you! I am going to give you eighteen months in which to read the rest of them."

(F) A District Court story:

A woman was recently in the dock of the District Court for having no TV licence. "Well Missis," barked the District Justice. "What have you got to say for yourself?"

"It's like this Justice," began the woman. "I have two sets of twins and three sets of triplets. I don't have time to think about a TV licence."

The District Judge rolled this evidence around in his mind for a while.

""Two sets of twins and three sets of triplets?" he asked.

"That's right Justice," said the woman.

"You know missus, it would pay you a lot better to watch a lot more television!" concluded the Justice.

(G) It is extraordinary how some unusual things about people come to light during cross-examination. Ignorant people often imagine if there is enough evidence to warrant someone being arrested and put on trial that that person must be guilty of the alleged offence. You often see this at its worst when a mob gathers outside a court and attempts to attack a person accused of murder or drug dealing on a large scale.

Recently I witnessed a few funny incidents in court. One middle aged man was being cross-examined and he gave the impression during his preliminary answers of being a scrupulous soul. He was asked by the barrister what his age was and he hesitated before answering.

"Come along," said the barrister. "I want to know your precise age."

"My precise age?" asked the witness.

"Yes," replied the barrister and then he patronised the witness and asked, as if talking to a child, "How many birthdays have you had since you were born?"

The witness replied, "I have had 10 birthdays since I was born."

The barrister wasn't used to being trifled with. "Don't insult this court by messing around. You have taken a sacred oath to tell the truth," the barrister said, his voice rising.

The witness was unruffled. "My birthday arrives only once in every four years. You see, I was born on the 29th of February. I was a leap year baby and I have had only 10 birthdays." The barrister quickly rushed on to his next question, while many people in the court smiled broadly.

(H) When I read biographies of law men it amazes me how some barrister got away with cheek which, if tried today, would land them in jail for contempt of court. One criminal case was going so badly that an ignorant Judge made the comment to the defending barrister, "I think you have a rogue on your side."

Quick as a flash the barrister retorted, "It is very good to know that my Lord, but your Lordship shouldn't call himself names."

(I) I love cases where old lags or 'incorrigible rogues', as persistent offenders used to be called, come up before a Judge and the extent of their life of misdeeds comes to light. There was one recently, where an old joker was had up for bigamy. He hadn't married once again, while still married to his first wife, he had married a further seven times! He had 40 children and when the charges were read out some of the younger children howled as if in protest. The Judge was mystified that the succession of wives bore little bitterness and all said they would take the defendant back if his Lordship did not send the defendant to jail. After the police finished producing prosecution witnesses, the old lag knew the game was up. He changed his plea to 'guilty'.

"I have one question before I sentence you," said the Judge. "Why did you marry all the women and then leave them in the lurch?"

The defendant cleared his throat, put on his most innocent expression and said, "I was only trying to find one that suited me!" He was lucky to get a sentence of only six months porridge and the promise from many of his wives that they would visit him. As he was being led away in handcuffs, between two prison officers, he asked, "Are there any women prison warders in Mountjoy?" Talk about an optimist!

The Smoking Room

Back in more enlightened times, ever workplace had its Smoking Room. People who smoked were usually easy-going with a good sense of humour. Jokes were plentiful and original wit was often dispensed.

It was coffee break time in the room and Martin, who fancied himself as a man of great integrity and always right in his opinions decided to grace our group with his judgement. On television the previous night was a gay rights activist by the name of Maurice. Martin was scandalised by Maurice boasting that the great love of his life was a Russian man. They would meet in different European cities for what he called "Romantic weekends". Martin was disgusted by this and called Maurice "a dirty bastard". Martin regarded himself as a working class hero.

On the other hand Charlie came from a middle class family, had gone to university, and did not buy into Martin's delusions.

"You know, Martin, one percent of the population are gay across all socioeconomic groups. That means since there are 700 people working in this organisation there are at least 7 men and women who are gay."

"True for you. True for you. I wonder who they are?"

He went off into a little wistful reverie and said again, "I wonder who they are?"

I tapped him on the shoulder and said, "Give us a kiss and I'll tell you." It got a good laugh.

Christmas stress was often relived in the Smoking Room. Even though, in the traditional family, women have a more stressful time than men the "right" gift was much debated. Niall, one of our regulars, brought the house down when he said: "A puppy isn't just for Christmas, you know. As they say in Korea, if you're not too greedy, there should be some left over for a curry on New Year's day."

After people came back from Summer holidays there were always anecdotes to share. Usually we went to sunny parts of Europe.

My wife and I met a couple for "Happy Hour" drinks in the garden of our hotel.

The woman, Mary, said, "Do you get the smell of this fellow?"

Harry defended himself.

"Now, hold on. I was dancing with a girl one time and she said: 'I love your B.O.' So I haven't worn powder, potion or lotion from that day to this."

It was an anecdote that went down well in the Smoking Room.

On another holiday we met a Dublin "Mammy" and two of her adult sons. We were staying in a four star hotel.

Jonny and Tommy were a study in contrasts.

Jonny had a beard and long hair. Tommy had a short back and sides.

Jonny lamented the fact that he had another brother at home in Dublin with a wife and two small children.

"The flat they live in isn't fit for human habitation. There is water streaming down the walls. Those kids have bronchitis from one end of the year to the other. I love those kids. Do you believe me?"

Yes, of course, we believe you."

"Because I'll pluck put my eye, tentacles and all, to prove to you that I love those kids.

I'll pluck out my eye, tentacles and all, to prove to you that I love those kids."

We managed to calm him down and to get him to leave his "tentacles" alone.

Round and round the smoke swirled as we indulged in the final vice to lose respectability.

The Spirit World

Where do I begin?

I was standing up in my local favourite Church of Ireland church and, together with the rest of the congregation, I was singing a hymn.

Suddenly I felt a wave of warmth from my left shoulder to foot. The next Sunday the same thing happened.

On the third and fourth Sundays it happened, I excused myself from my pew and went to two different parts of the church to see if the warmth remained. It did.

It is obviously someone who loves me and is now in our parallel spirit world. I thought for a long time as to who this spirit might be. T he answer came quickly. Who used to love to come to Church with me on Sunday mornings?

My mother.

In my fiftieth year of life I had a tough time. I was in hospital 3 times. Then on the first of January my wife's Aunt Kay died.

My sleep pattern was a bit askew so I decided to go to the Evening Service rather than the following morning's Funeral Service.

I went to the undertaker's funeral home and decided to have one last look at Kay's remains. In my mind I said to Kay: "They didn't do much with what was left of you, Kay. You were always much prettier than that."

It happened again. A wave of warmth established itself all down my left side. So I did what I had previously done in this situation – I moved to 3 different parts of the room to be certain.

Many people were not as blessed as I and I am grateful for these experiences which lead me to believe in the Spirit World.

A Great Character

If there was a star in our family, it was my father. But he was enormously blessed to be complemented by the kindness, common sense and business acumen of my mother. Often, in the early hours of the morning when I can't sleep, I think of the tragic comedy of my family.

And of my father's anecdotes.

I want to tell you a few things about my father:

Anecdote (1)

St. Patrick's Day: Mam, Dad and I went to the Mill House for a few drinks. I had coffee. Mam and Dad had 3 whiskies each. My father told us a story about St. Patrick's Day 47 years ago. He was working in a Midlands town and he was lying on his bed in his digs when he was told by the landlady that he was wanted at the front door. When he went down there was a Guard, with whom he had had friendly words, waiting at the door. They were both 'blow-ins' to Port, the Midlands town. The Guard said, "Would you put on your jacket and we'll go for a walk out the road? It's a grand St. Patrick's Day – sure it's like a summer's day." Mike consented and put on his jacket.

They walked about a mile out the country and Mike lamented the fact that St. Patrick's Day was a 'dry day', i.e. the pubs were not open. "It's amazing," he said. "When you think about it, isn't it ridiculous? All over America they are dyeing rivers green and serving green pints of beer. All over England the pubs are open and the Irish are welcome to enjoy a full day's drinking. But here in Ireland thanks to the church it's a dry day."

"Would you like a pint?" the Guard asked.

"I would," said Mike. So they took another road and headed towards the nearest pub. As they approached the pub they saw men skulking out bent double behind the roadside fences, trying to hide from the Guard. It was illegal to drink on St. Patrick's Day. A publican could end up in court and lose his licence for serving alcohol on St. Patrick's Day.

The Guard knocked on the pub door and the publican came out. They walked into the pub in silence and looked around at the quarter full, half full and full pints of Guinness – all abandoned. The atmosphere was heavy with cigarette smoke.

"Is there any place where Mike and myself could have a quiet pint?" the Guard asked the Publican.

"There is, of course," said the Publican, almost falling over himself with relief. "Come in to the kitchen." Mike and the Guard had 5 pints of Guinness each. The Publican allowed his customers to sneak back in when he knew he was not going to be prosecuted. On the way home that evening, as they walked through the pub one customer said to the Guard, "God bless you, Guard. May you be half an hour in heaven before the devil knows you're dead!"

That night there was a singing festival in the town hall and Mike won first prize singing, 'Robert Emmet's last farewell to his love' by Tom Moore.

The next Sunday morning the parish priest 'read' the Guard and Mike 'off the altar', as the saying goes. He referred to 'blow-ins' coming into the town and drinking alcohol on St. Patrick's Day. On the way out of church Mike and the Guard spotted each other and smiled. "What did you think of the priest's sermon?" asked the Guard.

"I'll drink to it! said Mike. Later they both found out the parish priest was an alcoholic who drank a bottle of whiskey a day!

Anecdote (2)

<u>Humour in Uniform</u>

My father was in the local Defence Forces (i.e. home guard) during the Second World War in Ireland. They were divided into two battalions and one was given the task of defending a small Irish town, while the other was given the task of attaching from 6am to 6pm one Summer's day. Because of a shortage of guns and ammunition they used hurling sticks (a lot like hockey sticks) and shouted "Bang! Bang!" whenever they shot anyone. The attacking battalion captured a bridge, blew it up in make believe, and left behind a few men to defend the position. A little old lady tried to cross the bridge but was told by the guard that it was blown up. She could see that it wasn't and remonstrated with them. They were adamant. So on her way back through the town, to cross the bridge at the other end, she spotted an officer who was sitting by the roadside smoking his pipe. She told him of the incident of trying to cross the perfectly intact bridge and being stopped because it was supposed to have been blown up. The officer nodded his head sympathetically and said, "I'd love to be able to help you but, you see, I was shot dead at 8 o' clock this morning!"

Anecdote (3)

"I was in a pub at the weekend – last Saturday morning in fact – when a lunatic came in and went berserk. He smashed every glass in the shop. And he frightened the shite out of everybody in the place. You should have seen all the hard men climbing under the counters – it was gas. It was a panic. All the hardchaws, these would-be assassins were pissing in their trousers with the fright. It was great gas watching them.

Then the squad car came and took your man away. If you had heard the spoof that began then!

"I was just going to break this pint bottle over his head!"

"I had this chair in my hand to batter him with when the Guard walked through the door!"

"I know," said his mate. "Didn't I see you with it?" if you had heard the hard men back each other up it would have made you laugh. And five minutes earlier they were under the counter pissing on themselves!"

Anecdote (4)

In the working class district in which I was reared there were some neighbours who were nice people and then there were the others. There were alcoholics, wife beaters, people who detested each other, a few suicidally prone people who eventually killed themselves and a lot of broken hearts.

Frank lived near us and followed in his father's footsteps by becoming an alcoholic and a wife beater. One night he came home drunk and demanded his dinner. His wife was as sweet as pie to him. She served him up his dinner and a few cans of beer. When he finished those she produced more beer and he continued drinking until he fell into a drunken sleep. When his wife, who had packed a suitcase full of Frank's clothes, attacked his drunken head with a frying pan. Frank woke up to find himself on the receiving end of a thorough beating. This was the long awaited day of his wife's revenge. She beat him black and blue, threw him and his suitcase out of the house and that same night she had the locks changed.

Frank didn't know what had hit him so he returned to his old neighbourhood. He asked Jim, an old neighbour, if he could sleep in the broken down van in the driveway. "You can if you like," said Jim.

If this was a movie we would now cut to another character: Donald. Donald lived with his brother and sister-in-law in the old neighbourhood. He was due to go to court the following day on a burglary charge. He told his softhearted, soft headed sister-in-law that he loved her and wanted to make love to her. "I'll be going to jail tomorrow and I won't have the chance to express my love for you for several months. It's today or never!" His soft headed, softhearted sister-in-law consented. They went to bed and made love. They were enjoying a post coital cigarette when Donald's brother burst in on top of them. He beat both of them up and threw Donald out of the house. Donald called on Jim and said, "I've had a bit of a row with my brother. I need some place to sleep tonight. I'll be going for porridge tomorrow. So can I sleep in the van tonight?"

Jim explained, "Well I've already promised Frank, who used to live across the road that he can sleep in it. But I suppose if he sleeps in the back you could always sleep in the front."

Jim related the above tales to my father Mike. "Do you know what Mike?" he said. "I was going to get rid of the old van – it's not much use to me lying in the driveway with no engine in it – but now I think I'll leave it there for the fucking tourist season!"

Anecdote (5)

My father worked as a Jack of All Trades for much of his life but in his fifties he was offered a job driving a minibus. He began working driving actors to film sets and to film locations. Being a character there was one incident in which my father made many people laugh.

Two actors were cutting down a tree as part of a film. My father walked onto the set and said:

"Woodman spare that tree
Touch not a single bough
In youth it protected me.
And I'll protect it now!"

Then he changed his voice to that of a Dublin hardman and said, "Hey Whacker! Make fucking logs of it!" Everyone was amused.

Anecdote (6)

My father had a wonderfully colourful way with the English language. Whenever he would fart he would say, "Good little arse, only for you, I'd burst!"

He came to see me in hospital one time and a tall nurse passed by. My father's instant comment about her was, "She has a nose you could slice bread with, a chin you could chop cabbage in a jug with and an arse as high as a sparrow's nest!"

Anecdote (7)

In my father's village there was a 'Big House' which was the residence of a large land owning Protestant family. One of the sons was a bit of a rake and poked every maid that ever went to serve in the house. They were dismissed to return home with a substantial sum of money as compensation when they became pregnant.

In the fullness of time the rake inherited the house and land and married. In his early forties he had a heart attack and died. He and his wife believed in spiritualism and reincarnation and other bizarre beliefs. Since he died without leaving a will his widow contacted the 'table-rappers' and they held a séance to fund out how he wished to dispose of his assets.

The story went that the séance convened in the usual way with his widow and others sitting around the table holding hands. Eventually after a bit of mumbo jumbo the rake was contacted. His name was Finian.

"Are you there Finian?" his widow asked.

"I have come a long way," came the reply through the medium. "I have left my new body to come back to talk to you. I have come a long way."

"I wanted to ask you something," said his widow. "Since you died without leaving a will I wanted to know what your wishes were regarding the disposal of your assets?"

"Do what you like with them. That life is over for me. I don't care what happens to my former assets. Please don't disturb me again. I must fulfil my mission in my new life. I had to come a long way in spirit travel to answer your call. Please do not call me away from my new life again."

"What did you come back as?" asked his widow, her head imbued with notions of reincarnation

"I'm a bull out in Africa," came the reply. "I'm a Charolais bull with balls as big as footballs and I'm having the time of my life servicing heifers! They're nearly as good as Irish maids!"

Anecdote (8)

Priests were very powerful in social status in rural Irish towns until very recently. They claimed to have the 'power'. One priest, in a Midlands town, some years ago, rode his horse into a village and tried to tie the horse to a lamppost. The horse did not like to be tied so he pulled his head every which way. As the priest's luck would have it a man came riding by on his bicycle so Father Gorey stopped him.

"Come here my good man," he said. "And hold my horse."

The man said, "Sorry Father, I can't. I'm on my way to work and I'm on my last chance. If I'm late I'll be sacked."

"Look," said Father Gorey. "I'm going into this house to give a man the Last Rites to help him on his way to Heaven."

"He doesn't have a job to worry about so, Father. I have. I need to keep my job. I don't get a pension until I'm seventy so I need to get to work in time."

The priest then became aggressive. "Hold this horse," he ordered, "or I'll stick you to the ground!"

The man got back up on his bike and as he cycled away he threw over his shoulder, "Stick the fucking horse to the ground, then you won't need anyone to hold him!"

Anecdote (9)

During the War or the Emergency, as it was known in Ireland, my father worked tarring roads. He lived in a dormitory which the company set up on the roadside near their work. It was a lot like the way migrant black workers live in South Africa. One ruse the men used to pull on each other was stealing food. One man solved his problem in an amusing, if stomach churning, way. He fried up his portion of sausages, rashers, eggs, tomatoes, mushrooms, black and white pudding and blew his nose in on top of the pan in full view of his friends. Then he asked in mock innocence, "Would any of you lads care for a rasher?" No one ever stole any food from him.

Anecdote (10)

Another of my father's jokes:
What's the difference between a man going into church and a man getting out of a bath?
One has hope in his soul and the other has soap in his hole.

Anecdote (11)

"Luigi was a chef in a big Italian restaurant when one day the waiter came in and said, "Luigi, there is a big fat American out there and he says he wants minestrone soup – not too hot and not too cold but just 'in the groove'."

Luigi said, "O.K."

Next the waiter came in and said, "Luigi, that big fat American wants a steak, not too well done and not too rare but just 'in the groove'."

Luigi said, "O.K."

Next the waited said, "Luigi, that big fat American out there says he wants apple pie a la mode – not too much cream, not too little cream but just 'in the groove'."

Luigi said, "O.K."

Next the waiter came in and said, "Luigi, that big fat American wants espresso coffee not too strong and not too weak but just 'in the groove'."

At this Luigi flared up and said, "You tell that big fat American to come in here and kiss my ass – not on the right cheek and not on the left cheek but just 'in the groove!"

Anecdote (12)

My mother was very house proud. She loved to clean and tidy things up. My father, on the other hand, was more casual about these matters. On one memorable occasion he reprimanded my mother's fussiness by saying, "A house is not a home unless one child can shite on the floor and the others make a slide of it!"

Anecdote (13)

In 1974 when Conor Cruise O' Brien was Minister for P_7T there was a discussion that Irish people might have to pay an extra T.V licence to receive the British channels. It was a political hot potato for a short season and eventually died off without any attempt at implementation. We were in a pub in Kildare drinking pints and discussing the possibility that we might have to pay it. A simple fellow in our drinking company brought the house down by announcing, "Bejaysus lads, if the Queen of England calls to my door looking for her licence money she'll go home sick, sore and sorry!"

Anecdote (14)

One of my father's stories:

<u>The Comeuppance of the 'Sack 'em ups'</u>

The 'Sack 'em ups' was the nickname given to body snatchers at the turn of the century in Ireland. Burke and Hare were famous body snatchers in London in the 1880's but Ireland had their equivalents the length and breadth of the country.

I was speaking to my father around an open fire in an inner city pub one evening when he told me the tale of the comeuppance of the 'sack 'em ups'.

Their trade was to rob freshly dug graves of their corpses and sell them to surgeons to be cut up for highly paying medical students. The surgeons paid the 'sack 'em ups' very well for the bodies they stole, having dug them up from the graves at the dead (pardon the pun) of night. My father knew one man who gained his seed-capital as a 'sack 'em up'. He sold several bodies to surgeons and bought land, a grocery shop, a pub and (guess what?) he also went into business as an undertaker.

At the turn of the century it was very important to give the dead a regal funeral. A man named Mike did so for his father upon the father's death. Mike was a poor working class man who owned a bicycle, a bucket and a cloth – he earned his living as a window cleaner. He cycled into Dublin from Blanchardstown early every morning so that he could wash windows before the shops opened for business.

Mike was cycling to work down Paradise Row when suddenly he was accosted by the constabulary.

"Come quick," they said. "Park your bike in Kevin Street Police Station and we'll bring you down to the Four Courts. We've got a couple of 'sack 'em ups' for trial. We caught them red-handed with a corpse in a sack going towards the College of Surgeons."

Mike acceded to the policeman's request that he become a member of the jury who would try the 'sack 'em ups'.

The case proceeded in court and the prosecution thought they had a watertight case. However, when they laid the stolen body out on the clerk's desk, Mike threw a 'wobbly' – the corpse was his father.

The Judge ruled that a jury member had a personal interest in convicting the 'sack 'em ups' and so the case was dismissed.

Mike ascertained the names and addresses of the two 'sack 'em ups' and when he had recovered his equilibrium and saw his father reburied he made it his business to shadow the two 'sack 'em ups'. He discovered the two of them owned and horse and cart and that they specialised in one particular graveyard.

Within a month one of Mike's neighbours died. She was given a grand funeral and late that night the two 'sack 'em ups' arrived at the cemetery to rob her body. They dug up the grave, emptied the coffin and rolled the corpse up in a sack. Mike saw all that happened. As the two body snatchers refilled in the grave with the empty coffin, Mike unfolded the corpse, hid her behind a bush and wrapped himself up in the sack on the back of the horse and cart.

The grave robbers – none the wiser – geed up the horse and started off for the College of Surgeons. They chatted amiably, looking forward to their reward as they passed over a hump backed bridge. They turned left over the bridge prompting Mike to declaim in a high-falsetto: "You should have turned right boys – that's where I live!"

It was the turn of the two 'sack 'em ups' to throw a 'wobbly'. They jumped off the horse and cart and ran up the road, screaming and shouting, frightened out of their wits.

Mike drove the horse and cart to a local farmer friend's barn. He had wanted a change of work from the window cleaning and now he had the wherewithal to begin.

"Do you know what?" Mike asked my father and without waiting for a reply declared, "I made a good living hauling goods for ten years with that horse and cart and no one ever challenged my right of ownership!"

Anecdote (15)

"Father Danny in Limerick was a bully. He used to ban the cinema from opening on Sunday, the pubs were shut because of him, there were no dances allowed. The only thing people were let do was march in sodality parades. There were 40 sodality confraternities and every one of the poor, unfortunate bastards had to march around Limerick City every Sunday and the tongues hanging out of them for want of drink.

He read me off the altar, one time, you know. There was a young couple I knew in 1945 and they wanted to get married. The priest's fee for a marriage was a minimum of ten pounds. She was pregnant and needed to get married but because the boyfriend only had seven pounds, Father Danny refused to marry them. The boyfriend approached the local Church of Ireland Minister. He married them for free and off to England they went.

Father Danny – a roaring alcoholic. I'd love to visit where he is buried before I die.

Me: Would that be to say a little prayer of forgiveness?

Mike: It would not. It's be in order to do a great, big crap on his grave!

Anecdote (16)

Mike: One of my pals, in my youth, was Jim Coyle. He was a dark fellow with black curly hair. The lads used to say to him, "Why are you so dark, Jim?" and he'd said "My mother was chased by a black man and he caught her and had his fun with her and that's how come I'm black."

His mother send him to the shop, one day when he was sixteen, for a load of bread. Wasn't the Recruiting Sergeant for the British Army in town and Jim took the King's Shilling and went off to India for eighteen years. He wrote to his mother and sent her money. After the eighteen years he was offered a generous pension. He took it.

He arrived home to his mother's kitchen and placed a loaf of bread on the table and said, "There you are mother – that's the loaf of bread you sent me for eighteen years ago!"

What could she do only laugh and hug and kiss him.

He was a great, witty fellow!"

Anecdote (17)

My father stayed in digs with two other men in Dundalk during the War. One of his fellow guests was a bit of a religious fanatic as was the landlady. The two of them went to Mass every morning together. Eventually they began an affair by tried to keep it from my father and the other man, Johnny. One day the fellow who was having the affair with the landlady announced he would not be going to work that day. "I have an infection in my eye and I have to go to the doctor."

On the way to work Johnny said to my father, "Do you know the eye your man has the infection in?" "No," said my father. "The eye of his prick. He'd better get out of there." The landlady had syphilis.

Anecdote (18)

After a neighbour burnt down our garden shed my father's response was classic:

"Well, fuck me, I love those dear hearts and gentle people who live in my hometown. If I catch the fellow who did that I'll kick his arse so high up between his shoulder blades, he won't know whether he is shittin' or spittin'!" How very different from the home life of our own dear Queen!

Anecdote (19)

My father worked, at one time making roads all over Ireland. Whenever the road was within 20 miles of home, my father cycled home every evening, it was the tradition to buy food from farmers' wives going to and from work. One of my fathers' workmates was a thief. He stole the food and brought it home. One morning a worker asked the foreman if he could hide a parcel of food in the foreman's hut. It was tied up in paper and twine. Sure enough, that evening, the parcel was missing. The thief brought it home and announced to his wife, "There's a few chops I bought today, put a couple on for my dinner".

She opened up the parcel and screamed when the contents were revealed: it was a dead cat!

Anecdote (20)

One time in the late 1950s the neighbours gathered in the back garden on a warm Sunday afternoon. Myself and the little girl next door were playing mammys and daddys. I walked around the garden and "came home" for my dinner. The little girl said "go back to work – your dinner isn't ready yet". This happened a few times and finally I got fed up and said, "Look, I want my fucking dinner now!". All the adults laughed and one woman commented "He is a real little man; he's the downcut of his father".

Anecdote (21)

In 1975 I paid forty pounds for a brown velvet suit for my wedding day. My father was scandalised at the price. "Forty pounds for a suit!", he said. "Before I'd pay that for a suit I'd paint my arse with tar and stick on feathers".

Anecdote (22)

One of my uncles had poor health and was forced to retire early. When he died he left behind my aunt and four children – two boys and two girls. My father took a paternal interest in my orphaned cousins. In teenage years, one of the girls began a special friendship with a black medical student. My father's conclusion was: "Well, she may marry him now – lips a yard thick and a mile long – what white man could compete with that? I mean, it stands to reason!"

Anecdote (23)

Dad told a joke about a fellow going to work for the first time in a hotel and coming home to dinner.

Dad: "Well son, how did you get on at your first day at work in the hotel?"

Son: "I got on well but I got sacked"

Dad: "Sacked on your first day! Why?"

Son: "I stuck my mickey in the potato peeler"

Dad: "What happened to the potato peeler?"

Son: "She got sacked as well!"

Anecdote (24)

My father once went into the gentleman's toilet in the Shelbourne Hotel for a piddle, as he was leaving an American man said:

"Excuse me sir, are you Irish?"

My father said, "yes". The American said,

"I thought so, you see, in America, we usually wash our hands after urinating".

My father said: "Well, in Ireland we usually don't piss on our fingers" and out he sauntered.

Anecdote (25)

My father, who was an old fashioned protestant and had no time for the Catholic Church, once asked a Reformed Church Minister if he thought it was a sin for Christians to smoke. They were in the sitting room of my father's house and the Minister noted my father's rack of pipes. "Should a Christian smoke?" he echoed my father's question before coming up with the answer: "Not only should Christians smoke, they should be on fire. On fire with love for God and their neighbours. That's my answer, not only should Christians smoke – they should be on fire with love!"

Anecdote (26)

My father worked distributing turf from the Phoenix Park during the war. Because of his excellent workmanship he was quickly promoted to foreman. One day at two intervals the manager sent down four men to begin work. My father shook hands with them and set them to work.

At lunchtime he approached the manager and said, "Those four men you send down to me this morning were very soft-handed men, not used to manual labour".

"That's right Mike", said the Manager. "Two of them used to be Church of Ireland Ministers and the other two were Catholic priests until recently". My father scratched his head and said: "Bejaysus, if only we had a second-hand Pope we could start our own religion!".

Anecdote (27)

My father had a vulgar tongue all his life. Sometimes he would pontificate about and debate with a person on the television.

My mother, on the other hand, was a very clean-tongued person who never used vulgarities. Often she would say to me, "Don't use bad language just because you father does it, doesn't mean to say that you have to do it too".

I tried to honour my mother's standards, especially in her presence. However, when my mother reached 60 years of age, she had intimations of mortality. She was in the sitting room and my father was in full verbal flight talking back to a politician on the television.

My mother paused and said to my father:

"Mike, would you do me a favour?"

"What's that, Mary?", my father said.

"Would you ever fuck!?!"

You could have knocked my father over with a feather.

Anecdote (28)

My father worked from the age of 14 to 79; often at hard manual work. Late one night on returning home from work I said to him: "How are you tonight Mike?"

He said: "I'm like the dog who shit in the tent – fucked out. And that is like the hairs on a blackman's left ball; it is neither right nor fair".

Anecdote (29)

My father loved to present a civilised face to the world. He shaved every morning; put on aftershave lotion; brushed his teeth, combed his hair and dressed well. One morning when he had been particular about his toilet he asked me:

"Do you mind if I ask you a personal question?"

I said: "no".

He said; "What would you give to be as good-looking as me?"

Anecdote (30)

I loved my mother and father very much. They were married for 50 years. My mother had a long, lingering illness for 5 years before she went to Heaven. It only took my father a week to die.

My mother was the wind beneath my father's wings. Even though I know they only went as far as God and that God is always very near, I miss them both.

I dreamt about them a good deal after their departures. I dreamt my mother wrote a book about me entitled: You are the flower of them all. I dreamt my father left me a letter that finished; "Why do we worry and fret so much about everything when God meets us at our point of need?"

Anecdote (31)

<u>This Is My Father's World</u>

This is my father's world
And to my listening ears
All nature sings
And round me rings
The music of the spheres.

This is my father's world:
The birds their carols raise
The morning light,
the lily white.
Declare their maker's praise.

This is my father's world
Oh let me ne'er forget
That though the wrong
seems often so strong
God is the ruler yet.

This is my father's world
Why should my heart be sad?
The Lord is King
let the heavens ring
God reigns let earth be glad

Reformed Church Hymn

(I read aloud this tribute at my father's funeral.)

Con Man Cop

By Detective Inspector P J Smith (Retired)
(Dateline: London)

Story (1)

In our beginnings is fashioned the pattern of our ends – a great moral truth which most of us happily appreciate, but which the average criminal fails to realise, or chooses to ignore, until it is too late and inevitable retribution sweeps upon him like a long-threatening and inescapable avalanche.

In my own beginnings – far back, when, as a very unsophisticated youth from the Channel Islands, I joined the Metropolitan Police Force – I embarked on a great adventure, on an exciting and ever-interesting career, which, when it ended with my retirement 28 years later, enabled me out of my specialised experience of criminals and their ways to compile an official "Who's Who" of that aristocrat of all crooks – the confidence trickster or "Con Man".

That black list, which was devised for Scotland Yard, but which now reposes in the criminal records department of every police force in the world, contains the photographs, descriptions, histories and details of the methods of operation of the many hundreds of confidence tricksters known to me personally. It is a Rogues' Gallery of the elite of Crookdom – men of intelligence, fascinating, indeed charming, proud of their "profession", inordinately jealous of their capabilities and feats, making capital from the greed and credulity of wealthy victims, harvesting with smiling audacity hundreds of thousands of pounds in a lifetime ...... and, by reason of that very flaw in their characters which makers them confidence tricksters, squandering their easy-made fortunes at casinos, race-courses, and the Continental playgrounds of the rich and fashionable.

That flaw? Fundamentally, it is laziness; a desire to have a good time without working for it honestly, to enjoy the best – or the worst! – and to let someone else foot their extravagant bills.

Truly, they are crooks in clover.

During the many years I spent at Scotland Yard my duties brought me into close contact with a great number of confidence tricksters, card-sharpers, and international crooks unanimously acknowledged to be the cleverest, craftiest and most resourceful of all criminals operating. Gradually, as my experience grew out of hard practice, I came to specialise in the prevention and detection of crimes of this nature, and I acquired a knowledge of almost every confidence man working in this part of the world. When a new man appeared on the scene it was not long before I became aware of his existence and "looked him over" just for future reference!

Audacious, ingenious, tenacious – those adjectives exactly describe the successful con man. The following story, based on actual fact from my case-book, will give some idea of how the super-crook with a tale to tell "trims" – or fleeces – his victims.

The manager of a famous hotel facing Hyde Park, when walking across the lounge, happened to see an American visitor talking with two smartly dressed men. True, in a fashionable hotel, there was nothing extraordinary about that. But glancing again at the strangers, who were deep in conversation with his client, he suddenly recognised one of them as a man by the name of Davidson, who was known to him as a notorious confidence trickster.

The manager quickly withdrew without attracting attention. He rang up the local police station and reported that he was suspicious and feared that an attempt was being made to victimise the American.

Shortly afterwards two detectives arrived at the hotel. Davidson, however, had left the building. But the second stranger still talked earnestly with the American in low, confidential tones.

The detectives intervened and asked the man from the States if he had had any business dealings with Davidson. No, he hadn't. In fact, he had just arrived from America with his friend – the stranger who now sat quietly and said not a word – and the other man about whom they inquired had simply passed the time of day with him in the lounge, and had then departed.

When questioned further, the American resented the intrusion into his private affairs, and curtly intimated that he had not made any deals with Davidson, nor had he drawn any money from his bank to transact business.

The detectives saw that nothing useful was to be gained by prolonging the interview, most obviously distasteful to the transatlantic visitor, so they took their leave, but not before advising both men to have nothing whatever to do with Davidson, as he was an undesirable character. They added the friendly counsel that if Davidson approached them further they should advise the manager of the hotel, who would immediately pass on the information to the police.

What the officers did not realise was that the stranger who had remained wordless during their brief visit was, in fact, a confidence trickster himself! The victim, as is usually the case, had been sworn to secret lest the profitable Stock Exchange transactions they had been so eagerly discussing should be jeopardised by indiscreet conversation. An old trick, but very effective! And, rather than risk losing the opportunity of making big money quickly, the gullible American purposely misled the detectives by personally vouching for his companion.

That attitude is typical. It is one I have found prominent in many victims I have met, and it reminds me of the remark once made to me by a trickster I had arrested: "The trouble is, guv'nor, he wanted to make money just as easily as I did. If you want my opinion, he's as big a crook as I am. Only, he's never been found out!"

Later, I will explain how the Stock Exchange trick is operated – but, to return to the American. It was true, up to a point, that he had travelled across the Atlantic with his so-called friend; but their association had only begun on the boat, when the stranger made a point of getting to know him, and ingratiating himself into his confidence. Upon arrival in London, the next stage of fleecing was set: Davidson – quite accidentally, of course! – happened on the scene. He talked, he knew a thing or two; he had money, and he knew how to make more money. As a big speculator on the Stock Exchange he could put his two new "friends" in the way of a good thing.

I wonder how many times that story has been told – and believed?

In this case the trick had progressed to the point where the American was about to hand over his money in order to make a big, quick profit on some wonderful investment. His avarice had concealed the fact fro the officers that only that morning he had withdrawn from his bank the sum of £5000 in Bank of England notes. It was in his pocket while his rejected helpers spoke to him.

As soon as the officers left the hotel, the other man – by name of Lawes, and a successful trickster behind all his clever social camouflage – jumped to his feet.

"I don't believe those fellows were real 'tecs'," he declared agitatedly. "I expect they're touts of a rival concern who have got wind of our business and are after our money. I'm going to put mine away." (He was supposed to have a stake of £10,000 in his possession to participate in the deal.) "You can do what you like with yours!"

The thought of losing a fortune was too much for the American. As Lawes made for the door, the victim got up and ran after him.

"I believe you're right," he assured him. "I didn't like the look of those men. They knew too much. Come on – I'm coming with you."

Lawes scarcely slackened his step. Outside, he hailed a taxi. T he two men jumped in. "Selfridge's," Lawes told the driver.

When they reached that store Lawes got out. "I'm going to put my money in the safe deposit here," he intimated. "It'll be safe. I don't know what you intend doing with yours."

As he spoke, he pulled out his thick wad of supposed Bank of England notes to the value of £10,000.

Excited, fearful, trusting, the American came up like a fish to the baited hook. "Here, take mine as well," he offered. "Put it along with yours in the safe deposit till we want it, old man."

And so £5000 of good and true Bank of England notes changed hands in an instant. Lawes told the American to remain in the taxi and wait till he came out. "Back in a jiffy," he called out, and he rushed across the pavement and into the store.

But he didn't stay there. He went right through and out the other side. A moment later he was gone – leaving his trusting victim cooling his heels in the purring taxi.

He did not come back. The American realised too late that he had been defrauded. When he eventually called at Scotland Yard I interviewed him. It was a sad and chastened man who told me his story.

He did not at first admit that he had been warned by the detectives. Knowing the facts of this particular type of swindle from A to Z, I was surprised to learn of a different finale from the usual. I questioned him and gradually came to learn the real history of the case.

Such is human nature!

I'm afraid that the American did not get too much sympathy from me, although, of course, he received every courtesy and assistance a zealous Scotland Yard officer could provide. It was not until some time later that we were able to arrest both of the tricksters concerned, for other offences. The American had by then returned home, and when we communicated with him and asked him if he would return to England to prosecute, he declined.

Again true to type!

It is suspiring how many victims do not wish to take criminal action against their fraudulent associates. Or perhaps it is not so very surprising. For, with his money lost forever, a man does not care to reveal to his friends how neatly he has been duped.

Clever psychologists that there are, the confidence-trick operators gain strength from the knowledge that that is their last line of defence.

I know of many who had been thus saved at the eleventh hour. I shall tell their amazing stories later in these reminiscences.

Story (2)

The lambs paraded themselves for a season of fleecing. The confidence tricksters swooped down to reap their harvest. And the police found themselves engaged in new warfare. London had to be cleaned up.

Off Jermyn Street, Piccadilly, there was a club which now no longer exists. It was the haunt of gangs of confidence tricksters, and it was my job to obtain an entry into their exclusive quarters. After considerable difficulty I got to know a member of the club. He was what we call an "honest contact". He was an American, a bit of a lad in his own way, with a passion for racing. He instructed me as a member, and thereafter I frequented the club for some weeks at all hours of the day and night.

I had to establish confidence, to be accepted as one of themselves. Had my real profession and intentions become known I would have had a most unpleasant time. But I went about free and unchallenged, and gradually became acquainted with the names and faces of scores of the most notorious and successful confidence men in the world.

That experience proved invaluable. It was instrumental in my being able at later dates to apprehend quite a number of my fellow club-mates.

One of the first to be disposed of was a particularly dangerous American named Frankie Dwyer. He was wanted by the American police, and his presence in this country was undesirable in view of the several cases of swindling reported against him. When I found he was a member of the club I arranged to interview him, with Inspector Leave, at an exclusive flat near Piccadilly.

That was a most unpleasant interview – for Dwyer. When we told him what our real business was he got such a shock that he had to be given a reviver. We arranged to wait for him while he completed his toilet, and as we sat in his luxurious room the door opened and a burly fellow, dressed in an expensive fur-lined overcoat, walked in.

"Come on, old man," he said to Dwyer. "We'll be late for the races. I've got the car outside."

Dwyer turned glumly. "They're taking me to Scotland Yard," he complained lugubriously, nodding in our direction.

His friend started. He flared up in a temper. "Look here," he bawled. "You can't do this sort of thing to a respectable American citizen, you know! If you don't leave him alone you'll be sorry."

Calmly, but forcibly, he was ejected down the stairs, and we took our prisoner to the police station, where he was charged as an undesirable alien. He was eventually deported to America, where his ultimate fate was attended to by the New York police.

His opulent friend, however, was destined to cross my path on two subsequent occasions. I shall call him Charles Denman. The last occasion on which I had "business" dealings with him ended in the Glasgow High Court, when he was sentenced to three years' imprisonment for obtaining money by means of a confidence trick. At the present time he is being supplied with free board and lodging by the United States authorities. But I shall deal with him in a later chapter.

With Dwyer out of the way, I continued to frequent the West End hotels and socials haunts of the con men, where the smart crooks met daily to discuss their latest coups.

Boasting is the confidence trickster's greatest weakness. It is the vulnerable spot in his armour, for a confidence operator loves nothing better than to tell the story of how he did So-and-So for £50,000, how he "put him in" and "trimmed" him. Bragging never does pay anyone – and least of all the criminal, who should know better than to air his personal secrets where not only walls have ears, but where their rivals may be listening with jealous interest and treacherous intentions.

At various restaurants, in the old days, I have often sat surrounded by as many as twenty or thirty confidence men while they openly chatted about their professional deals over champagne and cigars. When names were mentioned, seldom were the correct patronymic's used. They knew each other by descriptive nicknames, such as – Dictionary Harry, Cut-Face, Dave the Liar, Pretty Syd, Chicago Solly, the Count, Australian Jack, Australian Mac, the Bejeesus Kid, Worcester Red, the Fireman, the Red Herring, the Indiana Wonder, Yellow Pete. The majority of them were Australians and Americans. The Australian swell mobsman runs true to type; usually he graduates from the racing-tracks of that continent, from fake betting, pocket-picking, petty swindling, through the early stages of learning to "tell the tale" to the higher flights of professional acumen and ambition. They all gravitate to London like bees to a hive. For in London there are variety and vastness, wealth, a floating population of colonial and foreign visitors, and a social atmosphere which cannot be found elsewhere in all the world of crime.

At the time of which I write the confidence men had grown incautious and more than usually talkative, because of the almost complete immunity they had enjoyed from police intervention during the war years. They kept arriving in the country and finding their way to the haunts with a sure instinct. Many of them were total strangers to each other upon arrival, but soon they got to know each other as circumstances provided introductions or necessity threw them together. I spent a great deal of time in their not uninteresting company. I never forgot one of their faces; I memorised their mannerisms and descriptions until they were photographed on my mind. Even the intonation of their voices I recorded mentally. I was determined to specialise just as much as they were doing.

One night, I was on late duty at the Yard when two Australian officers were brought to me. They explained that earlier that evening they had found their way into a night-club – of which there were far too many then – and they had been induced to play cards. Of course, the inevitable had happened. They had lost. Indeed, they had lost all their money, including their back-pay, which had been accumulating while they were on active service. They were due to sail for Australia the next morning, and they asked if a police officer would accompany them back to the club and demand the return of their money.

It was evident that they had received the attention of a gang of crooks. But when they refused to assist in a prosecution of the individuals concerned they were informed that the police could do nothing for them.

From the description they gave of their erstwhile club companions, I was able to identify one of them as "Big Dan", a notorious card-sharper.

The Australians sat in my office talking over our war experiences, which had been so recent, and when they rose to go I casually told them that one of their card-sharping acquaintances, "Big Dan", lived on the south side of the Thames and made a practice of walking home from the West End over Waterloo Bridge in the early hours of the morning.

Nothing more was said about their loss. They looked at me, and I saw their eyes sparkle for a second and then dull down. One of them then asked with a slow smile: "By the way, what's the best road to Waterloo Bridge? We'd like to inspect it before we go home to Australia tomorrow!"

I pointed out Waterloo Bridge, and then said good night to them.

The next morning, shortly after my arrival at the office, I received a telephone call. The voice in the receiver was excited. But I was able to identify it as the voice of one of my Australian visitors of the previous night. He said he was ringing from a railway station on the way to catch the boat-train for home.

"Yes, I replied, waiting for the rest of the story.

The receiver spluttered. "I say, we happened to be hanging around Waterloo Bridge at three o'clock this morning when we saw 'Big Dan' coming along all decked up in a stiff front."

"Go on," I said, and I visualised "Big Dan", six foot two, sixteen stone, handsome, robust, active. "What happened?"

"Oh, I guess we just sort of pounced on him, hoisted him on to the parapet and threatened to drop him into the old Thames if he didn't come clean with our dough. You ought to have seen that darned crook change colours. He told us where the packet was lying in the breast pocket of his coat...... We hauled him up again and got our money back all right ...... Oh, we just want to thank you as a brother Tommy for all your help! Bye ......"

"Wait a moment," I cried. "What did you do with 'Big Dan'?"

A laugh broke in my ear. "Oh, we just plugged him!"

That startled me. "What?" I yelled back. "Did you shoot him?"

"Oh, no. I hit 'im with a leg of mutton!" (Meaning his huge fist.)

That Australian spoke the truth. It must have been a glorious sock, for I saw that unfortunate card-sharper in the West End a few days later, and he had the most beautiful black eye imaginable.

I often wonder what would have been my position, officially, if the Australians had carried out their threat and dropped "Big Dan" into the mud of London river! The act was by no means beyond them. I have seen too many "Aussies" do the most astounding things during the war. Taking all things into consideration, "Big Dan" certainly got off lightly ......

Story (3)

Early in the summer it was reported to us that another army major had been made the sorry dupe of confidence tricksters. We invited the victim along to the Yard and interviewed him, and he revealed that he had lost £2300 by what is known as the "Infallible Betting System". Not content with such a handsome haul, the crooks had made a further attempt to fleece him, this time to the extent of £9000.

His story to us was that the previous year, at an exclusive hotel, he had made the acquaintance of a South African who represented himself to be a wealthy planter on holiday. A very plausible claim, backed by the grand manner in a performance that would have given credit to many a famous stage actor! In truth, the wealthy one was a well-known confidence man with numerous convictions to his discredit. He had the usual paraphernalia of his breed, the same glamorous tale to tell, and the inevitable equally wealthy friends – in this case two men with strings of race-horses to amuse themselves.

They talked, idly to begin with, and as the conversation developed, one of the newcomers intimated that he and his friends were members of a syndicate which was in a position to use its influence to glean inside information concerning horses which would run in future races. Immense profits were assured anyone backing the horses in accordance with the syndicate's foolproof system.

It was then explained, in answer to the major's questions, that the horses were backed when they stood at long odds – say, at 16 to 1 – and the amount of money which the syndicate placed was so heavy that the price shortened to 10 to 1, or 8 to 1. That was the strategic moment to play their own game by hedging or paying off, so that they were bound to make a profit whether the horses won or lost.

Easy money could not surely be easier! The story, with all its embellishments, convinced the gallant major, who for several days had been royally entertained at the best hotels and at the flat of the ring leader, where a butler and footman paraded impressively. There was never the least shadow of suspicion on the gorgeous social landscape, and none in the major's mind. He handed over the £2300 to be invested in the wonderful scheme.

He never saw his money again. On the day of the race they all motored down to Goodwood to see their horse, named Ptah, run in the Stewards' Cup. It lost. When the major asked for his profit, which was assured on a win-or-lose basis, he was shocked to learn that his companions had not hedged their bet, as the price on the horse, far from going down, had actually risen.

The major returned to London, sad and dispirited – so disgusted at losing his money in such a manner that he did not even bother to keep in touch with his erstwhile friends. It was only when we heard the victim's story that the depth of the infamy was exposed to him. We advised him strongly to prosecute the men who had cheated him, and arrangements were speedily made to apply for warrants for their arrest.

After leaving the Yard, the major proceeded homewards across Berkeley Square. By a remarkable coincidence he met one of the confidence swindlers. There was a heated conversation which lasted for several awkward minutes; the major demanded there and then the return of his money and hinted that if this were not done he would not hesitate to call in the police.

The confidence trickster beckoned a passing taxi. As it drew up he opened the door. Then, prefacing his remarks with some lurid adjectives, he said: "You can do as you like. Take this cab, go straight down to Scotland Yard and tell them your story. They can't do anything."

His bluff was colossal. But he did not realise that the wheels were already being set in motion, and that something not too pleasant was in pickle for him and his associates. Had he been less brazen and been sensible enough to compromise with his victim, he might have saved himself and a number of his confederates from long terms of imprisonment; for the original complaint led to the discovery, during inquiries, of numerous other people who had been similarly fleeced by the gang, and we eventually arrested nine of the cleverest confidence men who have ever practised their shabby craft in this country. For us, it was a coup of coups, and it had the effect of damping the enthusiasm of other gangs who had been operating in London with impunity over a long period.

A few hours after our interview with the major we set off on our round-up; soon we had three of the crooks under lock and key. One was arrested at his home in the suburbs, in a most respectable street; another came to grief in his luxury flat off St. James' Street; and the third, the ringleader, who was known as Gibson John Davidson, was found with his family in a flat adjoining Manchester Square.

His apartments would have made a Hollywood star envious. They were furnished on an elaborate scale, apparently regardless of cost, and they contained furniture valued at about £70,000. Spacious and ornate, if ostentatious, they provided the perfect spider's parlour and must have trapped many unfortunate dupes blinded by their glitter.

When I called at the flat with another officer, the door was opened by a footman who, when we requested to see Mr Davidson, conducted us with a grand air down a long corridor and into a room at the far end. The door was shut on us, and we sat down to wait.

A minute passed, and nothing happened. "I don't like this," I remarked to my colleague. "You stay here and I'll pop outside the front door and keep my eyes open."

As quietly as I could I tiptoed down the corridor and let myself out of the flat. I closed the door carefully and stood back to wait. I hadn't long to wait, however, for a few seconds later the door slowly opened and a man whom I immediately recognised from the description I had of him, slipped out without hat or coat.

"Good evening," I greeted him.

He started. I could see he was taken aback.

"Mr Davidson, aren't you?"

"Oh, don't stop me," he retorted impatiently. "I'm rushing off to the chemist, as my boy has been taken seriously ill." And he made to walk past.

I shook my head. "Sorry! You must come with me. I've a friend waiting inside to see you." As I spoke I rang the door-bell, and it was answered by an astonished footman, who stepped outside with his mouth agape as I conducted his wandering master down to the end room. My colleague was about as astonished as the butler had been, and as Davidson had been. In fact, we were a most surprised party – with a strange mixture of feelings among us.

When the flat was inspected we found a remarkable assortment of gambling devices, including a roulette wheel, cloth and rake, a chemin de fer shoe, dice (genuine and fake), and scores upon scores of packs of cards. The most valuable find, however, was an address-book and memorandum which put us on the track of other victims of this audacious and highly successful gang. The book also obliged us with the names and addresses of various associates of the ringleader.

One of the crooks learned of the fate of his friends and tried to get across the France by a Channel boat. It was a vain attempt. A Scotland Yard man stationed at the port picked him up on our advice, and he was most indignant about being detained. He bluffed; then he threatened the officer with nothing less than dismissal from the Service for his outrageous conduct and officious behaviour. His protests died down quickly enough when a pocket-book which he had been seen to drop over the side of the ship was recovered and found to contain incriminating documents.

In the meantime, another of the conspirators had been caught, and the five prisoners duly appeared together in the Old Bailey dock. Leading counsel of the day ably defended them – but they were sentenced to five years' penal servitude each.

The extent of their illegal harvesting was amazing. It was revealed during the evidence at the trial that the had taken £25,000 from one of the witnesses, a City merchant, by means of Anzac Poker and the Infallible Betting System; another victim, an elderly builder, lost £16,000 to them through the same tricks, and yet another parted with £3000 in one night's play at Anzac Poker. Over the period of three years the stupendous sum of £250,000 had passed through the collective banking accounts of the five prisoners – yet at the time of their arrest they had not £1000 among them to their credit.

Verily, in most of those cases it is a matter of easy come and easy go. They make big money in a big way and spend it in a big way. I know of few confidence tricksters who have had the sense – despite the astuteness they display in a criminal manner – to bank some of the ill-gotten profits and retire comfortably from what must always be, by its very nature, an uncertain game, with nothing but disaster in the end.

Four of the other suspects in the betting swindle escaped our net for some time, but were all safely landed at later dates. One of them – named Teddy Naysmith – was not arrested for three years. I put a period to his freedom one day in the most unexpected manner while strolling along the Strand.

I had never seen him before, but I had memorised his likeness from photographs and had carefully taken note of various details about his appearance. I was not thinking of him at all when I saw him walking towards me on the Strand pavement. At least, when I first glanced at the approaching, dapper figure I did not connect him with the three-year-old case – until something flashed into my mind, memory worked quickly, and I realised that the immaculate stranger was none other than Teddy Naysmith, wanted by the police, flash crook, extravagant and blasé, a man who would go to extraordinary lengths to impress his "clientele", and who had even maintained a racing establishment at Epsom.

I decided to keep him under observation in the hope that he would lead me to his address. I turned around and followed him and saw him enter the old Haxell's Hotel – where the Strand Palace Hotel now stands. He went upstairs. So did I, at a safe distance. I stopped at the reception-office and had a quiet word with the manager, who came with me to Naysmith's bedroom door.

In answer to my knock, Naysmith opened the door and I told him I had a warrant for his arrest. He regarded me, grinning. Then he said: "I knew you were after me from the moment I passed you!"

"How was that?" I asked him.

His answer was what I expected, a revelation of the alert mind working behind his humorous eyes, of the essential psychologist within him.

"I spotted your eyes," he said. "And I saw the flash in them that was as good as flourishing a warrant in my face. Your build confirmed my opinion that you were a 'd' (detective), so I dodged as fast as I could into my hotel, hoping to lose you." He shrugged philosophically. "Got to make the best of it now, I suppose!"

And he came back with me as if out walking in the company of a friend.

Story (4)

I arrested a rogue once again. He regarded me as his especial nemesis, although he had never displayed any enmity. He always had had a fair deal from me and seemed to appreciate it like a good sportsman. I like to remember that in my war against crime I was as fair as the laws of the game would allow me to be, and I believe that the confidence men respected me. Indeed, often have they thanked me. Through it all, paradoxically enough, the cat and the mouse have been the best of friends!

The attitudes of the victims and near-victims has always intrigued me. Indeed, on many occasions it has been beyond my comprehension. The victim, of course, is usually too ashamed of his credulous part in the sorry transactions to be persuaded to expose the tricksters. Even the charitable prospect of saving others from a similar fate to his own will not always induce a "trimmed mug" to prosecute. He is more concerned about the money that has gone for ever – and about the fortune that he thought he was going to make so easily, but didn't! Perhaps, human nature being what it is, such behaviour is understandable. Yet those same victims who have made their complaints to me at the Yard, who have willingly, eagerly parted with, say, £50,000, would probably have hesitated to give me a shilling had I gone to their hotels and asked them for it! And I have often thought that the reluctance of the near-victims to display reasonable signs of gratitude for their escape is due to the overwhelming disappointment that they have suffered – the tantalising withdrawal of a tentative fortune, the dismal end to a glittering fairytale which has left them surrounded by the dead ashes of a Cinderella fantasy.

Of course, they are not all the colossal fools one might easily imagine them to be. One must remember that they have been morally and mentally intoxicated by the splendid acting of the confidence men, by the luxury, the lavish entertaining, the careless squandering of wealth for their pleasure. A clever confidence operator will spend months of time and thought, will cross the world like a millionaire on vacation, will spend thousands of pounds with the utmost charm and generosity humanly possible to exhibit, in order to set the stage for the last great scene of all – which is the only scene that matters to him.

The preliminaries are known as "putting him in" in order to "trim" him. They will rehearse speeches for hours and their tale-spinning for days on end. They are word-perfect before the curtain goes up. They will browse through books for information, for topographical details to establish the veracity of their stories, for antecedents and social contacts; they will pore over the financial columns of newspapers more assiduously than the most active speculator so that they may be conversant with markets and the movements of all kinds of investments; and they will subject themselves to laborious tuition in the social graces so that their manners will not betray them. They are essentially clever character-actors with an extensive repertoire.

One of the favourite "plays" in the confidence men's repertoire is the one known as "The Pay-Off", and which is an extravaganza spectacularly presented in a Stock Exchange setting.

Three men, and sometimes four, are required for the cast. The actor who finds the victim is known as the "Steerer" or "Lumberer"; it is his part to "mind" his newly found companion. The man who plays the principal part is known in the profession as the "player", and it is usually necessary to have another actor off-stage, watching points outside the hotel where the villainy is being performed, keeping a look out for such inquisitive and unappreciative persons as detectives, who are liable to give them "the bird"! This man is called the "Outside Man"; often he is an old grafter with a good working knowledge of the detectives in the district; he is the prompter, ready with his warning words as soon as the danger of a slip-up or a wrong cue becomes evident. If a fourth man is needed, he adopts the role of manager of the fictitious Stock Exchange and he takes his bow at the concluding scene with a banker's bag bulging with what are supposed to be rolls of bank notes.

The trickster uses various names for his "Exchange", and has all the necessary forms printed beforehand. The following impressive names are employed in the swindle: International Exchange, Anglo-American Exchange, International Brokers' Exchange, International Stock Exchange, Consolidated Stock Exchange, Continental Brokers' Exchange.

It is remarkable how many hard-headed people with solid bank-drafts fall for the swindle. When the trickster is operating the racing fraud he them becomes associated with the "United Turf Exchange," "International Turf Exchange," or the "Consolidated Turf Exchange," all of them as fraudulent and chimerical as the Stock Exchanges.

During my career I have acquired a large collection of the various "props" used by the confidence men in the play-acting – elaborate wallets, crested and monogrammed and all, and packed with spurious notes and documents; membership cards for the variety of Exchanges already mentioned; bogus shares certificates which look even more authentic than the real thing; cuttings from newspapers announcing windfalls to the confidence men, but cuttings which have been specially prepared by printing, in proper Press type-set, the paragraphs and headings in the vacant spaces to be found in the Stop Press columns of most papers.

One case in which the wallet figured came to my notice one sun lit day in May, while I was walking along the Strand, not on pleasure bent, but just to keep my eyes open in one of the favourite promenades of the swindlers. My luck was in, for I came on a notorious old rogue talking to two men, who, to my trained eyes, were obviously of his class. I watched them from a safe distance and saw them separate and walk in the direction of Trafalgar Square. I followed. Opposite the Savoy Hotel one of them turned off and entered the lounge, and within five minutes he came out again with a tall, well-dressed American.

A few minutes farther west the two men went into the Coal Hole public house and took seats at one end of the long bar. I kept them under observation, and had only a few minutes to wait before the other two crooks entered. In the meantime I had put through a telephone call to Scotland Yard for reinforcements. I knew they would not be long in coming to the scene.

The American and the three crooks huddled together over their drinks after the tricksters had greeted each other with great surprise and enthusiasm, as if they had not seen each other for a long, long time. And they talked in the low, confidential tones of conspirators. Just then my two colleagues arrived; we moved to the other end of the bar and sat down. Suddenly someone touched me on the shoulder and said: "What d'you think you're doing here? Working?"

I looked up to recognise the chief clerk of a well-known criminal lawyer, so I indicated the party at the far end of the bar and said we were rather interested in them.

"Tell you what," he exclaimed; "let me sit down near them and try to catch what they're talking about!"

He wandered off. We sat still – talking and watching. I saw him take out a visiting-card and scribble something on it; then he handed it to the barman, who came down to our end and quietly passed it across to me. One side of the card bore the lawyer's name, and on the back was written: "OK. They're ours. Get busy."

I often smile at the memory-picture of the amateur detective and the anticipation enlivening his features as he looked down and caught my eye. He was sitting there dramatising every movement, every word, and enjoying the thrill of it all. This was his Big Moment!

But we waited. And presently the American visitor and one of the crooks rose up and took their departure. I acted then. At the door I intercepted them and asked the American what his business was with the others. Of course, he was taken aback and hotly resented my intrusion, but when I informed him that we were Scotland Yard officers interested only in his welfare, he explained that the others had been discussing racing and had promised to put him on a good thing. In fact, he was then on his way back to the hotel for some cash, so that he could participate in a wonderful system of betting which, with the inside information his new-found friends certainly seemed to have, was guaranteed to show a handsome profit.

They had been telling him the old, old story. And he had believed every word of it. But for my intercepting him he would have parted with his money shortly afterwards.

We decided to take no risks. We arrested the three confidence tricksters there and then. There was a struggle, but an unavailing one, and they were escorted to Bow Street Police Station, where they were charged with being suspected persons loitering for the purpose of committing a felony. When searched, each of them was found to have a bulky wallet of the usual type in his possession, containing wads of tissue-paper cut to the size of Bank of England notes, with one genuine note on the outside and a rubber band holding the wad together.

There was an amusing sequel to the case. The American, whom we had taken along with us to Bow Street, proved to be a sheriff's officer who had come to England to study police methods! He had actually made a visit to Scotland Yard in connection with his official business. He enjoyed the joke against himself, and when the prisoners appeared before the chief magistrate the next morning the sheriff commented on the efficiency of Scotland Yard.

But, stranger still – when the three men entered the dock I saw to my amazement that their defence was being conducted by the solicitor whose chief clerk had acted the amateur detective in the bar the previous day. He was certainly a quick worker. Not only had he been instrumental in effecting their arrest, but he had then taken the opportunity of making business out of the adventure and turning it to the profit of his firm! I wonder if the prisoners ever knew of that piece of irony! They would have plenty of time to ponder on it, for they were all sent to prison, despite the eloquent pleadings of their solicitor. Their fingerprints revealed that they had had previous convictions against them.

When sentencing the men, the chief magistrate, remarked that it was a case of men setting out to perform what was known as the confidence trick, an operation that took some time. "This sort of thing," he added, "never seems to fail. All through the ages it goes on .... Even a police officer seems to have been a prospective victim, and in spite of his occupation, appears to have preserved a remarkable faith in human nature!"

Without wishing to enter into a controversy, I venture to suggest here that it has gone on all through the ages to as far back as the days of Esau and Jacob, when Jacob founded the "profession" by stealing his bothers' birthright through a piece of clever confidence-tricking. It has developed since those days, become an art, changed with the changing times since Isaac cried out in the anguish of the moment of revelation. "Thy brother came with subtlety, and hath taken away thy blessing." The mess of pottage is now worth as much as £50,000 a portion!

Story (5)

In due course I received promotion and was transferred to Paddington Police Station, where I spent three of my happiest years in the service engaged upon the investigation of every class of crime, from petty larceny to murder. Most of the work of a Division is comprised of routine duties of little interest to the average reader, so I will pass on, pausing only to recount the stories of two interesting cases which came my way at that time.

One evening, while working in my office at Paddington Police Station, an urgent telephone message was received from the Great Western Hotel, Paddington Railway Station: we were informed that two tricksters were being held there.

With another officer, I went to the hotel. Seated in a corner of the lounge, with a policeman and several hall-porters surrounding them, were two unhappy and dishevelled-looking individuals.

"What's happened?" I inquired, and a tall, curly-headed young Irishman stepped forward. In his pleasant brogue he told me that he was a wireless operator. While taking his seat in the Irish boat-train in Paddington Station he was approached by one of the two men who explained that he, too, was on his way to Ireland. They talked. The stranger thought that it would be a good idea if they travelled in the same compartment, and he added that he was expecting the delivery of a sporting gun which was being sent on to him at the train by messenger.

He kept a look-out for the messenger, and a few moments later he appeared. He was the second man of the dishevelled duo now dismally seated in the hotel lounge. He carried a long parcel, and after he had established the first man's identity he handed it over to him and presented a bill for £180 with the explanation that he had been instructed not to part with the gun without obtaining the payment for it.

The Irishman's travelling companion produced a piece of paper resembling a Bank of England note and said it was for £200. He handed it to the messenger only to be told that the messenger had no change. The train was due to leave; there was no time to go to the booking office, so the first man turned to the young Irishman and asked him for the temporary loan of £180 which he promised to repay just so soon as he could get the change from the guard.

Unsuspecting, the wireless operator counted out his notes and handed over the required sum. Just then the train started to move out of the station. The two strangers jumped aside. They slammed the compartment door in the Irishman's face and made a bolt for it. But Paddy's temper flared up. He jumped down from the moving train, chased the two men along the platform and caught up with them just as they were about to enter the station doorway of the Great Western Hotel. With a wild war-cry he hit the first thief on the jaw, knocking him down; then he threw the other on top of the fallen one, jumped on them, pummelled them mercilessly, seized them round the necks with his strangling arms and hollered loudly for reinforcements. His cries were quickly answered. The hotel hall-porters rushed to his aid, and the two thieves were soon subdued and placed under restraint.

When I saw them I immediately recognised them as two cunning old confidence tricksters who had been known to work similar tricks on travellers at railways stations on previous occasions.

They were taken along to the police station and charged; and the next morning the magistrate gave them their change all right. The young Irishman was the hero of the day. The magistrate congratulated him on the fearless manner in which he had tackled two persistent old criminals and so brought them to justice. I expect the lad never tired of his adventure in London and of the trouncing he gave those two desperate crooks. Certainly, single-handed, he made a mess of their looks. His Irish blood must have boiled over, with a vengeance ………

Story (6)

A notorious confidence trickster once said to me in a jocular moment that when he had made enough money from his "profession" he was going to found a family tradition and adopt a coat of arms. I asked him what his family crest would consist of. He grinned broadly and said: "A gold bar sinister on a field of purple clover, with the classic American motto underneath: 'A Sucker Is Born Every Minute!' Very fitting, don't you think, Inspector?"

I had to agree with a laugh that the merits of his social ambition were touchingly poetic.

"Very *touching*, guv'nor!" he said, winking.

So far as the unfortunate "suckers" are concerned, they have been prolific enough in London during recent years to put many an eloquent crook in clover for the rest of his life, if only those crooks had had the sense to husband their ill-gotten wealth. Among the many confidence tricks practised successfully, perhaps the most conspicuous has been that picturesque operation known to the police as the "Disbursement of Fortune Trick" or "Dropping the Rosary". More aptly, the confidence man dubs it the "Hot Seat".

This cunning trick, despite the publicity it frequently gets in the newspapers, seldom fails to come off. The *modus operandi* is usually the same – at least in general plan if not in finished detail.

The acquaintance of the prospective victim is made by the trickster who is known as the "steerer" on board a liner *en route* to England, or at an hotel, or at a resort or place frequented by sightseers. A friendship is formed, with the steerer invariably letting his newly found friend know that he is a person of some means travelling for pleasure. Craftily, without risking the least suspicion, the steerer gets some idea of his victim's bank balance, where has come from, how long he intends to remain in Britain, and any other personal details that may prove useful at a later date. In this manner the ground is prepared, not only for the fleecing, but also for the ultimate getaway of the crooks when they have rounded off the fraud. Nothing is left undone to ensure a successful operation.

In due course the trickster and his sucker might visit some of the sights of London Town. They are the best of friends, with not a cloud in their heavens. One day, while walking along a street, they observe a man ahead of them unwittingly drop something from his pocket. It may be a rosary, a wallet, a bunch of keys, a letter – anything, so long as it is of some apparent value to the loser.

One of the observers retrieves the article, hastens after the owner and returns it. In a rich Irish brogue the owner overwhelms the finder with his thanks. He explains that the dropped article was a gift from a Father O'Brien, or some such obvious Irish name, and that he would not have lost if for worlds.

The owner is, of course, Confidence Man No 2 – the steerer's accomplice. He is usually dressed in an old-fashioned suit of black cloth which gives the immediate impression that it is a relic of the long ago. He is rather quixotic in appearance, and when he talked, illiteracy marks his excited words. Nervous, shy, grateful – like a countryman out of his native element – he explains that his name is John Dillon and that probably they may have heard of him, as his name had appeared in all the newspapers recently in connection with a court case upholding his claim to £2,000,000, which had been bequeathed to him by a foreign uncle named Michael Dillon, who had died some time previously in the United States of America.

Garrulous, encouraged by the others' sympathetic interest, he then relates that the late Michael Dillon had emigrated to America very many years ago. He had finally settled in Bradford, Pennsylvania, where he had bought a small piece of land. During boring operations, oil had been struck on the land and sudden wealth had come to Dillon when an oil trust bought him out for £1,500,000. With his vast sum of money, the Irish emigrant had gone to Seattle and acquired property known as Dillon's Buildings.

All this golden fairy-tale had happened years ago. Michael was now dead and resting in peace, but on his deathbed he had told his spiritual comforter, Father O'Brien, that he had relatives in Ireland, and he asked the priest to trace them after he was gone. And so the humble and overwhelmed John Dillon came into the limelight from his impoverished obscurity. He it was whom the faithful priest traced and gave a rosary and advised him of the legacy awaiting his claim.

Part of the conditions of the legacy required John Dillon to give personally £20,000 of his inheritance to the Pope and £30,000 to the poor, irrespective of their creed or nationality, through persons who had means of their own.

A strangely moving story – a most impressive story – told with all the blarney of a sentimental Irishman.

The game of "Hot Seat" proceeds. The Irishman, still profuse with his thanks, invites the strangers to take a cup of coffee with him. He is a confirmed teetotaller, but if his friends will be kind as to accompany him to a nearby café he would be very happy, indeed, he would.

They toast each other in coffee, and the Irishman produces a newspaper cutting giving details of his legacy. This appears to be the final proof of authenticity, if such proof is required.

It illustrates to what lengths the cunning tricksters will go in an effort to impress. It is a genuine piece of newsprint, cut from the column bearing the open space for Stop Press news. The tricksters' canard is set up in proper printer's type and then imprinted on the white space reserved for late news. The back of the cutting is quite authentic, and the completed extract looks as real as it is possible to be. The reproduced specimen was made on the Stop Press column of a well-known London evening newspaper. I am sure the proprietors must be far from flattered when they realise to what base use the virgin white of their column has been put!

In the telling of his story the Irishman eventually comes to the part concerned with his journey to Italy to hand to the Pope the £20,000. The subject of the distribution to the necessitous poor is then mentioned. The Irishman suggests to his confederate – who, of course, is cleverly acting the part of the complete stranger – that he might care to participate in disposing of some of the fortune to the needy of his country. He is promised all his expenses, as well as a sum of money for his trouble.

Having reached this stage, the earnest benefactor then invites the views of the others on the best methods of allocating the gifts to the most deserving cases, and the steerer finally agrees to take, say, £1000 and share it among the poor people of his own home town.

It is now the turn of the prospective victim to be sounded. Sometimes he offers, with little prompting, to help in the distribution – especially if the prospect of making some financial recompense excites his sympathy. The acting of the fake simpleton from the Green Isle is so directed to give the quite erroneous impression that it would be an easy matter to deprive him of some of his embarrassing wealth.

I am afraid that in many cases the instinct of gain overrules the victim's natural caution. The play-acting of the crooks is so inspired that the victim usually agrees, or offers, to take some of the money and spread the blessing around. But ...... the Irishman is not just so witless. Having reached that point, he then suggests that his friends might give some proof that they are men of means, thus complying with the terms of the will, and that they can be trusted with the responsible task. He first asks his confederate how much financial evidence he can produce, and the accommodating fellow is willing to put up £10,000 as a guarantee of good faith.

Suiting his actions to his words, he then produces a bundle of dud bank-notes to the declared value of £5000 and shows a faked letter of credit, or some travellers' cheques, for the remainder of the sum.

The Irishman makes a pretence of examining the bank-notes. He acknowledges them to be for the correct sum; but he professes ignorance of the value of the letter of credit, and insists upon seeing cash, as he has no faith whatever in fancy bits of paper that are beyond his intelligence.

It is now the victim's turn to be asked about his means. As he is a visitor to England, he usually has to admit that his money is also in the form of a letter of credit. And once again the regretful Irishman refuses to accept this as evidence. He remains adamant, and the steerer and the victim go off to cash their letters of credit. The simple John Dillon now intimates that he will go and collect the money he is going to hand over, and arrangements are made to meet again in about half an hour at the same place.

Confidence Trickster No 1 goes off with his victim in a taxi, and the driver is instructed to stop at a well-known bank. Leaving his victim in the cab, the crook enters the bank and presently emerges with a bundle of notes supposed to represent the remaining £5000. The taxi now proceeds to the victim's bank — and this time real money is withdrawn on the letter of credit.

At the appointed hour the three men meet. The Irishman has a small attaché-case with him which, he is at pains to inform them, contains the several thousands of pounds he will hand over to them in due course. Before parting with the money, however, he suggests that they should show their confidence in each other by trusting one another with their money.

The steerer raises no objections. He hands over his two rolls of notes to the Irishman, who goes out of the restaurant with the dupe, leaving the attaché-case behind in the care of the steerer. The two take a short walk; the Irishman expresses his great pleasure in having met such a fine fellow as the man they have left behind, and he casually lets drop that he hopes to buy him a handsome present as a token of his appreciation.

The short promenade of faith is ended. They return to the restaurant. And the heir of Michael Dillon, deceased, hands back the rolls of notes to the waiting one.

It is then proposed that the victim should allow the other two to go outside with his money for a few minutes to show that he trusts them. He agrees. He hands over his money, is given the loaded attaché-case to hold, and is left sitting.

Well, the game has drawn to a close. It proves a long and uncomfortable seat — in all truth the "Hot Seat" which so aptly describes the piece of knavery — for the tricksters never return. After a disillusioning wait the victim usually becomes so suspicious that he is prompted to peer into the sacred interior of the case. Alas for human faith. All that is found is a bundle of old newspapers.

I have known the part of the Irishman to be played by a trickster dressed as an Irish priest. In such a get-up the crook could scarcely fail to impress; but such a role requires much great histrionic skill.

When the victim's seat has become so hot that he can bear the suspense no longer, he may advise the police of his loss — he may, but does not always do so, for he does not care to confess that he has been caught out so neatly by his own avarice or folly. In many instances the dupes have been deprived of every penny they have brought with them to England for their vacations; sometimes they are driven to appealing to their respective Government Departments for temporary assistance.

I have been told many a queer tale by the sorrowful victims when they have come to report the swindle. They have told me quite seriously that they have been hypnotised, or that the coffee they drank was drugged, or the cigarettes they were given were doped, or that they only parted with their money because their pockets were picked by the confidence men or force was used against them!

How silly – how sad! A few questions very soon elicit the truth, and the victim is astounded to hear, from official lips, the exact story of how he was picked up, set down and left to sizzle to his senses on the hottest seat of his existence.

Story (7)

One day I had a visit at Scotland Yard from a very agitated Jew who seemed almost on the point of collapse. He was quite incoherent at first, but he calmed down sufficiently to tell me that he had just been parted from a large sum of money. In a few moments I knew that here was another man who had been neatly "trimmed" by an exceedingly clever confidence trickster. Greed had once again met greed, and the cleverer had won the round.

The victim, who had hoped to add to his store of worldly goods, was a tobacconist. He owned a shop in the West End of London; he had a good bit of money safely tucked away, but that was no reason why he should not attempt to increase his wealth, especially as, in this particular case, it appeared that he was going to make something very quickly.

Alas, for appearances – and human hopes! That was the crafty bait. And he swallowed it just as it had been planned beforehand that he should swallow it.

This is the story he told me, sitting in my office rubbing his palms together and looking the picture of tragedy.

Late on the afternoon of the pervious day a well-built man, obviously a foreigner, walked into his shop. He was of the seafaring type, dressed in a conventional nautical attire of a blue reefer coat, blue jersey and trousers and peaked cap.

He asked for some tobacco and names a brand popular amongst sailors. He spoke awkwardly in broken English and then suddenly lapsed into his native Russian. That was the tobacconist's tongue. He was a Russian Jew – and immediately he was sympathetic towards his customer and they began to talk of Russia and other things of mutual interest.

The sailor explained that he had arrived a few days before in a Russian shop at London Docks. He became confidential, waited until another customer had been served and had departed, and then revealed to his countryman that he was greatly perplexed over a certain matter of great secrecy and would value his advice.

"If you tell me, I shall try to advise you," the Jewish shopkeeper suggested.

The stranger lowered his voice. His was a tremendous secret surely enough. He had brought to England a quantity of rich diamonds which he now wished to sell. But, for him, it would be very difficulty; he was a foreign sailor of no standing who was unversed in the art of handling big deals. He was a complete stranger, and had not the faintest idea of how to go about getting rid of his valuable stones. He maintained that the sparklers had come into his possession quite honestly, but as he was a foreigner who spoke very little English, there were many obstacles which prevented his making a profitable deal. Would his fellow-countryman give him some help?

"I have little English," the sailor confided. "It is so difficult to speak in London. I do not know how I can negotiate a good sale."

The Jew was intrigued. The story rang true enough and he wondered just how he could give a hand in the deal – and perhaps earn a decent commission for himself.

"If you care to let me see your diamonds," he hinted cautiously, "it is possible I may be able to find a purchaser. Yes, it is just possible."

The Russian sailor carefully looked about him and went to the door to make certain that no one was watching him. He then pulled up his woollen jersey, and from a body-belt he took out a chamois bag. Opening it, he emptied the contents into one of his large palms and the watching man gasped.

Diamonds lay there in the hollow of the stranger's hand – large and small diamonds – twenty or thirty altogether – and every one a sparkling beauty of flawless cut.

Even to the layman the stones were lovely and were easily recognisable as diamonds of great value. The man knew immediately he saw them that they represented a considerable amount of money. He thought quickly. This seemed his chance to make a profit without too much trouble. But he must be cautious – oh, ever so cautious.

"What sort of figure to you want for them?" he asked, as casually as his excitement would allow him.

The Russian shrugged and shook his head slowly. "I do not know. They are worth a great lot, but I do not know how much. Perhaps, if you could get an expert to value them. But we must be careful ......"

That suited the tobacconist perfectly. He would get an expert to judge them – someone who could make an accurate valuation of their worth. He had not the slightest intention of making an offer until he knew what he was buying. If he worked this deal well he stood to make a nice bit of money before the day was done.

He told his assistant that he was going out for a short time. He left the shop accompanied by the Russian seaman and walked along the street to where a jeweller friend of his had a business.

"What d'you think of these?" he asked, as the sailor opened his leather bag once more. "How much are they worth?"

The jeweller and the tobacconist spoke in English. The foreigner stood by, watchful but mute, apparently not understanding one word that was being said. His ignorance of the language prevented him from following the conversation between the other two men. When the man learned that the diamonds were worth a considerable amount of money he blessed the kind fates that had sent him this opportunity to bring off a profitable deal.

The seaman spoke, in Russian. "Will the jeweller buy them?" he asked anxiously.

The man hastily replied. "No, he is not interested. But I – well, I think I might be able to make you an offer when we return to my shop."

Back in the tobacconist's shop the man made an offer. The two men haggled for a few moments. But eventually the Russian agreed to sell his treasures.

It was then after banking hours. The man had not sufficient money on hand, and a cheque, in the circumstances was quite out of the question. It was arranged that the sailor should call back the next morning to conclude the deal.

Just as he was about to leave, the Russian hesitated. He explained that he intended having an evening's spree but that he did not want to carry the diamonds about with him. Could he leave them in safe custody somewhere?

Why, certainly! The man suggested that his jeweller friend would keep the diamonds. Back to the jeweller they went, the bag was handed over, the contents carefully checked, and a sealed package made, which was then locked away in the safe.

As soon as the sailor had departed the man went back to his friend. "Tell me," he asked, "what's your honest opinion of those sparklers? I mean, what are they really worth if I buy them?"

"They are of exceptionally fine quality. One of them, my friend, weighs nearly five carats. If properly handled in the right marked those diamonds should easily fetch a small fortune."

The man's excitement was intense. A rich profit was as good as his. But – he was reckoning without the simple sailorman!

The new day arrived. At the appointed hour the sailor returned, looking slightly the worse for wear. He and the tobacconist adjourned to the jeweller's. The diamonds were unsealed and checked once more in the presence of the buyer and the seller. They were put back into their little leather bag and the Russian slipped them into his pocket.

With an exclamation he withdrew them again. So silly of him! He had forgotten that he was selling them. And he handed over the bag to the shopkeeper.

The deal was concluded in a neighbouring tea-shop. Just before he parted with his money the man poured the stones into his hand and gazed on their perfection. He picked up the largest stone and drew in his breath. Yes, there was a fortune in that one stone. He was a very, very lucky man indeed! So thinking, he pocketed the stones and parted with his notes to the poor sailor from Russia.

He walked on air back to his shop. Then he hurried to Hatton Garden, to a diamond merchant of his acquaintance. He was still cautious. He did not reveal his entire hoard. Instead, he showed him only the prize stone of the collection.

"Can you dispose of this for me?" he inquired.

The merchant turned the stone between his fingers. He looked at it more closely, then looked at the Jewish tobacconist and raised his eyebrows. "What's the joke?" he demanded sharply. "This jargoon is worthless!"

The man started. A cold shiver ran over him. "But – it is true. It is real. I know it is. I have others, too. They were all checked up by a jeweller friend of mine. See," he explained feverishly, "look at them all. They were genuine. I paid a lot of money for them, too."

He poured out the other stones on the table. The expert examined them one by one. He did not take long to make his assay. He tossed them back on the table with contempt. "Pshaw!" he exclaimed. "Very pretty – very pretty! But duds, all duds! They are just worthless pieces of glass."

The man was sick with the shock. Back to the jeweller he rushed in panic, not knowing what or whom to believe. He threw the leather bag in front of his jeweller friend. "Look at them – examine them – what are they?" he demanded hotly.

The jeweller looked at them. It took him less than a minute. "These aren't the stones I examined for you yesterday, or this morning. They are just glass!"

The news was too much for the tobacconist. The thought of his lost money filled him with despair and sorrow. Down to Scotland Yard he tottered. When he was shown into my room he burst forth in a denunciation of the police for allowing such a rogue as the Russian sailor to roam the country at large, defrauding honest people like himself!

I took down the necessary written record of the man's complaint.

"But how did the diamonds become glass?" he kept demanding. "How were they changed? They were real at the beginning. They were real just before I gave him my money. Then they were just pieces of worthless glass!"

I was able to tell him just what had happened. It was very clever – and very simple. It was an obvious, and astute, case of "ringing the changes". The stones originally produced by the Russian sailor were genuine enough, otherwise he would never have allowed them to be examined by an expert. When he collected the little wash-leather bags in the morning from the jeweller's safe he dropped it – as if absentmindedly – into his pocket, then he hurriedly retrieved it with an apology and handed it over to the shopkeeper.

But it was another bag he handed over! In those few seconds, in the depths of his pocket, he had rung the changes. The bag containing the diamonds was left safely hidden; another bag, exactly similar in appearance, but containing the spurious stones, was substituted. Thus was the trick perpetrated with the slickness, the coolness of an audacious expert craftsman.

It did not take long to identity the Russian sailor. There were only half a dozen tricksters known to specialise in that particular type of confidence trick. But to put my hands on him was a totally different manner. Those international crooks, all of them foreigners, travel extensively – and quickly, when necessary – from place to place all over Europe, their passage facilitated by means of false passports. They do not remain for long on the one spot. They work carefully and quickly and pass on to fresh clover meadows.

However, I intended to get the Russian sailor this time. The net was spread and a watch kept. But three months passed and still he had not been traced. Then things began to happen.

From a certain source of information one day there came to me the news that two foreign conmen were frequenting a public-house in London. I was given the tip that it might be worth my while to pay a visit to this particular public-house. I went along with another officer and took up an observation.

For two days I waited and nothing happened. On the third day, after spending many hours in the pub, drinking beer I did not want, I saw two foreign-looking seamen enter and call for drinks.

Experience told me that the quest was not in vain. I had only a brief description to rely upon, but I was satisfied that the taller stranger was none other than the Russian who had defrauded the Jewish tobacconist. Nothing was to be gained by acting hurriedly. I decided to keep watch a little longer.

When the two men left the public-house we were not far behind them. They reached the main road and hailed a bus. We followed. They climbed up on to the top deck. We scrambled inside – and the bus proceeded on its way to Hampstead.

Presently the suspects came downstairs, the bus stopped and they descended. We kept carefully on their trail until they came to a halt outside a high-class tobacconist's shop.

So they were at it again! This, I thought, looked very significant; they were grafting right under out noses. It looked as if there were going to be some fun in a few moments.

I gave them time to get well ahead with their "business", then I walked casually into the shop and bought some cigarettes. My appearance disturbed the shopkeeper and his foreign visitors in an earnest conversation. The time for action had not yet arrived, so I walked out and took up my vigil again outside the shop.

Ten minutes passed. The door opened. Out came the shopkeeper, accompanied by the foreigners, and they all walked along the street and disappeared into a jeweller's establishment. The trickery was being operated according to the set plan. It was almost as if they were rehearsing, for our benefit, the scenes that led up to the cheating of the Jewish tobacconist. Only – another tobacconist was about to be caught!

The minutes passed while we watched. The three men left the jeweller's, and on the way back to the tobacconist's they called in at a bank. When they had returned to the victim's shop, my colleague went along to the jeweller's and came back with the information – or, at least, the proof, for we were already fairly certain as to what had happened – that they had asked for a test to be made of a quantity of gold dust.

Now was the time to act. We closed in and waited on the doorstep, ostensibly gazing at the goods in the window. We had not long to wait there. The foreigners made to leave the shop, but we barred their way and forced them back into the interior, shutting the door behind us.

We then explained that we were Scotland Yard officers, and I invited the shopkeeper to recount the facts of his dealings with the two strangers.

His story was to effect that the two foreigners had told him, in broken English, that they were Russian sailors who had recently arrived in England from Canada on a Russian vessel, and that they had a quantity of gold dust which they wished to dispose of for ready cash. As we had seen for ourselves, they had paid a visit to a nearby jeweller, who had applied the usual test and pronounced the gold to be real and to be worth about £3000. The tobacconist had offered to buy the gold for £2000, and he had actually withdrawn the necessary sum from his bank along the street. Indeed, the deal was completed, for just a second before our appearance on the scene the shopkeeper had handed over his money and had received in exchange the wash-leather bag containing the gold dust.

"May I see the bag, please?" I asked.

I opened it and looked at the contents. It looked to be the real stuff all right, but ….. So I asked the shopkeeper to send his wife back to the jeweller and ask for a test to be made.

She was quickly back. Breathless with excitement, she announced: "It isn't gold at all. It's only brass filings. It's worthless. You've been cheated!"

That was sufficient for me. We arrested the two pseudo-Russian sailors and searched them immediately. Another little leather bag was found, obviously containing the real gold, and also the £2000 in notes which they had received a few minutes earlier.

They were charged at the local police station with stealing £2000 by means of a trick. Later, they were paraded with twelve other men for identification, and the Jewish tobacconist who had laid the complaint picked out without the least hesitation the taller sailor as the man who had relieved him of his money three months before.

The Russians got their desserts in a British court of justice some time later. When they had served their sentences we made every endeavour to deport them back to Russia, but we found that the Soviet authorities refused to recognise them as Russian citizens and would not permit them to land on their territory. We had, alas, no alternative but to allow them their freedom. They could, if they wished, continue their criminal activities in this country!

It is not always easy to get rid of undesirable alien criminals. When their nationality is not in doubt their deportation from these shores becomes a mere formality. But it sometimes happens that a foreign country will refuse to accept their undesirables as their own nationals. In the circumstances it becomes impossible to dump them down in a land where they have no citizenship.

It may be wondered how men of this type are able to produce a quantity of valuable diamonds or a bag of real gold to assist them in their criminal play-acting.

There is a certain type of border-line criminal who will, for a substantial fee, afford financial assistance or give technical advice and "props" to those actively engaged in crime. This type of person is usually of the receiver class; although not willing to participate personally in a job because of the risk involved, he does not hesitate to work safely behind the scenes and take a large percentage as his "rake-off" when the proceeds of the crime are totted up.

The active criminal can always find the man to help him behind the scenes. He is the man, the unknown figure, the "sleeping partner", who, in ninety-nine cases out of a hundred makes crime possible.

The Master Mind never takes risks.

Story (8)

I have found that people awaiting trial and who happen to have a sympathetic doctor, sometimes have themselves admitted to hospital for alcohol or drug addiction.

A psychologist told me that one of my clients was suffering from depression. He was very down and needed assistance in coming to terms with the reality of his life.

He said to the psychologist:

"Even though I am in recovery, I am an alcoholic and drug addict."

The psychologist said: "You're a good man."

"I have been married and divorced three times."

"You're a good man."

"I have mad a career out of theft and deception."

"You're a good man."

"What is good about me?"

The doctor thought for a moment and then said: "I know. You're a good bad-example!"

Some of my confidence men fetched up in Dublin and the Irish police asked Scotland Yard for assistance. I spent a few pleasant months there and what follows consists of spliced together tapes.

Story (9)

'Did you know I was caught and put on trial one time?'

'Gosh imagine!' I said, and we tucked into a mug of coffee and a cigar each. 'Tell me about it'.

'I won the case fair and square by lying in the witness box. As I was about to take my leave Mr Justice O'Hoohig addressed me: "The jury have acquitted you. You are discharged. However, I think the only reason you were found not guilty was because of your prayers to the God of Good Luck. I hope you have learned your lesson."

'I was very aggrieved. I celebrated my acquittal in the usual manner but felt all the more indignant when I saw the following day's headline in the Ballyskerry Bugle. "Prisoner must have prayed to the God of Good Luck."

'I went to my solicitor and said, "I want to sue that judge." He said, "I don't see an action for slander succeeding. You can't sue a judge or counsel for anything they say in the course of a trial." "But the trial was over,' I said. "Will you have a go and see what happens?"

"I suppose," said the solicitor. "Justice O'Hoohig should have kept his mouth shut. I'll bang him off a letter." So he did.

To the Honourable Robert O'Hoohig,
Ballyskerry Circuit Court
Ireland
Personal and confidential

Dear Sir

It is our painful duty to write to you on behalf of our client, Mr Peter Bambrick. He complains that after you had discharged him you said, "The only reason you were found not guilty was because of your prayers to the God of Good Luck. I hope you have learned your lesson."

Our client complaints that, as the trial was over and he had been discharged, the words spoken by you were slanderous and not privileged. He instructs us to ask you to make a public apology and to pay a sum of money to charity. If you are not prepared to do so our instructions are to issue a writ and we would be glad to know if we are right in our assumption that the Chief State Solicitor's Office will accept service of proceedings on your behalf.

We are, of course, very sorry to have to write to you in this way, but it seems to us that it is right that the claim be put forward.

We are,

Your obedient servants.

Sue, Grabbit and Run.

'The Chief State Solicitor wrote back that he would accept proceedings. He did so and the case was struck out. We appealed but our appeal failed.

'I was completely dissatisfied. I found out where Mr Justice O'Hoohig lived. One night, a few months later two masked men broke into Justice O'Hoohig's house. They dragged him out of bed, tarred and feathered him and placed a placard around his neck that read, "You should have said your prayers to the God of Good Luck."

'For some reason best known to themselves the Special Branch called around to my house the following day and asked me to account for my movements the previous night.

"Since when do I have to say anything to the police. Go away, my good man, I don't like you."

"Do you know anything about Mr Justice O'Hoohig being tarred and feathered?"

"Not a thing but I'm delighted to hear about it. If you have sufficient evidence then arrest me. Otherwise go away, there is a draught and I'm sleepy – it's time for my afternoon nap. Close the garden gate after you, my good man. The streets are full of criminals."

'They came back a few days later and arrested me. I was put on trial again. Naturally enough I asked for a jury, swore blind that I had nothing to do with the assault and after all the witnesses, including two friends who gave me an alibi, were finished the judge summed up:

"Ladies and gentlemen of the jury, although this was a serious assault, you must not be in any way influenced by the fact that the victim was a distinguished judge. It would have been an equally heinous crime to commit against a street sweeper. Please consider whether the prisoner is guilty or not guilty according to the evidence."

'The jury returned after three hours with a verdict of not guilty. The judge looked very severely at the jury. "You are discharged," he said. "But in my opinion you are ...."

'Yes?' I said with a challenge in my eye.

'Discharged,' he said. 'Call the next case.'

'That was a bit of good luck,' I said to Peter.

'I have had some more good luck lately,' he said.

'Tell me about it,' I requested.

'I tried to buy a painting for my wife in the Soleil Gallery owned by Mr Oliver Marksman. He assured me that the Victorian watercolour sketch was by Mildred Anne Butler. I paid £500 down payment and promised to pay £250 a month until the painting was paid for. However, while I was in the process of paying for it, there was an auction in Adams Art Auctioneers during which Mildred Anne Butler paintings went for a far higher price than I was paying for mine. I hightailed it into the Soleil Gallery, paid the remainder of the money and collected the picture. I then consulted an expert who said that the painting I had been sold was not a Mildred Anne Butler painting at all. I had been swindled. I felt upset about the fraud, brought the painting back to the Soleil Gallery and after a row I got my money back.

'I made some enquiries about Oliver Marksman and found out he lived at 78 Park Lane. I also discovered he took off for six months every year to Florida. He was an Irish "snowbird".

'When I knew he had gone on his winter holiday I called round to his house. I rang the bell and a woman caretaker opened the door. I managed to persuade her to show me around the property and I noted that Oliver had left behind some genuine paintings and expensive antique furniture. I told the caretaker – I think she was a sandwich short of a picnic – that Mr Marksman owed me a lot of money and that I was going to sue him.

'I went and consulted the esteemed law firm of Argue and Bluster. I gave them the name and address under which I was working – I had taken a flat for a month – and told them that Mr Oliver Marksman owed me £100,000.

'I told them I knew he was staying in the Grand Hotel, Ballyskerry and that they should issue writs immediately. I then took the train to Ballyskerry and registered in the Grand Hotel as Mr Oliver Marksman

'I receive the solicitor's letter and went to a Ballyskerry solicitor's named Liars and Bastards, I produced the letter and said that I was staying at the Grand Hotel. I told Mr Liars that I owed the money but that I was off to America to live and didn't feel inclined to go to court. I said that the plaintiff could go and whistle for his money. I said to write a letter and accept liability but don't pay a penny.

'Then I paid Mr Liar's account, paid my hotel bill and left Ballyskerry.

'Back in Dublin I received a note from Mr Argue of Argue and Bluster. He asked me to call to see him.

"Good news!" he said as I sat down on the customer side of his desk. "The defendant has submitted to judgement."

"He'll do me out of payment if he can," I said.

'If he doesn't pay up we'll put in execution at his house. I'll ring his solicitor right away."

'He did so, put down the phone and said, "He has no intention of satisfying the judgement. From what Liars told me he has withdrawn his instructions and done a bunk."

"What can I do now?" I asked.

"I'll put in the sheriff as quickly as possible. We have leave to enforce the judgement. Hopefully there is enough stuff in his house to satisfy what he owes you."

"Good," I said. "Is there anything else I need to do?"

"No – just sign this authority. Thanks very much. You can rely on me to get on with this at once."

'Four weeks later I watched with satisfaction as the sheriff's men removed all the furniture and paintings from 78 Park Lane. As each truck was filled by the Sheriff's men a policeman stopped the traffic to let it out. The caretaker looked bewildered but put up no protest.

'Shortly afterwards there was an auction of paintings and furniture. I went along and paid a small sum for a Mildred Anne Butler painting. I got it for a song. A few days later I received a cheque for £75,000. In the accompanying letter Mr Argue said he was sorry the furniture and paintings did not fetch enough to satisfy the entire debt but after deducting the sheriff's costs and charges and their own costs the enclosed sum was all that was left. Would I send my instructions as to how they could recover the balance?

'I phoned up Mr Argue and said I was very disappointed at the amount recovered and that I would not trouble him any more.'

I smiled as Peter added, 'And I didn't.'"

As one of my colleagues put it: "you know PJ when the ruthless with experience meet with naïve with money, it is the ruthless who end up with the money and the naïve with the experience."

Story (10)

Sammy the Swindler

Sammy the swindler was a 30 year old young man who served his apprenticeship in that great university of crime – the average jail.

He fell in love with a raven-haired beauty named Sandra Purcell. They were planning to be married.

The bane of Sammy's life was his father who knew that Sammy was a confidence man. He used to quote the Holy Bible at Sammy, First Corinthians, chapter six:

"Do you now know that the wicked will not inherit the Kingdom of God?"

And Psalm 9:

"The wicked is snared in the work of his own hands. The wicked shall be turned into Hell."

And Psalm 104:

"May sinners be consumed from the earth and the wicked be no more."

When Sammy fell in love with Sandra she told him that she would only marry him if he went straight.

'Just one more sting?' he pleaded with her.

She relented to such an extent that she agreed to be part of the plot.

Enter the players:

Gerry the gambler had a nice life. He owned fifty betting shops and an equal number of florists. He did not work. He simply went from shop to shop letting his managers know that he was still in charge. Like Sammy he had been a criminal in his youth.

He spent most afternoons at home with a coterie of pals playing cards, drinking and smoking.

Sammy called to his house on the afternoon of the sting and found Gerry wary. Sammy had taken £100,000 from him in several card games. This amounted to Gerry's weekly profits from all his shops.

'I'm feeling lucky,' said Sammy.

'I have no intention of letting you play cards in my house,' Gerry told him.

'I was thinking of putting a bet on a horse.'

Gerry eyed him suspiciously.

'My horse runs in the first race at Fairyhouse.'

Gerry looked at the clock. It was 12.50. The first race began at one o'clock.

Gerry's house was in Glicktown on a tree lined avenue. It sported big picture windows.

'Sit down with your back to the window,' he ordered.

Sammy sat.

Gerry didn't want Sammy receiving a signal from outside. He knew the scam of ringing up a bookies and keeping a girl on the line until the race was won, then knowing the winner, placing the bet.

'I feel lucky,' said Sammy. 'Do you mind if I take a leak?'

Gerry motioned to one of his five pals.

'Follow him and make sure he doesn't get up to anything funny.'

Sammy went to the bathroom which was situated right beside Gerry's living room. He turned on the taps and locked the door. He then lowered the toilet seat, stood up on it and removed the bulb. He placed a small circle of silver cigarette paper into the socket, replaced the bulb and turned on the switch. He heard a "pop" which told him that he had blown a fuse. He took out the bulb again and after turning off the switch, removed the circle of silver paper and replaced the bulb.

He went back into the sitting room. He sat with his back to the window. He looked at the clock. It was electric and not now working.

'I feel really lucky,' he told Gerry and his friends.

Gerry eyed him suspiciously again. 'If you rob me again I'll kill you.'

'All I want to do is place a substantial bet.' Sammy was all affronted innocence. 'I would like to place £50,000 on Red Roses in the first race.'

Gerry turned on the radio. It didn't work.

'Will you take the bet?'

'I'll take the bet.'

Sammy handed Gerry fifty thousand pounds from his briefcase.

One of the men in the room phoned Gerry's headquarters.

'Red Roses won at ten to one.'

'How did you know that?' Gerry asked Sammy.

'I knew nothing. I just felt lucky.'

'You cheated.'

'If you want to welsh on the bet I'll be off but your name is going to be mud.'

Gerry went to the next room with Sammy's briefcase and filled it with five hundred thousand pounds. Sammy bid the bookie good luck and went for a walk.

He walked for three miles and made sure no one was following him. He arrived in a street that had four different coloured cars waiting for him to return to the car hire companies located in four different streets all over the city. He had actually hired five cars. The red car was the one he had seen in the mirror above Gerry's head flashing past at three minutes after one o'clock. It told him that Red Roses had won the race.

It took him a few hours to return the hired cars. Then he drove his own car to the beach and watched the sunset. Sandra would be along any minute.

He turned on the car radio. The newsreader announced:

'A car travelling at seventy miles an hour crashed in Glicktown today, killing the driver – Miss Sandra Purcell.'

He turned off the radio and wept and shook. The following day he went into Gerry's showcase premier flower shop. Gerry looked at him angrily but softened when he saw the bloodshot eyes, the unshaven face and the dishevelled hair.

'I would like to have two hundred pounds worth of red roses placed on Sandra Purcell's grave every week for the next fifty years. I would like to pay in advance.'

He handed over the five hundred thousand pounds. The gobsmacked girl behind the counter looked at Gerry for permission.

"Take the young man's order," he told her.

*   *   *

A Fond Farewell ....

The time had now arrived for me to think of retirement. All those years of adventure and unflagging interest since the day I left my native Guernsey had come to an end. And all too soon for me. However, I had qualified by service for a pension, and when my health finally broke down the doctors advised me to take a long rest and live far outside of London.

On the day before we were due to pack and move from the scenes we loved so well, my wife and I were coming down Haymarket when, approaching us, I saw two smartly-dressed gentlemen of familiar appearance.

They were two of my old confidence men – dressed up to kill. They saw me. They smiled. They doffed their hats and swept them down in front of them in a royal bow. In the past, when I had run into any of my "enemies" when off duty, or with no official grudge against them, their eyes seemed to say: "Good day, Inspector. Here's to the next time – and may it be a long time in coming!" But now a new look inhabited their eyes, for they knew already that I was going away. They seemed to say ....

Au revoir! Bon voyage!

They passed on, still smiling; sportsmen to the last, bearing no ill-will. I, too, raised my hat and my wife bowed .... To crooks who will always seek to browse in fields of clover ....

Au revoir!

Bonne Chassse!

The End.